ESCAPE FROM EGYPT

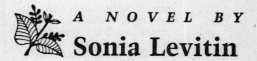
A NOVEL BY
Sonia Levitin

PUFFIN BOOKS

PUFFIN BOOKS

Published by the Penguin Group

Penguin Books USA Inc., 375 Hudson Street, New York, New York 10014, U.S.A.

Penguin Books Ltd, 27 Wrights Lane, London W8 5TZ, England

Penguin Books Australia Ltd, Ringwood, Victoria, Australia

Penguin Books Canada Ltd, 10 Alcorn Avenue, Toronto, Ontario, Canada M4V 3B2

Penguin Books (N.Z.) Ltd, 182-190 Wairau Road, Auckland 10, New Zealand

Penguin Books Ltd, Registered Offices: Harmondsworth, Middlesex, England

First published in the United States of America by Little, Brown and Company, 1994
Published in Puffin Books, 1996

9 10 8

LIBRARY OF CONGRESS CATALOGING-IN-PUBLICATION DATA

Levitin, Sonia.

Escape from Egypt: a novel / by Sonia Levitin.

p. cm.

"First published in the United States of America by Little, Brown and Company,
1994" — T.p. verso.

Summary: When Moses comes to lead the Israelites to the Promised Land, Jesse,
a Hebrew slave, finds his life changed by his growing faith in God and
his attraction to the half-Egyptian, half-Syrian Jennat.

ISBN 0-14-037537-6

1. Exodus, The—Juvenile fiction. [1. Exodus, The—Fiction. 2. Jews—History—To
1200 B.C.—Fiction.] I. Title.

[PZ7.L58Es 1996] [Fic]—dc20 95-43013 CIP AC

Printed in the United States of America

To my husband, Lloyd, for his steadfast love
and goodness;
To my son, Daniel, for leading the way;
To my daughter, Shari, for her insight and joy.

Acknowledgments

With special thanks to my teachers,
whose wisdom and kindness have been my inspiration:

Rabbi Richard Levy
Rabbi Chaim Menz

And special thanks to Rabbi Hayyim Kassorla for
his generous help in reading the manuscript.

CHAPTER 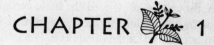 1

"You! What are you are carrying in that basket?"

Jesse quickly averted his eyes. He looked down at the thick legs and sandaled feet of the overseer and subdued his thoughts. Anger must never show. Jesse had learned this since earliest childhood; it was the way a slave survived.

"Just some vegetables from our common garden, my lord," murmured Jesse, making his voice pleasant and devoid of resentment. "Perhaps my lord would like some for his table?" Jesse reached into the basket and brought out a bunch of fresh green onions, their white tops glistening in the bright afternoon sun.

The overseer's hand darted out. He was Horus, second in command. Now Jesse raised his eyes, saw Horus's belt with the heavy gold buckle, the fine linen of his tunic. Gold and silver rings gleamed on his fingers.

The overseer grasped the onions, then threw them down into the dust. "I have plenty," he said with a laugh. "What lean harvests you Israelites produce, and after we give you everything — water and soil and time to plant. It's a disgrace!"

"I'm sorry, my lord," said Jesse, ducking his head.

He waited until the Egyptian walked away, the whip swinging at his side. Jesse sighed, a light sound, like the wind singing through the palm fronds at the canals. He was hardly aware of this habit of catching, holding, and gently letting out his breath, though he knew well the little compensating gestures made by those close to him. His mother had a way of sucking in her lips to choke off speech. His father pulled his shoulders down, even when he carried no bricks on his back.

Jesse lifted his head now, and also his steps. Enough of this! He slipped his hand into his waistband, where a gleaming gold buckle lay against his skin, warm and satisfying. He had been working with metals for only a few months, and it was winning him praise.

"You have the touch," his master, Sinuhe, the ornament maker, had said. Sinuhe was kindly for an Egyptian, round-faced and nearly bald, and his skin always gleamed with a light patina of pure olive oil. "We shall teach you to work with gems by and by," he had promised. Then his eyes had narrowed in warning. "All your work must be left in this basket and accounted for — none taken to your dwelling overnight — do you understand me?"

"Yes, my lord," Jesse had murmured, hands pressed together in the pose of obedience. "Thank you, my lord."

This afternoon Jesse had disobeyed. With a swift, calculated gesture, he had slipped the gold buckle into his waistband. His hand was steady, though his heart hammered, not only because of his audacity, but because he saw Jennat's dark eyes upon him.

Jennat, the beautiful ward of In-hop-tep, worked beside Jesse learning gold- and silversmithing. Jennat's mistress had chosen her to learn these skills. As for Jesse, someone had interceded to bring him to this post. He did not know who, or

4

at what price. One did not ask, but accepted opportunities. To work indoors and learn a skill was the highest goal of a slave.

For the first weeks, Jesse had struggled to avoid gazing at Jennat. Jennat was lithe and slim as a reed. She moved with the grace of a queen, her long legs caressed by her wide, filmy tunic, which parted tantalizingly when she walked. In the fashion, Jennat's large, almond-shaped eyes were accentuated with deep blue kohl. One glance, and Jesse felt breathless.

Jennat was half Egyptian, half Syrian, a higher ranking captive than he. She would likely become the concubine of a wealthy man. It was foolish and wrong for Jesse even to imagine the silken touch of her skin or the scent of her glossy dark hair. But Jesse could not control his thoughts, especially in the nights. Then, over and over again, he would recall the delight of Jennat standing close beside him while Sinuhe instructed them. Sometimes her breath brushed his cheek, and the scent of her hair overwhelmed him with desire.

Jesse had calculated taking the gold buckle to give to his cousin Avi. But it was also a test. One cry from Jennat, and he would be doomed. If she betrayed him, Jennat could win favor for herself. But as Jesse grasped his prize, he saw Jennat's color deepen. Quickly she averted her eyes and moved nearer the teacher, inventing a question to keep him occupied.

The memory of Jennat's conspiracy filled him with joy. She must care for him, or at least not despise him!

He hurried now, to tell his cousin Avi. Aunt Channa would have prepared something festive to eat, perhaps a stew, for Avi's birthday. Later they might go to the canals and lie among the cool reeds and spy upon the Egyptian maidens who came to bathe in the moonlight.

The sound of horses shattered Jesse's calm. Shouts rang out. Three Egyptian boys, bent over their steaming mounts,

5

whipped them on into the slave camp. It was their usual sport.

Jesse tried to dodge behind a low wall, but the horses, with their heated bodies and blazing hooves, came bearing down upon him. Dust blinded him. Jesse heard the fearful cries of animals and the shouts of the boys: "Ho! Faster! Faster — look at that idiot trying to outrun us!" They roared and laughed. The boys were tough from the games and competitions that filled their days, and they hungered for a fight.

In the next instant Jesse lay on the ground, shaken. The side of his face felt numb, then oily to his fingertips. The boys were gone, but they would be back, Jesse knew. There was blood on his hands. He heard a cry. A woman lay just beyond him in the dust. She had been walking with a cache of precious eggs in her apron. The broken eggs dripped like pus down the front of her robe.

The woman's eyes reflected first terror, then shame. Jesse looked away, but he had seen. In the attack, the woman's kerchief had slipped from her head, and now she clutched at her nearly bald skull, trying to hide her humiliation. The Egyptian masters often took the hair of their Hebrew slave women to make the wigs that they prized.

Jesse moved toward the woman, his heart pounding with rage. His cheek stung. "Are you all right, Ima?" He asked softly. He used the title *Mother* respectfully, as was the custom in addressing any married woman.

"Oh, the eggs! The eggs! Lord, save us, how can I make it up to my master?" With trembling hands, the woman placed the cloth back on her head; then she stood up, leaning on Jesse's arm.

"I will find you more eggs, Ima," Jesse said. "Come, don't be afraid."

She brushed the egg slime off her robe, leaving trails of dirt,

6

and now she looked Jesse full in the face and exclaimed, "Jesse! Son of Nathan and Devorah, can it be? You've grown a hand's breadth, I swear, since I saw you last. Where have you been?"

Jesse laughed slightly. "I've been learning metalcraft in the household of Memnet the Egyptian, wife of In-hop-tep."

The woman made a mouth and rolled her eyes. "Ah, you are coming up in the world. No wonder you don't spend time in our fields anymore."

"I do my share," Jesse objected. "Often, at night, I pull weeds and make furrows. I would not shirk my responsibilities, Ima."

She reached up and patted him on the shoulder. "I know." Then she frowned, seeing the blood on his face. "Let me dress that cut for you quickly. It won't do to scar that fine face." She reached out with the edge of her shawl.

"Don't bother," said Jesse as she dabbed at his cheek. "It will heal. I have tough skin."

The woman's eyes became gentle. "You're a good boy. Just the age my son would have been."

Jesse knew the story. Everyone had a story — a tragedy or a miracle. His was a miracle. He was still alive.

"They found my boy," she said. The bitterness was like acid in her voice. "They took him. We did not even have time to circumcise him. They took him from my breast on the third day."

Jesse nodded slowly. Always the same grief flooded over him, filling his chest, rising to his throat. At such times he hated himself for working in an Egyptian household, eating from the table of Jennat's mistress. It made him want to fight, as his cousin Avi did. Avi's body was sinewy and knotted with muscles from wrestling and running. Such pastimes, of course, were forbidden to slaves, but Avi took his chances.

7

The Egyptian boys were back — on foot this time, swaggering.

"We have come for the eggs," said the tallest of them. He stood at eye level to Jesse. He was about Jesse's own age, sixteen or seventeen, obviously the leader.

"I — my lord, I regret . . ." stammered the hapless woman.

Jesse leapt forth. "It was an accident," he said quickly. "I broke the eggs in my awkwardness, Master. I'll run to my own mother's house and fetch fresh eggs, only don't, I pray you —"

" 'Don't'?" The leader grinned at his companions. " 'Don't,' he says to an Egyptian? There is a quota due to us," he continued. "It must be fulfilled. Maybe you can put the broken eggs back together again, eh?"

"Maybe he ought to eat them," called out another. "It's a pity to waste good food!"

Cruel laughter filled Jesse's ears as the boys surged toward him and grasped his arms. They pushed his head down to the ground. He felt a heavy weight on his neck and another on his back. "Eat those eggs, slave. This will teach you to waste Pharaoh's food! All that we have comes from Pharaoh, isn't it so? Enjoy Pharaoh's eggs!"

Gravel tore into Jesse's cheek. He smelled the raw dirt, felt the blows on his back as the boys chanted, "Eat! Eat! Eat!" He tasted eggshell and mud, and he tasted his own hatred. If only he could feel the force of his fist against an Egyptian jaw — it might be worth a hundred lashes.

Suddenly Jesse was pulled up by the shoulder, and then to his horror, he heard the clink of metal on stone.

The gold buckle lay exposed at his feet.

In the turmoil of the next moments, as Jesse heard the overseer approaching, his mind went numb with fear. He looked down at the hem of Horus's garment.

"So." Horus's voice was soft, almost caressing. "What mischief is this?"

Gleefully the Egyptian boys accused, "Look, look, a thief. He has stolen from Pharaoh's treasury. All belongs to Pharaoh, and this slave —"

"Where did you get this buckle?" The overseer's tone was soft, but his hand went to the handle of his whip.

Jesse forced strength into his voice. Fear was a slave's undoing. "My mistress," he said loudly, "Memnet, wife of Inhop-tep, gave it to me."

"Liar! Why would a slave be given such a treasure?"

"It was because I — I pleased her, my lord." The inference was clear. Jesse held his breath. Either Horus would laugh in the way of men when it came to such matters, or he would deal with Jesse as a liar and a thief.

A stronger voice intruded. "What's this? A feast? I need fifty slaves for quarry duty — you were to select them for me, Horus — do you recall? Is this one of them?"

Jesse knew that gravel tone well. The head slave master was known for his flashing temper. He swiftly meted out punishments, then vanished like a serpent in a pool of reeds. His name was Meri-Aten, but the slaves called him Emsis, meaning "Crocodile."

"Yes, of course," barked out Horus. "He's young and strong, tall as a grown man, and look at those shoulders."

Meri-Aten's heavy hands fell upon Jesse, probing his muscles. "He'll do," said the Crocodile. "Might last a month or two. What is your name? Where is your hut?"

"I am Jesse, son of Nathan and Devorah. I live close by, between the marshland and the road."

"You will report at dawn to the quarry," said Meri-Aten. Jesse smelled foul garlic and onions, and the man's sweat.

"Yes, Master." Jesse's breath caught in his throat. He could

9

survive it, he thought, if he were careful. But his disgrace and the loss of his position in the great house of In-hop-tep would demean him forever. His mother would be worried sick. How could he inflict this upon her?

"If you are not in line in the morning . . ." Meri-Aten made a gesture. Jesse knew what it meant.

"I will be there," he said, his head bowed.

When they had gone, the woman scurried out from the bushes. "Oh, Jesse," she wailed, "you poor child! Your poor mother! The quarry — men are maimed there. My own husband —"

"Hush, please, Ima. Let me go now."

The woman swooped down and snatched up something from the ground. In her hand lay the gold buckle, miraculously forgotten by the Egyptians. "Your treasure," she said, half in awe, half in derision.

By the time Jesse reached his hut, the vegetables were limp in his hand. He stepped carefully over the puddles, squinting against the late afternoon sun. Buzzards swooped low over mounds of trash. Flies and mosquitoes hummed around his head. One price of spending his days in the Egyptian sector was having to smell the putrid decay of the slave quarter anew each night. It settled in his nose and throat, overpowering and sickening.

How could he tell his mother about his punishment? She had lost too much already. They had always been close. Devorah never berated him, as his father did. Where Nathan was always finding fault, Devorah was gentle, though firm. At night, sometimes Jesse heard her praying for him.

When Jesse was a baby, his mother had hidden him cleverly with Gentile women. Devorah paid them with her jewels and by mending their garments at night. She had lost two other boys before Jesse was born.

Jesse found his mother sitting in the doorway of their hut on a broken chair, half concealed in shadows, nursing the baby.

"Ima!" Jesse greeted her with a special smile.

"What happened to your face?" Devorah cried.

"Nothing, nothing. Just a slight fall." Jesse dipped a cloth into a crock of brackish water and wiped his face. He would tell her later about the quarry — or perhaps he would think of a way not to tell her at all.

His mother beckoned him to come near. She kissed his forehead and rested her hand momentarily on his hair, lustrous and curling and dark. His hair was her pride; her own was thin and dull.

Devorah smiled. "You brought us some vegetables! I can smell the onions and the peppers. I told your father I am going to kill that old chicken in the next day or two. If it runs about any longer, there will be nothing left but skin and feathers." She gave a snort. "He keeps giving them to the overseer, hoping for favors — what favors? Our deaths?"

"Now, Ima, don't be angry," Jesse soothed. "You will make my sister Shosha cry." The words "my sister Shosha" still sounded sweetly unfamiliar to his ears. The baby was seven months old, and beautiful, sucking with her tiny pink mouth, so perfect it looked as if it were painted.

His mother held the baby over her shoulder. A loud belch rang out, and they both laughed. "Here — will you hold her?"

"Not now, Ima." Jesse raised both hands. "I must go and find Avi and congratulate him on his birthday."

"Avi was here looking for you," she said. "He left a short time ago."

"I'll go then," Jesse said, but his mother stopped him.

"Wait, my son." She laid the baby down in her wicker basket. "I want to talk to you."

"Ima, let me go. . . ." Jesse began, impatient.

"Avi brought news," Devorah said. She motioned for him to sit down at her feet. With a sigh, Jesse complied.

"Avi says a stranger came into camp from the wilderness. He's been talking to the leaders — your uncle Rimon and all the others. He says he will redeem us."

Jesse took in her words. They only filled him with pain. "So, a stranger comes," he said heavily. "Others have come. We've heard talk of redemption. Pharaoh's walls have ears. Each time we speak, he despises us more."

"Wait! This is not the usual wanderer. This man is different. He speaks of wonders and miracles. He says —"

Jesse laughed. "Oh, yes, miracles, Mother. Is he going to drain the mosquitoes from these holes? Will he give us roofs over our houses, so that when it rains —"

"Jesse, listen. You must believe. We have prayed for help, and this man —"

"Spare me your prayers, Mother," Jesse cried. "I'm not a child anymore. How often I did believe. You sang me to sleep with your dreams. When morning came, there was the same mud and stench and always the whip. I can't dream anymore."

Devorah seemed to sag, her body falling to the side, breath whistling through cramped lungs. Jesse felt the bitterness he had unleashed upon her, but he could not stop. "My father is right about one thing: the Egyptians wipe their feet on us. We must bow our backs, or be destroyed."

"*My son!*" Devorah exclaimed incredulously. She stood above him. "You must love your captivity," she said accusingly. "How can you give up hope? This could be our only chance for freedom."

The last word was a cry. Jesse trembled. His mother had such faith. He hovered between contempt for that faith and utter amazement. How often she had spoken to him of Abraham, calling him always by the sacred name, "Abraham, our father," and of the promise that someday his descendants would claim their own land.

Now she appealed to him with reason. "Listen, Jesse, they say this man is quite old. Rumor has it that he even killed an Egyptian once, and fled to Midian. Would he, a wanted man, dare to return unless he were sent to —"

"Very well, Mother," Jesse said. "Believe what you will. I hope you are right." He paused, pondering. "What does Uncle Rimon say about this?" Avi's father, Uncle Rimon, was the head of their clan. It was Rimon who led them in prayers for redemption. If the time were ripe, surely Rimon would know it.

Devorah threw up her hands. "I don't know. He says — you know Rimon. Always has to be certain, to turn a thing over this way and that."

"I see." Jesse turned. "I'm going now, to Avi."

"It isn't only a matter of believing." His mother held him back. "It means that we must be prepared. If this is the plan of our God, Adonai —"

"But I *am* prepared," said Jesse. "I live a good life. I do my work. I'm learning a craft."

"With the Egyptians." His mother spat her contempt. Now he gleaned the purpose of this discussion. It had come up before. His father said he must seek every advantage the Egyptians offered. His mother disagreed. "You would have him sell his soul?" she had once cried.

"What good is his soul if the boy is dead?" his father had shouted back.

Now, remembering his new assignment, Jesse lowered his

13

eyes and bit his lip, much as he did with his taskmasters. An innocent expression usually paid off.

"I know there is a girl working beside you, a Syrian." His mother bent toward him. Her strength was gathered now in her voice and the set of her jaw. "You know what is expected of you. Your cousin Talia turns fourteen next month — the age of betrothal."

Jesse struggled to keep his demeanor calm. How dare she spy on him! How did his mother know his secret thoughts?

He retorted coolly, "I don't know any girl."

"They say she walks about half-naked. Don't take me for a fool, Jesse. I know what it is to be tempted, how young men desire foreign women."

"Mother, I haven't done anything!"

"It would be best for you to have other work," she said firmly. "We must find a way to free you from that household."

Fury rose in Jesse now, and he flung back the only weapon he had. "Don't worry, Mother," he retorted. "I won't be in the household of In-hop-tep any longer. I've been ordered to report to the quarry, starting tomorrow."

He strode off, struck by his own savagery.

Talia, as usual, was at her cousin Avi's house. With no sisters or brothers of her own, Talia had spent her childhood wandering from cousin to cousin, seeking playmates. The habit had not died as she became womanly, much to Avi's amusement. "She's smart for a girl," he always said, "and pleasant to look at, anyway."

Avi and Talia were outside, cutting and stripping reeds for Aunt Channa's basketry.

Avi leapt up, his face turning crimson, embarrassed to be seen at woman's work. "Jesse!" He clapped Jesse on the back so hard that Jesse stumbled forward.

"What a greeting." Jesse laughed. "Next you will knock me flat on the ground." He thought of the poor woman and her eggs, and then pushed the image from his mind as Talia called out eagerly, "Jesse! Cousin Jesse! Let me see you. Are you well? How is the baby? And your parents?"

"Very well," said Jesse. Talia seemed to have sprung into womanhood overnight. Her lips were full and red, her eyes lustrous. And she wanted him. He could see it in the quick flutter of her lashes whenever he came near. He was pleased, but also embarrassed.

His aunt Channa, to make matters worse, called out loudly, "Jesse! How is my handsome nephew? Come, I am putting a bit of pottage on the fire special for Avi's birthday."

"Many congratulations, Avi," Jesse said, with a touch to his cousin's shoulder.

He waited until he saw that his aunt and Talia were engrossed with their tasks, Talia with the reeds and Channa at the usual woman's drudgery, pounding straw and mud into mortar. All the women's hands were cracked and blistered from the work.

Jesse took Avi aside and whispered, "I have brought you a gift. I made it myself." He reached inside his waistband and brought out the gold buckle. It gleamed in his hand.

Avi stared at him and quickly grasped the buckle, his face reddening with pleasure and surprise. "What a handsome, worthy gift," he exclaimed. "But Jesse, how could you manage it?"

"I got caught," Jesse said quickly. "It means I have to work in the quarry."

"Those pigs!" Avi clenched his fists.

Jesse shrugged. "Maybe it will strengthen me. My mother says you came with news. Another prophet." He laughed.

A commotion interrupted them. The men, done with their labor, came into view, all walking with the same heavy gait, as if their legs were chained. They came to rest near a sparse growth of acacia trees. Uncle Rimon's voice rose above the others, and Jesse heard the word "treachery."

In accord, Avi and Jesse ran to the group of men, uncles and cousins and second cousins, an entire clan of relatives, distant or near. They squatted on the ground, and the circle widened to take them in. As youths, they were free to join and listen, but seldom allowed to speak.

Jesse sat down near his uncle Rimon. Rimon was strong and grizzled, with a curling beard and bushy hair. "Solid as a tree trunk," Devorah said of him. She was proud of her brother's leadership. Uncle Rimon reached out and patted Jesse's arm and smiled in greeting. The touch filled Jesse with pleasure.

Cousin Seth's eyes bulged as he spoke, and specks of spittle formed at the corners of his mouth. All his front teeth were gone. "We don't have enough to keep us busy here, day and night?" He pointed to Jesse. "Nathan, Jesse's father, is still at the pits, working all night because a load of bricks was smashed. Punishments we have enough."

Jesse felt sickness in his belly. How like his father to take the blame, to endure the extra labor.

Uncle Rimon tapped his finger to the side of his head. "This newcomer is sunstruck." He laughed. "Are we a flock of sheep to be led to the slaughter? *He* has nothing to lose. *He* is tight with the Egyptians. And besides, his father-in-law is a Midianite. He can always run back to them. We will ignore him."

"That's right," muttered the men. "That's right. We must keep ourselves low." They glanced about, uneasy.

"What are they talking about?" Jesse whispered to his cousin.

"The old man wants us to ask Pharaoh to let us go." Avi was breathing heavily.

"Go?" Jesse repeated. "From Egypt?"

"He says we can escape."

Jesse felt blinded for a moment, realizing he was looking into the setting sun. Everyone knew it was impossible to escape from Egypt.

Jesse looked at his cousin's face. It was flushed with excitement, and the eyes were wild with desire.

"This old man," Jesse said. "What is his name?"

"Moses."

And Moses was tending the flock of his father-in-law, Jethro, the priest of Midian, and he came to Horeb, the mountain of God. And the angel of the Lord appeared to him in a flame of fire out of the midst of a burning bush....

"Moses! Moses!"

"Here am I!"

"Do not come near. Put off your shoes, for the place on which you are standing is holy ground. I am the God of your fathers, the God of Abraham, Isaac, and Jacob. I have seen the affliction of my people who are in Egypt. I have heard their cry. Come, I will send you to Pharaoh, that you may bring forth my people, the sons of Israel, out of Egypt."

But Moses objected. "How can I go? If I say that You sent me, the people will not believe me. I speak poorly; surely You would choose a better man to speak for Your people."

CHAPTER  2

Even before she came fully awake, Jennat sensed that the time of anxiety was past. A gentle breeze blew through the open portal and across her room. The air was laden with the faint scent of lily and papyrus, surging with life.

Jennat turned and stretched on her mat, carefully lifting her head from the wooden headrest. She slept with no clothing, and only a thin cotton sheet for a cover. Now she wound the sheet around her body and went to kneel at the wide-open window as she whispered her morning prayer of thanksgiving:

> Hail to you, O Nile,
> Sprung from the earth,
> Come to nourish Egypt.
> Hail to you, Hapi,
> God of the river,
> Creator of all that is good.

Water birds chattered from the rushes. Yes, overnight the inundation had begun, and the dry season was now past. It meant life, food, and harvest, and river traffic.

Again last night, Jennat had dreamed of those dark eyes, Jesse's eyes. For weeks Jesse's gaze had become bolder, more scalding, until the day he took the buckle, challenging her outright to betray him. What did it mean?

Once, when they were working with several strands of gold, their hands had touched. Another time, as Jesse was leaving, she watched him running to meet another Hebrew, and she heard him laugh, and that laughter had filled her with a surge of joy.

When Sinuhe, the teacher, was occupied at the firing, or when he stepped out for a glass of beer, as he liked to do, Jesse would talk softly to her. At first his words only made her laugh. He talked teasingly, his body light and nimble and his eyes flashing with jokes. "Ho, now, last night I went down to the river, and guess what? The young crocodiles were dancing, yes, to the music of a lute. Come out tonight — you will see it. Listen, I will weave you a hat from the rushes, and maybe a skirt, too."

She had pretended to scowl and scorn him: "Ridiculous boy, what you won't do to get me into trouble!"

Later, there were serious moments. Small stories, whispers of hard times when the flood almost swept away the Hebrew village, when soldiers came crashing into the squalid hovels, looking for babies, for boys.

As he shared these stories, Jennat saw something new in Jesse's eyes. "They took our neighbor's little one," he whispered. "They carried him to the wall."

"The wall?" Jennat stared at him. She'd heard rumors, horrible stories, too ruthless to be true. "Surely you are mistaken. The Egyptians only try to protect themselves. They fear rebellion, so they must be wary. But I know they are not cruel men. They have children of their own. I have heard my master explaining it. . . ."

Jesse had only looked at her and murmured, "Poor Jennat. So innocent."

Now she had not seen Jesse for two weeks. The days dragged, days of anxious waiting, both for the river to swell and for Jesse to return.

Today the river lay swollen; perhaps it was an omen, and Jesse would be back.

By the gods, she must hurry! With the floods begun, her master would be ready to travel, and he had promised, this time, to take little Seti along. She must help prepare the boy.

Jennat rushed to the tiny anteroom, with its screen and bathing platform. She poured cool water into the heavy copper wash basin, inlaid with bright-colored faience beads, and she carefully washed her hands and face.

A moment's envy crossed her thoughts. Her mistress, Memnet, bathed from a washstand decorated with real gems — turquoise and green jasper. Jennat shrugged. It was true, she loved beautiful things too well. She must continually thank the gods for her good fortune, to be living in this household, as Memnet and even her dearest friend, Shepset, often reminded her. Jennat knew that her keep, even after all these years, depended upon Memnet's moods.

She had been found by In-hop-tep on one of his many travels, a burdensome half-Egyptian child trailing along with a peddler's caravan. The headman had sold her for two gold coins, glad to be rid of this skinny, sunken-eyed four-year-old, too young to provide either service or pleasure.

Now Jennat dried her face with a linen cloth, then rubbed her arms and feet with scented oil. Her hair, as she saw in the mirror, was still fairly neat, thanks to her care and the padded headrest. Still, Mement would insist that she have her hair dressed before the feast. It would take hours to achieve the perfect ripples and tiny braids that her mistress insisted upon.

Everything belonging to Memnet must be perfect, or one would rue the day!

Jennat dressed quickly in her tunic, adding a thin shawl to cover her shoulders. As a little girl, she used to run about happily naked. Memnet would show her off to her friends, crooning, "Look, isn't she pretty?" Then Memnet would enfold Jennat in her arms and pop sweetened nuts into Jennat's mouth.

Lately, if Jennat didn't rush to obey, or if a guest murmured praises, Memnet suddenly became enraged. "Get out of my sight!" she would scream. Jennat would run to the river for solace. Two choices seemed to beckon: to drown herself in the river, or to let herself be carried far away.

But then she remembered the adages learned in childhood: "Lucky the people whose king is Pharaoh! Serpent and dragon, creator and protector of the Nile . . ." Why, Pharaoh himself stepped to the shores of the Nile each morning and blessed these waters. Twice in her life Jennat had seen Pharaoh from a distance, resplendent in robes of gold, heavily encrusted with jewels. Remembering this, Jennat was lifted again to optimism, murmuring the refrain: "Lucky the people whose king is Pharaoh, god incarnate."

A commotion from the room across the tiny courtyard propelled Jennat outdoors. Eight-year-old Seti, with his black Nubian nurse, stamped his feet. "No! No!" he screamed. "I bathed only a few days ago — leave me alone. Father promised to take me to the ships with him. I must go."

Seti writhed in the nurse's grasp and, seeing Jennat, implored her, "Jennat, tell her to let me go. I'm to see the ships today, and if Father leaves without me, I will slice off my ear with a knife."

Jennat struggled not to smile at Seti's wild threat. "Look, Seti," she said patiently, "I'll go and find out when your father is leaving. I'm sure he is still in his quarters. He always takes a long breakfast and works with his scribe. Now, go quickly into the bath. I'll bring you some fruit and tell your mother you have already eaten. Then you will be sure to be ready when your father leaves."

"Very well," Seti said. "But you must bring my favorite," he said testily. "Plenty of figs — and a pomegranate, too."

"Certainly." Jennat smiled. Eight-year-olds, she knew, had to have the last word.

Still barefoot, Jennat pattered across the courtyard to the storeroom, where from the various baskets she took a handful of dates and one of figs, as well as two pomegranates. She sliced and arranged the figs and pomegranates on two flat plates, along with the dates and several biscuits. She hurried to bring Seti's breakfast, then to serve her mistress.

She found Memnet half reclining on her cot, holding a hand mirror decorated with a carving of Bes, the god of household and of toiletry. Behind Memnet stood her hairdresser, chattering as he deftly tied another small braid with a thin gold ribbon.

"Might be best to insert a small hairpiece there," the man said, pointing. "Quite the style, milady."

"You have already two pieces at the crown, haven't you?" Memnet said sharply.

"Indeed," said the hairdresser, proceeding with the next sectioned strand. "These pieces last forever, and one can't have too many, with the styles as they are."

"Jennat!" Memnet called, seeing her. "I'm starved. What kept you?"

"Forgive me, Mistress, if I overslept," Jennat murmured.

Memnet peered at Jennat, then back at her mirror. Her eyes were already painted with kohl, the dark blue lines intersected with a translucent green shadow. She took a biscuit

23

and a fig and consumed them quickly. "Where is Seti? Why hasn't he come to greet his mother this morning?"

"Nurse took him to bathe," said Jennat. "His father wishes to —"

"I know perfectly well what his father wishes!" Memnet snapped. She turned on the hairdresser, teeth clenched. "Stop it! You are tearing my hair out at the roots, man! Is this what you do, in order to sell me hairpieces, then?"

"Begging your pardon, Mistress," the man murmured, sweat breaking out on his brow.

"Finish that braid, and leave me be," commanded Memnet.

"But milady, the fashion . . ." stammered the man, for a section of Memnet's hair remained loose, curling slightly down her back.

"I will make the fashion here!" cried Memnet. Struck with that thought, she smiled. "Yes. Leave it so. You'll see that the other ladies will copy me." She waved Jennat to sit down at her side. "Am I right?" she asked, her expression triumphant. "What do you think, young one?"

"All the other women will copy you, Mistress," murmured Jennat. "It is very becoming. Your hair is thick and glossy. It sets off your fine skin —"

"Enough," said Memnet. "I don't need to be flattered." She put down her copper mirror and peered closely at Jennat. "I wish to speak to you, Jennat."

Jennat bowed her head. "Mistress," she murmured.

"You are fifteen," Memnet began.

Something in the pronouncement, and in Memnet's tone, sent a sudden chill across Jennat's body. She glanced up, wondering whether the sky had clouded over, but no, it was bright.

"High time for you to be given to a man."

"Mistress —"

"I am speaking!"

Jennat folded her hands together under her shawl and kept her head down. A man. She had not thought overly much about men, not until lately. Not until Jesse came into the household.

"I see you have washed and scented yourself already," Memnet said with a slight smile. "Come. You may use a bit of my powder to put some blush into your cheeks." Memnet leaned forward, and with a small spoon scooped some pink powder from her cosmetic jar, then brushed it gently into Jennat's cheeks.

"Not bad," she appraised. "I have decided," she said, "to give you the opportunity of a lifetime. I'm sure you will understand what this means to your future."

Jennat held her breath. In every life, she knew, there comes a moment of turning. Her friend Shepset had had such a moment when her father sold her to be trained as a dancer. Wait! she wanted to cry, needing a moment to compose herself. But Memnet continued, speaking swiftly, as was her way.

"I am giving you to your master, In-hop-tep, as concubine. This means you shall be the second woman in this household. Not a wife, mind you, but you shall have certain ... ah ... privileges. You shall move to the larger room, nearer your master, and you shall be dressed in a way fitting your new station. In-hop-tep likes women who are perfumed and adorned. I will give you Nurse's daughter for a personal servant. She will prepare you for your master, and she will help you when you ... uh ... you are growing with child."

Memnet paused, and Jennat held her breath, too amazed even to gasp. Dreamily Memnet went on. "You will give sons to In-hop-tep. You will pray to the gods to make you fertile. And I shall pray, too, and bring sacrifices, for as you provide

25

your master with babies, so shall I and my beloved little Seti be" — the last word was barely a whisper — "free."

Disconnected visions raced through Jennat's mind. Master! Concubine! Babies!

She could picture only In-hop-tep's knees, bony and coarse, and his hands, those long, clawed fingers that pinched and prodded and snatched whatever they wanted, without mercy or tenderness.

"Isn't this the long way around?" asked Shepset. "Why didn't we go directly to the perfumer's?"

"I thought it would be nice to walk by the river," replied Jennat. "It gives us more time to be together. Besides, my mistress wanted us to dig out some lotus blossoms, so they'll be ready for the festival." Jennat kept her voice low. The slave-boy walked several paces behind them with his baskets for packages; still, slaves often managed to eavesdrop and to trade information for special favors.

"Am I to dance for the party?" Shepset asked.

"Of course," said Jennat, glancing at her friend's lithe body and lovely face. "Memnet especially asked for you. We're having nearly a hundred guests, five musicians, six dancers, cakes and wine and meat . . ."

"All this for a little boy's eighth birthday?" Shepset looked amused.

"The birthday does coincide with festival time," Jennat said. "And Seti is everything to her. Memnet would keep him a child forever if she could. She makes plans, always, to keep Seti with her. Now she has even used —"

Jennat glanced over her shoulder; the slave-boy plodded on, heedless of their conversation. "She is giving me to In-hop-tep," Jennat whispered. "She plans to announce it at the fes-

26

tival. An auspicious day." A sudden ache caught in Jennat's throat, and she put her hand to her mouth.

"You'll be In-hop-tep's wife?" Shepset exclaimed.

"Hush, my friend! Keep your voice low. No, not wife. Concubine. You know what that means."

"How well I know!" Shepset said, clasping Jennat's arm. "You will be provided for as long as you live. Jennat, if you please him, if you bear him many strong children, he will buy you jewels. Oh, Jennat. I'd give anything to belong to someone!"

"Belong?" Jennat cried. "Don't you understand? My mistress wants me to bear all her burdens. She hates her husband's touch."

"How do you know that?" Shepset exclaimed.

"I see how she looks at him. In-hop-tep is old. Harsh. Sometimes, seeing me, he pinches me hard. For no reason."

"By the gods," gasped Shepset. "A pinch does no harm, even a beating — how well I know. Jennat, listen to me. You have a chance to be the second woman in the household of a wealthy man, a trader who owns ships and cargo. Everyone knows his name."

Jennat bit back the tears. "I thought at least you, my friend, would understand."

They walked a few steps in silence. Dust and mud collected on the hem of Jennat's robe. She pulled her shawl closer around her shoulders, covering her throat and breasts. From the corner of her eye she saw an occasional Israelite woman with a ragged girl-child, coming to the shops to trade with their meager produce and handicrafts.

"Look at them," said Shepset in a low tone of disgust. "They are so ugly — no jewels, and those clothes!"

"They are poor," said Jennat. "How can they help it?"

"They are ashamed of their bodies," Shepset said. "They

even cover their heads. The priests told me that they bring sickness, Jennat. You should stay far away from them."

It was true, the Israelites were a strange people, even more mysterious to Jennat than the Syrian or Sudanese visitors who sometimes came to In-hop-tep's house. The Israelites spoke their own language and taught their children stories about strange deities that nobody ever saw.

But Jennat muttered, defiant, "The priests don't know everything. I've heard that our soldiers don't let their boy-children live. I've heard —"

"Look, they are not like us," said Shepset. "They have children as readily as frogs lay eggs. To them, one more or less is not so important."

"How can you think that?" Jennat exclaimed. "Every mother loves her child!" But the words caught in her throat; she had never seen her mother. Perhaps she, too, had been simply abandoned at birth.

"Ah, you defend them." Shepset's long, dark lashes fluttered, and now she smiled slyly. "Tell me, do you miss that Hebrew slave who used to work beside you?"

"Don't be ridiculous," Jennat snapped.

"Before," Shepset continued, "you were always complaining. 'He looks at me! He stares at me like a hungry panther!'" Shepset laughed. "Don't be angry, Jennat. I'm only teasing. But tell me, is he really so handsome, this Israelite?"

Jennat felt her cheeks redden. "He looks like the sun-god, Ra," she whispered. "The one in the niche by the fountain outside the house. His hair is all wavy and shining."

"Oh, by the gods," said Shepset. "You are actually in love with this — this slave?"

"I'm only fearful for him," Jennat whispered.

"What do you fear?"

"I don't know. I had a dream. I was at the riverbank, and

28

there was a crocodile. It turned and spoke to me, quite like a human, and it said, 'I have swallowed him whole.' "

"What an extraordinary dream!" exclaimed Shepset. "What could it mean?"

"That he is in danger or — dead," whispered Jennat. Now she spoke what was in her heart. "I have this terrible feeling, Shepset."

Shepset stopped walking. A cluster of palm trees invited rest. "Sit down a moment," she said, settling herself on the ground. "It's so hot. What kind of feeling, Jennat?" Shepset reached for Jennat's hand. "Your hand is so cold!"

"I — I'm afraid," Jennat said, drawing her hand away. "Oh, Shepset, you must swear not to tell anyone." She glanced back and saw that the slave-boy was taking his ease, reclining on a low wall some distance away, waiting.

"I swear by Thoth, god of divine secrecy, may he smite me dumb and blind!" Shepset rattled off.

"All right," said Jennat. She leaned toward her friend and, breathing heavily, told her about the gold buckle. "If they caught him stealing, he could be" — she lowered her voice — "already dead."

"Sometimes it's only a matter of taking the right hand," said Shepset.

Jennat shuddered. "His hands are — amazingly gentle. Gentle and strong. The way he works with the metals ..." Jennat sighed.

"It sounds as though you are in love," Shepset said knowingly. "Listen, I have been there a dozen times, at least."

Jennat smiled slightly. "Love? Is that what you call it?"

Shepset tossed her head. "I cannot help it that my dancing arouses men. It is my talent."

Jennat gazed at her friend, graceful and limber as an antelope. It seemed true indeed, that the goddess Hathor had

29

given Shepset the special grace to turn men's heads, to make them generous when they came to worship.

Now Jennat recalled the look on her mistress's face when she had said her final words. "I want no more children, Jennat. I want my body to remain lithe and slim," Memnet had declared. "Jennat, take the oil and rub my feet while we speak. And be tender."

Jennat had knelt at Memnet's feet, rubbing in the warm oil, and she realized now that Memnet had wanted her to assume this slave posture, to remind her that she was already bound.

"You are pretty," Memnet had crooned, stretching her slim arms above her head. "And you are young. Even younger than I was when In-hop-tep married me. Already he gazes at you with desire. I've seen it. That makes it all the better for me. He will take you and gladly."

Now Jennat repeated it to Shepset, word for word. "My mistress will use me," she said bitterly, "to bear sons for In-hop-tep, so that she can keep Seti for herself."

"Be content, Jennat," Shepset whispered. "You are lucky. We must live for today! We are both lucky to be beautiful, to be desired. What about ugly girls?" She shuddered.

Jennat smiled at her friend. "You'll never have to worry about your looks," she said.

Shepset stood up, reaching for Jennat. "Come, let's go to the perfumer's, and afterward, we can buy some sweets for ourselves." Shepset reached into her belted tunic. "I was given some extra coins," she said flirtatiously, "by a very pious man!"

The stalls beckoned with their smells and sounds and the commotion of buying and selling. Beads and bangles and spices and furniture, painted bedsteads and chairs and mats, all attracted their gaze, and Jennat felt calm again, ready to enjoy the marketplace. Shepset was right: live for today!

"I will probably have a new gown for the party," she told her friend. "My hair will be done in a multitude of braids. I will have new sandals, maybe painted . . ."

They paused at the perfumer's stall and purchased the waxy scented cones, enough to fill two baskets to the brim. Then they moved to the stall where sweets were sold, and they viewed the baskets of honeyed nuts, the jars of stuffed dates, and the strings of dried, sweetened locusts.

A low murmuring rose to a higher pitch, a uniform groaning, intruding upon Jennat's thoughts. She looked up. Across the road, now approaching the river, came a small band of laboring men, bent under the overseer's whip.

The male slaves toiled with boulders, six men tied to one stone, straining like beasts, their mouths open, tongues hanging out. Daily they hauled the huge boulders to the Nile, where they were cast upon rafts to be towed upriver, building materials for Pharaoh's citadels.

"What's the matter?" Shepset asked sharply. "You look as if you'd seen a cobra."

"I — nothing. It's just the — Israelites."

"Don't watch," said Shepset. She selected several honeyed locusts and held one out to Jennat. "Here. Enjoy it. Look, Jennat, you can't let everything bother you —"

"I —" Jennat began to walk as in a dream. It was one of those moments of premonition; perhaps the gods had indeed led her here today. Now, as she took a step forward, then another and another, it seemed so.

Even from this distance, she knew it was he. His body was bent nearly double, the muscles of his back rippling with the enormity of his effort. For a moment Jennat thought she had deceived herself; all men in toil look alike.

Then his head lifted. His eyes, once large and gleaming, were small slits, puffed with weariness, the flesh around them reddened, perhaps from blows.

"Jesse," Jennat whispered.

Suddenly something broke. An iron counterweight had torn loose somehow, and was hurled up into the air, striking Jesse. In the next instant, he lay on the ground, blood pouring from his skull.

The overseer, Meri-Aten, gestured and raged at this delay. Dockworkers and quarrymen rushed to the victim. Someone loosened the ropes from Jesse's shoulders; someone else ran for water.

"On with it!" shouted Meri-Aten, willing to let Jesse bleed to death on the ground; he could be replaced.

"Quick!" Jennat shouted to the slave-boy, her fist raised in the gesture of command. It was a sign she had never used before in her life, and her tone, too, was strange in its severity. "Go and fetch the master's physician. Go!"

The slave-boy stared at Jennat, dumbfounded. He mumbled, "Master's own physician, for a Hebrew?"

"Don't you dare to argue with me!" Jennat shouted. "I am to be second mistress of the household. Obey me, and hurry, or I will have you whipped until the blood runs from your back!"

She heard the catch of Shepset's breath. A new person, it seemed, now lived within her, a woman capable of anything.

CHAPTER  3

Pain pressed upon Jesse like a weight. The sky blurred. Sounds rang in his ears . . . the voice of a young woman, indignantly commanding, "Fetch the physician of In-hop-tep!"

Jesse glanced toward the sound, saw an angel in white, and thought he was dead, entering paradise.

He couldn't move. He lay in a pool of something warm and thick. Just before he swooned, he realized that it was his own blood.

It was dark when he awakened, with the cool of evening all about. Pain was his first awareness — in his head, ribs, shoulder.

He groaned, then heard the sound of scurrying feet, a cry.

"Oh, Jesse, you're awake!" cried Talia. "The physician said you might never waken again — I've been praying for you. The doctor said you must drink more medicine."

Talia went to a shelf, brought forth a beaker, and held it to Jesse's lips as he half raised himself from the mat.

"Drink," she said, watching him. Her eyes were puffed from lack of sleep or perhaps, Jesse thought, from crying.

"What is this?" Jesse asked, appalled by the color of the stuff.

"It will heal you. Opium and herbs and powdered crocodile."

Jesse braced himself against the vile taste, drank it down, and immediately felt relief from the buzzing in his head.

"Uncle Rimon came and prayed over you," Talia said. "We thought you were going to die. Your mother wanted to send for this new prophet, Moses, but Rimon wanted to come himself."

"My mother wanted Moses?" Jesse was astonished. "Is this man supposed to be a healer, then?"

"He has a staff, they say. It works wonders. You know how it is. Rumors fly." Talia bent over him and whispered, "If you had died, Jesse, I would have thrown myself into your tomb, as the heathen do."

Jesse shook his head. "How can you say such silly things, Talia? You sound like a child."

"I'm not a child," she replied, flushed and trembling. "My father was speaking to your father about us. Ever since we were little, I always knew that I would become your —"

His mother, Devorah, appeared suddenly, and she rushed to lay her cool hand on Jesse's forehead. "Jesse, you've had a terrible fever. It's broken now, praise Adonai."

Next, his father's loud voice rattled through the hut. "He's alive? Fool that he is, it's a wonder he wasn't tossed into the river to drown. Can't do anything right, even under the whip."

Jesse's father, Nathan, pushed Devorah roughly aside and squinted down at his son. "So you'll be flat on your back for a month, likely, and of no use to anyone."

34

"Nathan, the boy is hurt," said his mother.

"He causes these things," said the father. "It's a wonder he hasn't brought Pharaoh's wrath down upon us all. Didn't I tell him, time after time, to keep his eyes down, his head forward, and his thoughts to himself?"

"Yes, you told me, Father," Jesse whispered. Scorn rose, like a taste, into his mouth. He spat into a small linen cloth and saw the bloody stain. His father, it seemed, would rather have him dead. Well, once again, the old man had been defeated, Jesse thought with contempt.

"I'll bring you some broth," murmured Devorah, and she soon returned with a cup of hot soup. As she spoon-fed him, baby Shosha lay by Jesse's side, smiling and waving her little fists, and Talia sat nearby, watching.

"How long have I been ill?" Jesse asked, pushing away the cup at last.

"Ten days," said his mother. "Everyone has been here to see you — all the relatives." She paused. "Talia's mother sent this linen coverlet for you, and this cushion. You must visit them as soon as you are on your feet, my son."

"Yes, yes," Jesse said absently. Then a sudden warmth came over him, serenity mixed with joy. Jennat! Her name sang through his mind, even as Talia approached and laid her hand gently on his arm.

"I stitched this pillow myself," Talia whispered. She straightened the cushion under Jesse's head, and as she bent over him, Jesse breathed the essence of spices, and he felt a flash of attraction for his cousin. Still, his mind was on the half-Egyptian girl, how she had raised her fist and her voice for him. Even as his face burned with guilt, Jesse began to form a plan. He must visit Jennat.

Somehow, too, he must restore himself to the good graces of Jennat's mistress and be allowed to work with Sinuhe

35

again. Since early childhood, when Jesse had seen Egyptian ladies on the street, decorated with all their fine jewelry, he had been entranced. He used to lie under the reeds at the river, watching the way the wind touched the leaves, and he imagined forming such shapes in gold, bringing nature's magnificent variety into lasting, tangible form. How wonderful, to create things of beauty! He longed to work with gems, as Sinuhe did, to know how to gather the greatest luster from the heart of a stone, and how to make a setting to flaunt its unique spark.

Nathan had rubbed his hands together in glee at Jesse's good luck. For the first time, father and son had had the same goal. For Jesse, every day of learning from Sinuhe was a day of joy.

Still, his father goaded him. "Keep your eyes continually on the master, emulate him, work beyond his orders or his expectations," Nathan instructed him daily. "Learn! Make yourself valued. Someday, Jesse, if you heed what I tell you, you may even be called to work a design for Pharaoh. Listen to me!" and he would grasp Jesse by the back of the neck and give him a vigorous shake. "Even a slave like you can stand in the presence of the king!"

Jesse sat with the others, watching the flickering campfire. The flame was their signal to assemble.

Uncle Rimon stood before them, speaking softly, so that people had to strain to hear. Several men stood guard, watching for informers, spies whose betrayal could make life unbearable for them.

Rimon paced and swung his arms as he spoke. Jesse saw the deep frown between his heavy brows. "I know I was one of the first to discredit Moses. But I made a mistake."

36

Men whistled through their teeth, amazed.

Rimon's beard quivered. "It's a fool who never admits to a mistake," he asserted. "Look, I think we have to take this man Moses seriously. He says he can lead us out. He asks only for our patience."

"Another prophet," called out Jacob, an elder, with disgust. "How do we know he isn't another liar?"

"Each time he visits Pharaoh, he proves himself," said Rimon with quiet dignity. "Moses has courage. And he has a staff with which he can work wonders."

"So far the only wonder is that we are still alive," retorted Jacob. "We are Pharaoh's possessions. Life has always been hard, but at least we've known what is expected of us."

Aram stood up, fist raised. "This Moses is a deranged fool," he said. "He talks about seeing a bush that burns but is not consumed. I ask you, does this sound like a leader?"

"It could happen," Rimon said softly, arms crossed, firm. "Sometimes there are wonders, signs."

"We got such a sign!" shouted Yossi. "Now we must gather our own straw to make bricks, yet our quota is just as high as before. Our women know not a moment's rest. Is this our escape, then? To die of exhaustion?"

"Moses has a plan," Rimon responded. "He asks Pharaoh to release us, so we can pray in the wilderness to our God. Pharaoh refuses — it is part of the plan."

"Aha," cried Jacob, almost laughing. "Very clear. If he knows Pharaoh will refuse, why does he place us in jeopardy with his meaningless requests?"

"The bricks that took us an hour to make now take two!" cried a woman. "Soon they will use our flesh for mortar!"

Men leapt to their feet, grumbling and gesturing. "We all said we would remove ourselves from this rabble-rouser. You,

Rimon, said we must ignore him. Now I say we rout him out! Kill him! Get him from our midst!"

Rimon faced them all, his beard trembling, eyes penetrating. He had led them for twenty years; times of trouble brought all the men to his doorway for help and counsel. Now he stood before them, staring them down.

"You," he pointed to one, then another. "You always came to me. You trusted me. Rimon the wise, you called me, Rimon our father. Now hear me! I tell you, we lose nothing by holding our peace. Do you love being slaves so much? Is the whip so kind? Are your little ones so expendable?"

People averted their eyes and gazed into the fire.

"Listen," Rimon said, his voice enfolding them, cajoling, "I have seen this man Moses. I have looked into his eyes. Believe me, he is not an ordinary man. In his face there is humility so deep, so pure . . . and he speaks words that are plain, simple. Let him speak for us. What do we have to lose?"

"We can lose our very lives!"

Rimon walked before them, his stride long, his head bowed. Then he looked up and faced them. "Since I was boy," Rimon said, "I have prayed for redemption. All of you have taught your children the same prayers. They invoke the name of Abraham; they invoke the promise. Suppose the time of redemption is now. Suppose the prayed-for leader has come. And we expel him!"

His last sentence was a shout, falling over the group like the hiss of the master's whip.

He went on. "Moses is willing to risk his life for us. Don't you see? Pharaoh could cut him down in an instant, yet he does not. This alone must tell you that Moses has special protection. If it be true — and think for a moment's moment that it could be — then, if this man Moses is really sent by Adonai, how dare we resist?"

The fire crackled; the wind raised small clouds of sand around their feet and blew smoke into their eyes.

"Look," Rimon continued, his tone almost gentle now, "Moses is no stranger here. You all know his brother Aaron. His sister, Miriam, is a good and charitable woman. How many of you can thank her for helping to save your little ones? They say it is she who saved Moses as a baby — but that is neither here nor there. For now, I only ask that you wait. Make your bricks, gather your own straw, say nothing, but meanwhile, let us prepare ourselves. We must collect what food we can, strengthen ourselves, select leaders —"

Yossi rose again. "I say we heed Rimon. He has never betrayed us."

"Rimon has always been a good leader to the Reubenites."

"Rimon . . . Rimon . . . Rimon." They murmured his name; the mood changed. Jesse saw his cousin Avi standing among a group of men linking arms, calling their refrain, "Rimon . . . Rimon . . . ," and he envied his cousin that pride. His own father sat at the edge of the group, gossiping and taking gulps from a goatskin flask.

"Friends — clansmen" — Rimon lifted both arms — "we have little to lose. What's a bit of straw more or less, laid in the balance, against freedom?"

The word *freedom* held its own magic. All movement ceased; faces glowed with dreams.

"Now, a story for the children," said Rimon, relinquishing his place. "My sister, Devorah, will speak."

Devorah came forth, proud, her slim frame etched against the flickering light. The men shifted, and some left the circle entirely. Stories were for children; they had come for information.

Jesse watched as his mother took her place. She was the

queen of storytellers. When she spoke, all the children, and many of the adults, sat spellbound.

Devorah led the children in a song. Then she told of Father Abraham and his wife, Sarah, conceiving a child in her old age, then of Abraham's great-grandson Joseph, once a mighty man in Egypt, second only to Pharaoh himself.

"Joseph foretold our captivity," said Devorah now, her voice rising. "He also foretold our release, saying, 'When at last you leave Egypt, my children, bring my bones with you into the promised land of Canaan.'"

Jesse squirmed, partly from the discomfort of his rib, still not completely healed, partly from irritation. Devorah had always been a playful mother, different from the others. She used to make him giggle. She spoke of strange, magical things, so that at times he couldn't tell what was real and what was not. And now, this talk of redemption. What use were her fables? They only inspired false hope. He touched the side of his face, the tender scar.

As he grew older, Jesse used to argue with her. "If Adonai wants us to have our own land, why are we slaves in Egypt?"

"We can't always understand His ways. Our ancestors came to Egypt looking for food. There was a famine in Canaan —"

"But why did they settle here? Why not return to their homes when the famine was past?"

"They liked Egypt. They were attracted by its fertility and" — she frowned deeply — "its glitter. So we stayed — alas. Then it was too late."

Jesse knew the history — or was it a story? He could never be completely sure. The Israelites had been invited to remain in Egypt, Pharaoh's guests. After several generations, however, things changed. A new pharaoh feared the growing tribe of Israelites. They were clever; their women were most fertile. What if, in a war, the Israelites were to join Pharaoh's enemies?

Now Devorah told the same story, squinting, as if to see back to those distant times. "At first, we were welcomed here. Then came the usual conscription, the same as for all the other Egyptians, to work on the canals and the roads during the wet season. But a new pharoah came, who feared our numbers. Then the Egyptians put masters over us. They built special villages, with walls, to separate us. And then—"

"Jesse! There you are." Cousin Avi, panting, flung himself down beside Jesse. Since Jesse's accident, he had come to visit nearly every evening. "Are you well? Can you wrestle yet?"

Jesse grinned, shaking his head. "Don't dare touch me," he said, holding up both hands. "One embrace from you, and you'll crush my ribs again."

Avi glanced at the bright scar on Jesse's face, an upward line from eyebrow to scalp. "I see you've removed the bandage."

"I'll bear this sign for the rest of my life," said Jesse. "Pharaoh's gift." He grimaced.

"Well, the truth is, the accident kept you alive," said Avi. "Did you hear it? Three more died this week, collapsed from that labor. You would not have lasted another week, my cousin. Talia tells me you were worn to the bone when they carried you here that day."

"Talia exaggerates," said Jesse. "But I must say, she has been a good nurse to me, bringing me soup and cakes every day. But it was Jennat who saved my life, Avi."

Avi nodded soberly. "It is true. Nobody ever heard of such a thing before, the physician of a powerful man being brought to the side of a slave."

"I must go to her," said Jesse. "Will you come with me?"

Avi slapped his thigh and gave a laugh. "Ho! You're a bold

41

one suddenly. What are you going to do? Knock at In-hop-tep's door in the middle of a feast?"

"What about a feast?"

"Are your ears stopped?" Avi exclaimed. "Everyone knows it's the third night of festival, and the birthday of In-hop-tep's son as well. In-hop-tep is giving a banquet for a hundred guests."

"Ah, you see how my prayers are answered," said Jesse delightedly. "What could be better? Come, Cousin. My mother will be talking for hours."

"Can you walk so far?" whispered Avi, giving Jesse his arm.

"I'm going," said Jesse, "even if I have to creep on my belly!"

A dozen or more torches lit the courtyard. From a distance, Avi and Jesse watched as the young servant girls greeted guests at the gate, offering them lotus blossoms and cool drinks.

"Welcome! Welcome to the home of In-hop-tep," they called.

"Where will you find Jennat?" asked Avi. "What a fool's mission this is. You think she will come running out to meet you?"

"It's possible," said Jesse with a smile.

Jesse held his side; every breath brought a stab to his ribs. He moved behind a cluster of palm fronds, and Avi came beside him.

Several ladies appeared, laughing and talking. Behind them came serving girls bearing cups, capes, mirrors, and cosmetic boxes. The party would last until early morning, and each woman came prepared.

Strains of music drifted out. Men laughed, their voices expanding with the power of the wine.

"More wine!" someone called, and three male slaves, dressed only in loincloths, soon emerged from the courtyard, making their way to the storehouse.

Jesse flung off his robe and stood naked to the waist, his body gleaming in the torchlight.

"Jesse, you must be crazy," Avi sputtered, catching him by the arm, but Jesse broke away. The slaves returned, two of them balancing a huge keg on their shoulders, the third trotting behind. With a glance at Avi, Jesse rushed after them. One more young man in a loincloth would be all but invisible, Jesse thought, among this company of revelers.

The three moved inside the gate, threading their way between party guests, and once inside, Jesse stationed himself beside a pond decked with water lilies. He had never seen such splendor. Floral wreaths decorated the arches. Maidens with perfume cones in their hair walked to and fro, serving the guests. Several dancers hurried by, with bells on their ankles and wound into the many braids in their hair. The dancers' costumes were nearly transparent, and the girls were young and beautiful.

Through an open portal, Jesse gazed at the festivities on the women's side of the complex. Ladies sat at small decorated tables, alone or in twos, eating the delicacies that slaves heaped upon their plates. From a raised platform, half reclining on a couch, Memnet oversaw the proceedings, directing slaves and servants with a flick of her wrist.

Jesse allowed himself a sidelong glance. The slaves with the wine had disappeared. Aghast, Jesse realized that he stood alone in the courtyard, the only man among the still-arriving guests. He felt a hand on his back, fingers pressing deep into the flesh. "What are you doing here?"

43

Jesse whirled around. His heart clapped in his chest. It was Sinuhe, the master ornament maker, grasping him by the shoulder. His face and eyes glowed, obviously from an over-abundance of meat and wine.

"Mistress Jennat told me that you could no longer work in the household," he said. "A pity. You have a gift for metal-smithing."

"Thank you, Master," said Jesse faintly. He wondered what Jennat had told him.

"After you left," the man continued, "we had a little excitement. One of the Nubians was caught sneaking about — later I discovered that a gold ornament was missing. A buckle. We questioned the fellow — he lied, of course, but eventually he was made to confess." Sinuhe wiped his brow and smiled broadly. "It provides a good lesson for all the Nubians."

"Was the ornament found?" Jesse asked, barely breathing.

"No," said Sinuhe. "The rascal had thrown it into the river, by his own confession. Well, you must be back to work," said the master, and Jesse nodded. It was the first time an Egyptian had ever spoken to him thus, man to man, almost as if they were equals.

It made his heart pound and lift; he could imagine what it might be like to walk the streets with one's head high, to be free from fear.

But another thought sickened him. Whatever awful fate had befallen the Nubian, Jesse knew the man was innocent, while *he* was guilty. It's not my fault, Jesse told himself. Such injustice happened every day. It was part of life in Egypt. But he could not shake off his guilt.

"You idiot!" came the hoarse whisper, close to his ear. Jesse turned and saw his cousin Avi, now also naked to the waist, grinning at him. "What now? You are becoming quite the adventurer, little cousin," Avi said, admiration in his eyes. "You used to be afraid of every little thing."

"Now I am only afraid of big things," said Jesse grimly. A servant walked past with a tray of wafers and fruit. The man was suddenly racked with coughing, a common malady among those who lived near the river. The tray shook dangerously in his hands.

"Let me help you, brother," said Jesse, taking the tray from the shivering man.

"To the —," the man sputtered, "women's —"

"Certainly, certainly," said Jesse, bearing the tray high on his hand as he turned toward the women's quarters. He kept his head down. It would not do to be recognized by one of the usual household staff. In his thoughts, like a song, a single word repeated itself: *Jennat*. Jennat. He would find her somehow.

Until this moment he had not even admitted it to himself. He loved her. Why else would his heart be beating so? Why else did his legs feel like reeds bending under the wind?

He glanced about at the women, all talking, eating, laughing, some watching the dancers, some calling for their slaves to bring them sweets or to fetch cool water for their hands and feet, for the air was heavy with heat and drink and dance.

Where was Jennat? Jesse glanced toward the platform where Mistress Memnet now stood, clapping her hands and calling to her servant boys, "Go and fetch more water for our guests. Hurry! Everyone must be cool and comfortable before the next part of the show!"

Jugglers and acrobats stood at the side of the platform, waiting to be announced. "The jugglers! The jugglers!" shouted young Seti from his mother's couch. In his lap was a small dog, dressed in a bright-green vest and with a jeweled

45

collar around its neck. A birthday gift, no doubt, Jesse thought, one among many. He felt a surge of disgust at the sight of the pampered boy, his face and belly rounded from too much food.

"Let's have that tray. What's the matter with you, man? You're walking in circles."

Keeping his eyes averted, Jesse set the tray down and moved on. Jennat. Where was she? He heard a laugh, whirled around, but it was someone else.

And then he heard, ". . . given to the master. It is to be a surprise, a great secret, but Memnet and I are closer than sisters, and she told me Jennat will be given tonight."

Given? Given to In-hop-tep? Jesse felt dizzy and ill. He staggered out to the courtyard and slumped against the brick wall.

Avi approached. "Well? Did you find her?"

"She's not there," Jesse said dully.

"Look, we'd better get out of here."

"She must be in the anteroom, being prepared for —" Jesse could not get himself to say it.

"What room? What sort of preparation?" Avi, though he was older than Jesse, had never been inside one of the great houses and did not know the things that happened within them.

Slaves would bathe Jennat and dress her hair, then clothe her in transparent robes. Then they would bring her out, before everyone. All the men would gaze at her as if she were a prize calf or a she-goat. The men would laugh and joke, and In-hop-tep would claim his new possession.

Outside, Jesse leaned against his cousin. His face was coated with sweat, and his ribs ached with every breath. "Wait," he told Avi, trying to catch his breath. "I'll tell you in

a moment," he gasped. "You were right, we shouldn't have come."

Someone screamed. "Blood!"

The word echoed through the compound from every corner. "Blood! The water's all bloody, by the gods! The cup, the pail, the very river — all running blood!"

And the Lord said to Moses, "Take your rod and stretch out your hand over the waters of Egypt, over their rivers, their canals, and their ponds, and all their pools of water, that they may become blood; and there shall be blood throughout all the land of Egypt, both in vessels of wood and in vessels of stone."

And the fish in the Nile died; and the Nile became foul, so that the Egyptians could not drink water from the Nile.

CHAPTER  4

Trembling, Jennat allowed herself to be bathed and dressed, her hair brushed, and her fingernails painted.

"Beautiful," whispered Ipuia, the bronze-skinned young woman who was to be her personal servant now. "Mistress, see how your hair shines! Ah, your skin is soft and fragrant; your master will love only you. You will be the mother of fine sons; I shall pray to Hathor for you every night."

The flattery annoyed Jennat. But Ipuia would probably keep her promise. Jennat often saw her going to visit the temples.

Goddess of love, Hathor was Jennat's favorite of all the deities. Hathor's face was reflected in the ripples of the Nile, and her voice sang through the reeds, urging lovers to meet under the stars. Jennat had prayed to Hathor to preserve Jesse's life after the accident. "Let him live," she had whispered, and then, lost in sudden rapture, "Let him come to me." She had fixed her eyes upon the image of the goddess. The small idol seemed to burn the palm of her hand. Jennat held her breath. The goddess laughed, then whispered seductively, "What will you give me for him?"

"I shall make you a necklace of gold," Jennat had promised. "I shall give you the best of the meat, and fragrant smoke; I shall name my firstborn for you."

Blasphemer! It struck her now what she had done. She had not fulfilled her promises. She had not provided the gold necklace; instead, she had made an armband for herself. As for naming her firstborn... Suddenly Jennat saw it clearly. Hathor was punishing her for arrogance, for her failure to keep her promises. "Name a son for me? Very well! I will force you to have a son from a man you despise."

Jennat stood rigid while the servants arranged her gown and perfumed her hair. Near midnight Memnet appeared. She held out a small basket to Jennat.

"This is for you," she said, smiling.

Jennat gazed at her mistress, then took out the gift, wrapped in fine linen. Quickly she opened it and saw one of Memnet's own pectorals, of garnets and gold, a beautiful, costly ornament.

"Mistress!" she cried, falling to her knees in gratitude. "It's beautiful. How can I ever be worthy?"

"Give him his desire," said Memnet, still smiling, though her eyes were cold. "Each time you bear a child, I will give you a treasure. But if you do not . . . ."

Jennat held her breath, shaking her head against the thoughts that, if they crowded in upon her, would overwhelm her. She knew the consequence of failure.

"It is time," Memnet said, her eyes hard, lips firm.

Jennat hesitated.

"Come! Rise!"

"Mistress," Jennat began, "I — am not worthy." Words rattled out, unbidden, unrehearsed. "If you would consider — my service to you — should not be cut short by this. . . . Mistress!" she suddenly cried, dropping to her knees. "Let me stay with you. I'll serve you faithfully all my life. I won't ask for anything — just let me stay a maiden. Give me not to this man — I beg you!"

Jennat lay with her head touching the floor. She felt her body contract, as if she were an insect or an animal, but she didn't care. Sobs shook her now, and she became aware of a scurrying, a clucking of tongues as the other women — Memnet's friends, servants, and slaves — watched in amazement.

Memnet spoke. "Get up. Stop this nonsense. Any sane creature would be honored. Get up!" A sharp kick landed just below Jennat's breast, and another in her ribs, knocking the breath from her body.

"Get up. If I have to send you to him black and blue, so be it. I was wrong to give you these jewels. Creatures like you don't understand kindness. They told me so — my friends all scold me for being too soft. No longer!"

Memnet grasped the pectoral from Jennat and clipped it onto her own breast. "You'll get nothing until you earn it. Nurse! Prepare her."

Ahouri, the old Nubian nurse, her dark face crumpled and strained, wiped Jennat's face with a cool cloth. "Come, child," she murmured. "It's not so bad. It's the way of all women — you will be content — wait and see." Ahouri wore large silver discs dangling from her ears and a necklace strung with countless silver pins. She placed the flat of her hand on Jennat's belly, where a red bruise had formed. "Ah, gently now. You must learn to let your body go. Let it soar — do you understand?"

"Yes." Jennat breathed deeply, slowly, in and out. It was a trick she had taught herself many years ago, when as a little child in the caravan, terror overcame her. She would roll herself into a ball, eyes shut tight, then gradually unfold her body

51

beneath the sky, looking up at the stars, forcing herself to breathe slowly, deeply, to imagine that she, too, lay twinkling and safe against the black depths.

Ahouri brought a goblet filled with rich amber liquid. "Drink this," she crooned in her full, foreign accent. "It will help you to be calm. It may even give you . . . joy."

Jennat drank, feeling the coolness, then the heat of it.

"Drink it all, my mistress," said the nurse. "It is good."

Jennat sipped slowly, then faster, until the cup was drained.

Now Jennat raised herself, stretched out her arms, and lifted her chin. "I'm ready," she said, and Ahouri called her mistress.

Memnet took Jennat by the hand. With them came several of Memnet's friends. They smiled and blushed, charged with the drama of this event.

The small procession moved through the courtyard into the hall where the men were celebrating, the most important persons seated on couches, the others on floor mats at small tables, eating sweetmeats, clapping to the beat of the lithe young dancers, aroused by the wine. The smell of wine engulfed Jennat, and the strong scent of men's sweat, balanced by the perfumed hair of the dancing girls. Six girls bent their backs in rhythm, dipping their heads nearly to the ground, clapping small silver finger cymbals. They swayed and churned their hips and bellies. Their arms reached and beckoned; their eyes were bright. Jennat met Shepset's gaze. Her friend showed no sign of recognition; this was her profession, and she was good.

The beat intensified as Jennat approached the platform where In-hop-tep reclined upon deep cushions with several of his cronies. Three slave-girls stood behind them, ready to refill their goblets. Heat blazed from the men's bodies. In-hop-tep's eyes were lustrous with desire.

"Wife," he breathed, rising to meet Memnet, and he nodded and bowed. His cheekbones stood high, and his brows protruded sharply. "You bring me a gift to mark our son's birthday, to celebrate the festival."

Formally Memnet announced, "I bring you this young woman, whom I have raised to please you. May she be desirable to you. May she give you . . ."

A strange dullness came over Jennat, a dream state, as if she existed not in this place, but high above it, without feelings, without past or future, like a dragonfly pinned to the ceiling.

In-hop-tep reached out to pluck away the light shawl that covered Jennat. He would reveal her to his friends, much as he would display a fine new piece of furniture.

"Blood!" A cry rang out. "Blood in the river!"

Trays of food crashed to the ground. Guests leapt up and scattered. Servants fled in terror.

"Blood! Oh, the Nile is filled with blood. Merciful Hapi, save us from this plague!"

The air was heavy with the smell of decay. Dead fish floated upon the river and lay on the land. Dark froth formed at the water's edge. Servants ran far into the fields, digging for fresh water. What beer had been stored was dropping dangerously low. Thirst prevailed, and rot, and fear.

Without water, life slowed to a near stop. Ships stood at their moorings, listless. Work on the roads and monuments ceased; even slaves need water to survive. Braziers sizzled; nothing could be boiled. A pall of smoke hung in the sky.

Households fell silent. Without water to drink, words seemed too much of an effort.

Memnet sat rocking her son, Seti. At her feet, the small dog panted, its tongue quivering up and down. The little dog ran out and drank of the poisoned water from a pottery dish forgotten in the courtyard. Two hours later the dog gave a single, sharp cry, then toppled, dead, its legs up in the air.

In-hop-tep stood on the docks cursing the murky water. Day after day he entreated the priests for remedies. They argued and urged him, a man of wealth, to bring sacrifices to Hapi's temple, to purge the river of this plague. And In-hop-tep counted out coins and trinkets; he searched his wife's jewelry box and took away earrings and nose rings and bracelets and brought to them to the priests, and then he damned the priests as betrayers, for the river remained polluted as before.

In-hop-tep had run out that night with the others. Later, when he returned, Jennat lay in her bed, her body bunched together, tight. She had felt him looking down upon her. He pulled back the sheet. The night air assaulted her flesh. Then she heard his retreating footsteps.

Until dawn Jennat had lain awake, whispering her thanks to Hathor. She had been spared. Now six days had passed. Shepset, subdued, came to visit her.

"But they say that in the villages of the Hebrews," Shepset said, "there is fresh water."

"Nonsense," replied Jennat. "How could there be? They draw their water from the same river we do."

Shepset shrugged. "They have a new god. One who wreaks these punishments upon us. Why? Because we have sinned," said Shepset. "The priests say that Hapi was not given proper sacrifice this year. Do you remember how scant the presentations were? All of us are guilty, so say the priests. We do not pray with pure hearts. We think only of ourselves, not of the gods. We must humble ourselves, we must beg them —"

"I have prayed every morning and evening of my life," objected Jennat.

"Maybe you prayed for the wrong thing, trying to avoid your duty," Shepset said sharply.

"How do you set yourself up as my judge?" Jennat exclaimed. "You have nothing to worry about. Your life is fixed. You will always have a home in the temple, and you will be fed and pampered and adored. It's easy for you to criticize."

"I am only saying," Shepset retorted with a shrug of her shoulders, "that if each of us does her duty, the gods will be pleased. When they walked here upon earth, they kept everything in harmony. Now it is up to us. You should not have shunned your lord, In-hop-tep. He is a big giver to the temple of Hapi, a friend of the priests."

"You are blaming me for the blood in the Nile?" Jennat leapt up, biting her lips in her fury. "How dare you speak to me so?"

"Not you, not only you," Shepset cried, wringing her hands. "Don't you see? Everybody is forgetting the gods, learning new ways. We must cling to the old, the true —"

"Why would this Hebrew god want to punish us?" Jennat asked, settling herself down. She was too exhausted, too thirsty to argue. She picked a nearly dry pomegranate from a dish and began to suck the seeds. The sourness filled her mouth for a moment, relieving thirst.

Shepset replied, "They want to go into the wilderness to worship their god. Pharaoh, of course, won't let them. Why should he let his workers go?"

"So their god has punished all of us?" Jennat shuddered. "A vengeful, horrible god. What is his shape?"

"They say he has no shape or face, but is formless," said Shepset with a nervous laugh. "Can you imagine?"

"Odd, these Hebrews," said Jennat. "Primitive — a god without form? How can they speak to him?"

"Who knows? They are a tricky people. Their leader, Moses, has a staff that turns into a serpent."

"Ha!" said Jennat scornfully. "Pharaoh's magicians can do the same, I'm sure."

"The difference is, Pharaoh's magicians are kindly; they don't want to kill us," said Shepset. "I told you the Hebrews are dangerous, Jennat. You don't like to listen to me, but I mean only well for you."

Jennat shivered. In the past day or two, she had felt fever coming — a sudden burning, then chills. "I am listening to you now," she said. "If it's even possible that the Hebrews have caused this, then I say, let them perish, every one."

That night she was nearly asleep on her cot when In-hop-tep came to her. She heard his footsteps and the thud of his staff on the floor. Then she felt his weight beside her.

He spoke. She lay silent. He uncovered her. She did not move. The scent of him, foreign and acrid, filled her nostrils, made her gag. His murmurs changed to grunts and groans, and Jennat had visions of a snake encircling her body, squeezing the breath and the life out of her heart.

She gritted her teeth and pressed her eyelids tightly together. She raised herself up beyond pain. She clung to that vision of sky and star, until at last In-hop-tep left her alone.

Then she slept, defeated and exhausted.

Presently, from the depths of sleep, she felt a sensation, a stirring, and she jumped, fear clawing at her heart. In-hop-tep — had he returned? Her hair, loosened of its braids by In-hop-tep's greedy fingers, now clung to her cheeks. Her limbs felt weak, her armpits wet. She half raised herself and heard a whisper.

"Jennat! Jennat!"

She knew the voice; she had to be dreaming. She poked her finger into her mouth and bit. Never, in dreams, is it possible to feel a bite!

Jennat leapt up and went to the open window. "Yes?"

"It's me. Jesse."

"Jesse? The Hebrew? Go away!" And yet the pain in her chest was not from rebuke or hatred, she knew. It was that sweet pain of relief and longing. Suddenly what In-hop-tep had done to her body didn't matter so much — or at least the horror of it was diminished.

"I came to see whether you are well. I'm told there is no water here." Jesse held out a goatskin flask, cool and firm.

"Water?" Jennat's voice rose nearly to a squeal, and Jesse laughed and hushed her. "Drink," he urged. "It's all for you."

Jennat drank. The cool water soothed her throat and filled her with gladness. She felt wide awake for the first time in days.

"Will you come out?" Jesse whispered. "I must talk to you."

"Must?" Jennat smiled to herself, feeling powerful.

"Please," Jesse whispered. "Only for a moment. Nobody is about. They are all sleeping. I've been waiting for hours."

Jennat pulled her robe close and climbed out the open portal. The grass felt cool against her bare feet. The evening air was light with breezes, and now that her thirst had been slaked, Jennat wanted to laugh and run.

Outside in the courtyard, she turned and slipped through the gate, then ran and ran, not toward the river, which had always been her sanctuary, but up the small incline where two sycamore trees grew, and where she could look down upon all that belonged to In-hop-tep, as if she were the victor and he only a slave.

Gasping, holding his side, Jesse followed. Jennat stood leaning against the tree trunk, laughing. "You run like a wounded hare," she said.

"I am a wounded hare," he replied, smiling slowly.

"Oh. I forgot. Are you feeling better?"

"Now I am," he said, staring at her. She could see him clearly by the light of the moon. There was something magical about being alone together.

"Why did you come here?" she asked.

"You saved my life once," Jesse said. "Also, I wanted to see you. I was here the night of . . . the festival. The night the river turned to blood. I had hoped—"

"You were here? What did you see?"

"Enough. I know that you were to be given to In-hop-tep. Jennat"—he looked away—"has he come to you?"

"No!" she said in a high voice. She shook her head. Then she covered her face, for tears streamed down her cheeks.

She felt Jesse's hands on her face, brushing away the tears. He kissed her fingertips, her hands, and he moved to place his mouth upon hers, but she turned away, her heart pounding violently.

Nobody had ever caressed her before. Perhaps as a baby she had known her mother's touch, but she could not remember. This new sensation filled her with alarm and excitement, and partly she wanted to run away, to plunge into the river to become cool once more.

"Jennat, I came to warn you," Jesse said. "Bad things are upon us, and worse things may yet happen."

"Why?" Jennat pushed away from him. "What have we done to be punished so? Why is your magician, Moses, making us miserable?"

"It is not Moses," Jesse said. "Jennat, I don't understand these things. They say Moses asks Pharaoh to let us go, and Pharaoh refuses, so these plagues come to teach Pharaoh —"

"Who teaches Pharaoh?" Jennat cried. "Pharaoh is our lord here on earth! How dare anyone come before him?"

"I know only what I hear. Half my people say Moses is crazy, and they want him gone. The other half say Moses is powerful and has come to save us."

"Save you?" Jennat exclaimed. "From what?"

"From . . . this," Jesse said, his hands outspread, following her gaze to the houses and fields and canals below. "From being enslaved. They say we can be free, with our own land —"

"Nobody is free," Jennat argued, twisting away from him. "What a strange idea. We are all servants of Pharaoh, just as he is the prime servant of the gods. Without this order, how could we live?"

Jesse shrugged and frowned deeply. "I don't know," he said. "But my mother says our God meant for us to live in our own land."

"But why would anyone want to leave Egypt? The river is our life, our strength. The land is so beautiful."

"Yes," Jesse breathed, staring at her. "It is beautiful."

"All the temples are here," Jennat went on. "The gods live here. Why would anyone want to leave their protection?"

"Jennat, we have our own God."

"Then bring him here, and stop this nonsense!" she snapped.

"He does not live in our pockets," Jesse said. He nodded toward her gown, knowing she kept a small idol tucked in her waistband, as most Egyptians did.

Jennat laughed. "Then where does this one live, the one you are running to?"

Jesse shook his head. "My mother says He lives wherever

we dwell, and also within us. She says that He governs all things, the affairs of heaven and the earth —"

"Oh, yes, I heard all about that," said Jennat. "No shape, no face. Jesse, how can you believe such nonsense?" She put her finger to her lips, as if to cancel her own laughter. "How could a single god do everything alone? It makes no sense at all."

"He is powerful," Jesse replied.

"Then ask your god to cleanse the river!"

"I can't," Jesse said.

"Because yours doesn't really have any power," Jennat snapped.

"Look, I didn't say I'm a great believer — I tell you only what I hear, and I tell you it might get worse, and I came to let you know I will bring you water, and even food if I can. I don't want you to suffer."

"Don't talk about things you don't know," Jennat said, quoting Shepset, even imitating her stance. "Who is suffering? Not I."

"Good, then," he said, his arms folded across his chest.

"Look, Hathor has power."

"My mother says that the things we make with our own hands have none."

"Of course they do!" cried Jennat. "How else does the world remain in balance? You will be punished, Jesse, for these words and these thoughts."

"I will not be punished. Look, I am here with you — this is not a punishment." He laughed. "Come," he said. "We'll go and find some pomegranates. I know where there is a fine grove."

"They are gone," said Jennat, sullen. "Since your evil magician ruined the water, all the trees are stripped bare."

"It was not a magician," Jesse argued. "It was our God, Adonai."

"If this is true," said Jennat, her eyes narrowed, "how can you worship such a cruel being? The children are sick. Poor Seti hardly moves from his couch."

"Look, you know nothing about cruelty," Jesse retorted. "The Egyptians have killed our children for years, drowned them in the river, bricked them up in the walls."

"That's a lie!" Jennat cried. "It's just what the Hebrews say; there's no truth to it at all!" Angrily Jennat confronted him. "You claim power for your god, and none for mine. Well, if Hathor has no power, how did you come to me tonight?" Immediately she put her hand to her mouth, as if to push back the words.

But Jesse had heard, and he grinned and let out a low sound, like a cat that licks itself, fat and satisfied. "So you wanted me," he said. "You even prayed for me! Here I am, fair one!"

He spread his arms and walked toward her. An image of In-hop-tep flashed in her mind, and now the full knowledge of what men called by the name of *love* assaulted her. Her stomach rebelled, writhed, and she doubled over, sick. She glared at Jesse, sputtering, "Leave me alone. *Leave me alone!*"

"Jennat! Forgive me, I didn't mean . . ." He sounded so sorry that for a moment Jennat thought she could forgive him anything, even his maleness.

But no. He was the enemy, in more ways than one.

Jennat grabbed the goatskin flask, and with it she ran down the hill.

Frogs began to climb out of the river. They leapt upon the land, swarmed into houses through doors and windows. Frogs infested the food bins, clung to the walls, laid their eggs and multiplied. One could not set down a foot without stepping on a frog. Frogs jumped into people's beds, wet, slippery, stinking frogs.

Jennat shuddered with revulsion. She clung to little Seti, who screamed his terror of the frogs and would not be comforted.

After the frogs came the lice.

And Jennat hated the Hebrews and Moses and Jesse for these plagues.

CHAPTER 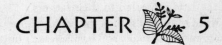 5

Lice rose out of the very dust, invading clothing and mattresses and bins of flour. The vermin appeared in people's hair, under their fingernails, in all the creases of their bodies. Peasants suffered as much as princes; even Pharaoh's household was infested with lice.

Daily, spies carried the news, buzzing and humming into the waiting ears of the Israelites. Everyone knew what was taking place behind those walls where Pharaoh and his ministers and magicians met with Aaron and Moses.

Moses and Aaron, the two old men, pleaded, argued, threatened. To threaten Pharaoh! It was a wonder that Pharaoh allowed them to live. For days, weeks, and months, they pleaded. "Let my people go to worship their God in the wilderness. If you do not let them go, Adonai will send yet another plague." And Pharaoh, hard, would reply, "I know not this God of yours, called Adonai. I am the lord and power here. Get thee from my sight."

The Israelites watched from their houses; all work on Pharaoh's storehouses and cities had ceased. News traveled from mouth to mouth, swifter than flames in dry brush: "Moses is meeting Pharaoh by the river to give him warning," and then, again and again and again, "Pharaoh refuses to let us go."

Several of the leaders, like Uncle Rimon, had discovered Moses' true intention: once Moses got the people out of Egypt, there would be no returning. They would go on to Canaan, the land promised to their fathers.

A dry wind moaned through the leaves of the two tamarisk trees that grew in the rocky soil beside Jesse's hut. His parents and Talia's parents, Efrem and Shira, had been talking for hours. They were joined by several distant cousins who listened silently. Devorah's face was all but concealed by the head scarf she wore, and her eyes peered out brightly, as from a cave.

"Every time Moses speaks with Pharaoh," muttered Efrem, "things get worse for us."

Talia sat beside Jesse's mother, shivering. She had grown thin, Jesse observed, and her eyes were ringed with dark shadows. Her parents, Efrem and Shira, occupied a stone bench, low to the ground. They were oddly misnamed. Efrem, whose name meant "fruitful," was a dried-up twig of a man with a small, slim face. He constantly chewed bits of straw and bark. Shira, whose name meant "song," had a voice filled with complaint. Her arms were cushions of flesh, and she panted at the slightest effort. Now Shira scratched the folds of her arms, behind her ears, under her breasts. "This pestilence!" she whined. The lice that had infested all of Egypt did not stop at the boundaries of the Israelite homes; everyone itched. "The decay of fish and frogs," she wailed, "has spawned these vermin."

"No," said Devorah quietly. "You know better. It is Adonai, punishing Pharaoh."

"Why does he punish us also?" wailed Shira, scratching her head.

Jesse stiffened. Jennat had made the same accusation.

"How can you worship a god so cruel?" The taunt left him no peace.

"Lice have no brains," scoffed Nathan. "They keep no boundaries." He slapped at the back of his neck.

"You must bathe yourselves twice a day," said Devorah calmly. "Use balsam and camphor leaves."

Shira sniffed, unconvinced.

"It will soon be over," said Jesse's father, Nathan. "The question is not whether Pharaoh will *allow* us to go, but whether we will follow."

"You mean the community will be divided?" exclaimed Efrem.

"Since when have we all agreed on anything?" Nathan asked with a laugh.

Jesse shuddered. It had not occurred to him that there might come a moment of choice. He glanced at his mother. In the dim light of moon and stars and a single torch, Jesse could see the white cotton thread of his mother's spindle whirling faster and faster as her words flew out.

"For now we must be patient," said his mother. "When the time comes, we must act quickly, without looking back. You know the story of Lot's wife," she said. "It is the story of our people. When Adonai calls, we must be ready."

"What, leave everything behind?" wailed Shira. "I am not so brave, Devorah. Nor so foolish. What if we find nothing to eat and try to return here? Someone else will have moved into our houses; what little we have scraped together will be stolen."

"Well, I saw Miriam today," said Devorah, vigorously tugging the thread into a ball. "She says we must not lack faith now." Her voice rose, and she brushed back the cloth from her head, exposing her wide, clear forehead. "It is a precious moment. If we miss it, this chance will never come again."

"Talia is my only child," murmured Shira, "the light of my

65

eyes. Shall I bring her out into the desert, to die there? At least here we have food. Can you imagine what it is like to have no food for your child? What about you, Devorah? What will happen when your milk dries up, and your tiny Shosha cries from hunger — what will you do?"

Talia went to stand behind her mother, with her hands encircling her mother's face. It was a childlike, tender gesture that made Jesse's eyes sting. He reached for his little sister, Shosha, taking her from their mother's lap. Devorah glanced up at Jesse, smiling slightly, then she continued, her voice low but resonant.

"What is our future here, in Egypt?" she demanded. "Here, nothing changes."

"Only from bad to worse," said Efrem in his taciturn way. He changed his opinion as often as the clouds turned in the sky.

Jesse's heart plunged. Traitor, he accused himself. He could sit here among his kin as if he were loyal, when he had been going day after day to Jennat, bringing her water and food and balm for the sores that the vermin inflicted.

Gradually Jennat had warmed to Jesse and learned to trust him. They talked. They argued, and she was aghast at his suggestions that her idols were mere clay. But then he would make her laugh, and several times he had coaxed her outdoors in midday, when everyone was asleep, and they had gone for a dip in the Nile, which was once again fresh and clear.

Her master, In-hop-tep, had claimed her, she finally confessed haltingly.

"Curse him!" Jesse had shouted, sickened with rage.

Jennat's eyes glittered with unshed tears. "It doesn't matter," she said defiantly. "He has my body — I have my own thoughts."

66

"Your thoughts," Jesse whispered. "Do you think of me, Jennat?" He felt overcome with love and longing.

"I think you are like a wild hawk, you come and you go — what if In-hop-tep sees you speaking to me? What would I say?"

"Are you still working with the ornament maker?" he asked.

Jennat nodded. "It is my one pleasure, and my master allows it. He even speaks of trading my creations — a bracelet I made, with turquoise inlay."

"If I were a student again with Sinuhe," Jesse proposed, "we could be together again every day."

"You expect me to arrange that?" Jennat exclaimed.

"If you wish it," Jesse said. "Wouldn't your master grant you one small wish — an assistant, to help with the heavy work, firing up the furnace, polishing stones?"

So Jesse had laid his plans to draw nearer to Jennat, even while his family spoke of escape.

Nathan held up his finger for attention. "We have to move very, very carefully," he said. "Let's not rush into something. Aaron drips honey from his mouth, but don't forget, he is a priest — he knows how to win a crowd."

"I never trusted Aaron," said Shira, scratching her head. She picked out a louse and cracked it between her fingernails. "These priests only want a following. And what have they done for us all these years?"

"At least here we know where our food is coming from," said Nathan, nodding, "and we have a place to lay down our heads. If we are cunning and watch the masters, we can rise to high position. Jesse, my own son, can tell you how it was in the household of In-hop-tep."

Jesse realized that all eyes were upon him now, according

him respect. The name In-hop-tep carried weight. "It's true," he murmured. "It was a splendid house."

He heard his mother's sharp intake of breath.

"Here we know what we have," his father continued, gesturing strongly. "In the wilderness, where Moses is so eager to lead us, who knows what wild beasts and evil men will fall upon us?"

"What is so wonderful, suddenly, about Egypt?" Devorah cried. "Have you forgotten all our pain?" She clutched her hands underneath her chin. "For years we prayed and cried out, we sat together just like this, in small circles, dreaming of deliverance. And now — now that it is at hand, you waver and yammer, 'Egypt this! Egypt that!,' blaming Moses and Aaron, even finding fault with the plan our God revealed to us. How can you forget our destiny?"

Jesse held his baby sister close against his chest. She smelled sweetly of the ointment his mother had prepared, and, amazingly, her skin was clear and smooth. He felt torn between his mother's passion and his father's caution. Every day the battle between them heightened, and also the battle within Jesse — to go or to stay, to dream or to submit.

Jesse breathed deep, filling himself with courage. He seldom spoke out when the adults were assembled, but his father had drawn him in. "When I was working in the home of In-hop-tep," he said, "I found out that the Egyptians are willing to let us work beside them if we want to learn. They think of us as arrogant," he said, "unwilling to learn their ways."

"Their ways are foreign, evil," cried his mother, but his father broke in.

"Exactly! I have always said, we must learn to survive, wherever we find ourselves. The place is not important. A person of cunning can rise to high position anywhere."

"Like Joseph, our ancestor," said Jesse. "You told us the

story, Mother, how he became viceroy, highest in the land next to Pharaoh." Jesse felt his mother's eyes upon him, felt her fury, yet he did not retreat. For the first time, he knew the strange joy of being allied with his father and saw his father's gaze of pride. "The Egyptians need us," Jesse concluded.

His father nodded and beat his fist into his hand, "Yes! Yes, of course they do," and his voice rang with confidence, almost as authoritative as Uncle Rimon's. "Let our kinsmen go. Send them away with singing! Those few of us who remain will rise in importance. You'll see how their bearing toward us changes when we are few in number."

"They will appreciate us," said Efrem with a dry cough.

Jesse took a long breath and said, "And maybe now that Pharaoh has seen Adonai's might, he will treat us better. He will never kill our boy-children again."

They all fell silent. This was the crux of their pain: the murder of their sons. They could live with labor and hardship — these existed everywhere. Jesse was struck with his own clarity, ashamed and exhilarated both at once.

"You think . . . ?" Efrem began.

"My son is right," said Nathan proudly, clapping Jesse on the back.

Devorah broke off her thread. The spindle lay still in her hands. "When the time comes," she said quietly, "we will go."

Nathan rose. "Since when do women make such decisions?"

Shira spoke out weakly. "Caution doesn't mean lack of courage," she whispered. She drew Talia close, stroking her hair as if she were a baby.

Devorah threw down her spindle. The ball of cotton thread rolled to the ground, gathering dirt. "Betrayers," she spat. "I'm ashamed of you all."

"Listen, woman," Nathan snarled, not to be outdone in front of the others, "you are a storyteller, a dreamer. When Adonai speaks to me personally, then we'll talk."

In the night, strange ideas circled in Jennat's head, like buzzards circling meat. Plagues were part of life. They were the punishments of the gods for deeds left undone, or for evil thoughts, or simply the consequences of the gods' own petty rivalries.

Every child knew this. Seth, for instance, the Egyptian god of darkness and storms, always liked to cause havoc. It was useless to question the dealings of the gods; they simply acted, and it was up to mortals to figure out how to appease them.

Jesse had said that his Adonai was different. He had laughed at her small idol, calling it mere clay, "mouth without breath, body without heart!"

So Jennat had even tried praying to this invisible deity of Jesse's. Why not? She prostrated herself and promised obedience and savory smoke. But still little Seti was terrified, and still the plagues continued — some attacking the animals of the field, so that their dead carcasses lay abroad, bloated and covered with flies.

Talk continued — arguments, pleas. "Let the people go!"
"I am Pharaoh."

Hail came. It ruined the standing barley crop and the flax. Hordes of locusts settled over the land, eating all the wheat and spelt.

One day, at dusk, there came a knock at the back gate. Ipuia went to answer, then ran to Jennat.

"It is a beggar woman, asking to see you, Mistress," said Ipuia.

Jennat, sitting with Seti, trying to divert him with a game of *senet*, smiled at the boy. "Think about your next move," she said, "while I go and see."

Jennat rose, sighing. Lately beggars swarmed over the land, many made homeless and impoverished by the plagues. She shivered. Jesse did not come much anymore; it was dangerous to go out. One never knew what to expect, the sudden onslaught of biting insects, or charging beasts, or boils that raised blisters on one's body. Each time Pharaoh had relented, promising Moses whatever he wanted "if only you will ask your god to take away this plague!"

When the plague was gone, Pharaoh went back to his old ways. Thus the kingdom teetered from one calamity to the next.

At the back gate Jennat saw the figure of an old woman clad in black, her face covered with a heavy veil.

"How can I help you, old mother?" Jennat asked gently, knowing she could give little, perhaps a handful of corn and a few drops of water.

"I have no place to go. They have banished me from the temple. My own mother won't bear the sight of me."

The stance was that of an old woman, but the voice... Jennat bent closer. "Shepset?" she whispered. "Is it you?"

Weeping followed. The woman's hands emerged from behind the black robe, blistered and scarred. "Don't look upon my face, dear friend," Shepset pleaded. "My hands are hideous enough. It happened all in a single night. In the morning, when I rose, I felt the scabs on my face, the pus running down, and then, I looked in the mirror —"

Shepset fell to the ground as she sobbed.

Jennat went to her. She took the disfigured hands into her own. Slowly, gently she pushed aside the hood and the veil. A cry caught in her throat, and she thought she would scream at the sight of this face, utterly changed now, encrusted with scabs.

"By the gods," she breathed. "Oh, my friend, you must come in to me. I will help you — come. No more weeping."

But even as she brought her friend inside, Jennat despaired of any way to hide her or to help her. Then she thought of Jesse.

CHAPTER  6

A strange sense of desolation lay over the land. After the storms came stillness, a quiet retreating, a slow rebirthing.

Hail had shattered the trees. Trees lay split in pieces, but within the damp bark grew fungus, and between the fungus crawled bugs and insects; larvae grew.

Jesse and Avi and their friend Omar picked their way across the fields down to the marshes. Occasionally they saw the skeleton of a cow or goat sticking out from a mound of sand.

The outing had been Omar's idea. Jesse was at first shocked, then eager — why not? Everyone had been confined far too long, experiencing or watching catastrophe. It was time for some fun.

"We'll go fishing," Omar had proposed, arriving with net in hand. "Maybe catch ourselves some baby crocodiles. Why not? If we're really going to leave Egypt, might as well enjoy some hunting first. And if not, we'll be back to work soon enough."

When Jesse told his mother he was going out, she gave him a long look, filled with reproach. Ever since that night of talk, when Jesse had sided with his father, her words to him had been sparse and peppery.

"If you must go," she said, "at least bring back something to eat."

"I always do," Jesse said curtly.

"The trees are stripped of their fruit," she complained, as if it were his fault. "The locusts have devoured everything. If the cursed Pharaoh won't bend, all of Egypt will be destroyed."

"The hail did not touch us," said Jesse, "nor the locusts."

"And still you would disobey Adonai?" his mother demanded.

"I do not disobey Him," said Jesse. "I only question — "

"Who are you to question? Scarcely more than a child — how dare you question your elders and even your God?"

Jesse turned. "Mother, I'm going."

"And stay away from that girl," she snapped.

"There is no girl," Jesse retorted.

She made a sound, deep in her throat. "But I heard you telling your father you want to go back and work for the Egyptian. What is the matter with you, Jesse? I don't understand you anymore," she said, pulling at her kerchief. "I can't control you anymore."

"The boy's nearly a man," called Nathan, striding past. "Going fishing?"

"Yes."

"Bring back food," said his father.

Abruptly Jesse had left.

It was a relief to be with Avi and Omar out in the open air, even though the land looked ravaged. It had been several months since the plagues began; everything had changed.

They went down to the marshes, alive with birds and insects. Barefoot, they waded in the cool water.

Avi pointed.

Jesse squinted past the leaves, into the speckled sunlight. A short distance away lay a sleek-coated hippopotamus. Something bobbed in the water. Beside the mother, a hippopotamus calf rose to the surface, letting out air and water with a mighty grunt.

The boys laughed softly. "Want to catch it?" Avi suggested. He raised his spear, ready for conquest.

Jesse hesitated. "No," he whispered back.

"Why not? It's great sport!" Avi rubbed his hands together.

Jesse shook his head. Too much death had left him somber when it came to killing as a sport.

"Let's get some fish for our supper," Jesse said. He waded out almost to his waist and lowered his net. Small silver fishes flashed beneath the water.

"How quickly the fish have come back," Avi exclaimed, lowering in his net. "No sooner was the plague of the river past, than the fishes reappeared. My father says this proves the miracle and the power of Adonai. Of course, I respect my father," he continued, "but they say Pharaoh's magicians were able to make the same wonders."

"Their staffs also turned into serpents?" Jesse asked.

Avi nodded. "They caused blood to flow in the Nile. They created frogs."

"Why would they want to cause more blood in the Nile?" Jesse asked, but Avi only shrugged, and Jesse wished he could spend time with Uncle Rimon and hear the truth.

Rimon was always occupied with meetings and making plans, going from house to house, relating events, telling people to get ready. What must it be like, Jesse wondered enviously, to be the son of such a man? He gazed at Avi, who was testing his knife on the reeds.

"Maybe magic looks the same as a miracle," Jesse said

thoughtfully. "If I knew the right words and the right ways, maybe I could make a frog spring out — but it would be different from a miracle."

"How so?" Avi asked. "The important thing is the deed, not the way it's done."

"I don't know . . . ," Jesse murmured.

Omar cried out, "Yii!" A large fish flipped and struggled in his net. Omar seized the fish with both hands, pulling it from the water. The fish fought and writhed.

With a quick motion, Omar struck the fish on the head with a rock. It flipped once more, then died.

"Let's cook it," Avi said.

Jesse's stomach growled. He and his family had food; their goats still produced milk, and their gardens yielded a little, and they had stored up grain for bread and beer, the staples of life. They had learned this lesson well, from Joseph, their patriarch. Store up grain in times of plenty; then in the lean years you will survive.

Still, survival usually meant that one's stomach grumbled much of the time and hunger lurked in one's dreams.

"I'll pull some wild onions," Jesse said. "And I brought a goatskin of beer."

Omar laughed approvingly. "Good. We'll have a feast."

"Avi! Jesse!" A voice rang out from behind a screen of rushes, a girl's voice, fresh and eager. "Where are you? Listen, I know you are there — come out!"

Avi laughed and rolled his eyes. "It's Talia. Just like when we were children — she followed us."

"Here!" called Jesse, half annoyed, half pleased when she emerged, her face wet from the dew that still clung to the rushes, her cheeks flushed.

"Uncle Nathan told me you'd gone fishing," she said, her

eyes upon Avi, then sidelong at Jesse. "Hello, Omar," she said, as if she had not seen Jesse at all.

"Hello, Talia. You're just in time to clean this fish for us." Omar laughed as he held it out to her, tail first.

"I eat what I clean," said Talia.

"Then we'd better catch more fish," Jesse said, picking up his net. Talia lifted the hem of her skirt, ready to follow him into the water.

"Stay on shore," Jesse said brusquely. "You shouldn't get wet."

"Why not? Girls don't melt."

"Stay there," he said. "I'll toss you some fish." And so saying, he scooped up a net full of five little fish and tossed them at her. One smacked her on the side of the face, so that she ran, squealing, to the others.

Laughing, Jesse gathered up his small catch of baby catfish. "I'm sorry," he said, smiling at Talia.

She smiled back. "Thank you for the fish," she said demurely.

Jesse sat down, hands clasped around his knees. Talia stood behind him. In the next moment he leapt up, feeling something cold and slippery down his back — and he knew instantly, as he yelped and lunged after Talia, that it was the fish head and entrails, odorous and sticky, with which she had repaid him.

Screaming, laughing, worn out from the chase, Jesse and Talia finally sat down with the others. Jesse's chest heaved, and he felt refreshed, young again.

Omar and Avi had made a small fire and set the fish upon a hastily made grid of green sticks. While they waited for the fish to cook, they sipped the beer in turn and chewed the sweet, pale slabs of palm heart that Avi cut from a fallen tree.

When the fish were done, Omar carefully divided them into portions, placing each on a large leaf. A flock of wild geese rose from the reeds, beating their wings and crying out as they took flight.

"Do you know," Jesse began, chewing the savory fish, "we have never had such a peaceful hunt as this."

"Delicious," said Talia, nibbling at the crisp skin.

"It is true." Avi nodded. "Usually some Egyptian thugs would be upon us, taunting and looking for a fight."

"You men are lucky," said Talia. "You can fish and hunt anytime. The Egyptians take their wives and daughters with them to fish. Why don't we?"

Omar's eyebrows lifted in surprise. "You are admiring the Egyptian ways?"

"I suppose there is some good in them," retorted Talia, and Jesse knew it was more for the love of argument than for the love of Egyptians.

"I suppose that Adonai's punishments have improved them," said Omar. "They will no longer bother us, I think."

"And we can live peacefully in Egypt?" Jesse asked.

"By heaven!" Avi exclaimed. "Can't we talk about anything else? Day and night, it's all I hear. People come to my father and sit and talk and argue: 'Pharaoh is letting us go!' 'No, he isn't.' 'Yes, he is.' 'He will.' 'He won't.' It's all I hear. And the tales get more wild every day. Now they say the Egyptians will beg us to leave, that in fact they will pelt us with gold and jewels."

"Come, now," said Jesse, laughing. "Won't that be the day!"

They finished the fish and wiped their hands on the leaves, and then they dug underneath fallen palm trees for dates. They found an abundance of dates, and they consumed them and lay back drowsily, the sun on their faces, and they talked and joked.

It came upon them suddenly. First there was only a sound, like the distant whistling of a reed pipe. Then a wind came up, hurling debris all about like a mighty hand. In the next instant it was as if a lid had dropped upon the earth. Darkness was complete.

Talia screamed. Her voice was close to Jesse's ear. She clung to Jesse while the wind whipped her hair and her tunic around her body. Her cloak flew off and disappeared.

"Come! Quickly!"

Hastily the three boys piled up branches and leaves and other debris for a windbreak. Jesse pulled Talia down. The four of them lay huddled together. The three boys held their robes aloft, contriving a kind of tent; still the wind and sand raged above them, and they closed their eyes against the harsh blasts of sand and stone that pelted them from every direction.

"Oh, God, oh, God," moaned Omar. "What is this now, this darkness? Why has darkness descended on this land?" Sand blew into Omar's mouth, muffling his words.

"It's Moses and Pharaoh," Talia said. "They still fight. God is punishing Pharaoh."

Talia lay between Avi and Jesse, and the two held her, as if she might blow away, and she clung to them. "We're going to die," she cried, sobbing, then coughed and choked. "I know we'll die. Oh, my poor mother. How she'll weep and tear her clothes. I'm her only child. I don't want to die, Jesse!"

Hours and hours went by. They could not distinguish night from day, except for the bitter cold that assaulted them, then waned, but still the storm and the darkness held them prisoner.

As Jesse lay with his companions, eyes sealed against the wind, he thought of Jennat's words: "What sort of god is this, who can be so cruel?" Talia's words, too, rang back at him: "God is punishing Pharaoh."

79

And the sudden thought flashed upon him, like a beacon. Adonai does this not only to punish Pharaoh, but to prove Himself to us, His doubting children.

Never, as in that moment, had Jesse been so certain of anything.

The darkness held for three days and three nights.

Jesse, Talia, Omar, and Avi staggered home. And Jesse was met by his father's wrath.

Furious, Nathan grabbed Jesse by the hair, as he had not done since Jesse was a child of ten. He led him away from the house, as if to slay him personally like a beast, a sacrifice.

"How could you take a young girl like that into the marshes? What must her parents think?"

"She followed us!" Jesse objected loudly.

"Did you sleep with her?" his father demanded. "Did you touch her? Did you?"

Jesse saw his mother in the doorway, watching, her hands clutched together. She looked worn and old; she looked as if she had given up every tender thought.

"I did nothing!" Jesse yelled.

His father's hand struck him across the cheek.

"Never raise your voice to me!" Nathan roared.

Jesse confronted his father. They were of equal size, and Jesse's shoulders were broader, his arms heavy from labor. He had youth on his side, and resentment at the unfair accusation. He clenched his fist. Then he put his hands behind his back.

"Well, it's no matter now," grunted Nathan, wiping his face. "The thing is done, one way or another. You are promised now, betrothed. You will marry as soon as we can get it done."

"What do you mean, Father? I tell you I didn't — "

"That is the way it is," Nathan said. "You know if you spend the night with a woman, you must marry. Or would you make your cousin out to be a harlot?"

His mother appeared. "We have already spoken to Efrem," she said. "Nothing you say will change it. Come, now, my son. After all, this has been our plan for years. It should neither surprise nor displease you. Talia is lovely, and more, she is good. She fears Adonai. She will be a fine mother for your children." Jesse caught his breath and held it, almost resigned. He knew that his destiny was with Talia. He also knew that his desire for Jennat would continue to torment him.

Swift-footed young boys ran as messengers from one small village to the next, and from house to house. They banged on doorposts and heralded, "Meeting! Come to the meeting! Everyone, all Israel. At the base of the hill, at the third hour of afternoon."

"Why? What is happening? Who is speaking?"

"Moses."

At first Jesse couldn't see a thing. He stood amid the thick throng of people, most of them Israelites, but a few of mixed race and from different lands. It had taken some time for Aaron to quiet the people. Jesse strained to see and to hear. Shouts pierced the air, relentless yammering and arguing and complaining.

Aaron, Moses' brother, waited.

At last an uneasy silence fell over the crowd.

Then Jesse heard the voice. It was not loud, and neither

high nor low, but moderate, clear, and slow. The voice seemed to resonate, covering the people with a blanket of sound.

Moses said, ". . . and so, Pharaoh commanded me to go from his sight, saying, 'Don't dare to see my face again! The day you appear before me, you will die!'

"Now hear me. Adonai has asked me to speak to His people and warn them. One more plague will come against Pharaoh and Egypt. After that, Pharaoh will let us leave this place. He will actually drive us out of here. Now go. Go to the houses of the Egyptians, your neighbors . . ."

Jesse strained forward on his toes. He could not see. The man in front of him was tall and heavy, and Jesse was wedged into the throng with scarcely air to breathe.

"There will be a great cry of anguish throughout all Egypt," Moses announced, "such as there has never been before and never again will be. . . ."

The man in front of Jesse shifted to one side. And now Jesse glimpsed the face of Moses from afar, and he was dazzled. Jesse was dazzled not by any beauty or fineness of features, for Moses was old. His skin was leathery from desert heat and cold. His neck was thick and corded, from laboring with the herds. Moses' beard was gray, long and coarse, and his hair hung loose to his shoulders in the fashion of shepherds and hunters. His long, heavy robe was worn. The sleeves were pushed high, revealing arms that were extraordinarily muscular and firm.

So this was Moses, Jesse thought, an ordinary man — yet a feeling clutched at his heart, a sudden and intense feeling of kinship. Something blazed from those dark eyes, a fire within, a depth of knowledge, a well of sorrow and of fatherly love. Jesse felt it, more powerful than any embrace. Even from this distance, Moses' eyes seemed directed upon him, Jesse,

82

and the words from Moses' mouth found their way into his being, shaking him utterly.

"These are the things you must do this night."

The people listened. Not a sound stirred the silence.

"Take a lamb for every household ... slaughter it in the afternoon. Take a bunch of hyssop, dip it into the blood, and smear it on the two doorposts and on the beam above the door of the houses. The Lord will then see the sign on the doorpost and pass over your houses, and there will not be any death among you when He strikes Egypt."

Fumbling and frightened by the threat of death, the people scurried. Women ground wheat into flour. Children fetched water from the well. Animals bleated and screamed; lambs were selected and slaughtered; pans were brought to hold the blood that drained from the neck cavity.

"Can we sup with you?" Efrem and Shira rushed toward Jesse's mother as she bent over the basin. "We have no more sheep to slaughter," Shira said, embarrassed.

"Of course," said Devorah, wiping her hands with a cloth. "We are family. Come, help me gather some hyssop, as Moses said."

Talia ran to Jesse. "Did you see him?" she asked excitedly. "Did you see Moses? His face?"

"I cannot forget his face," said Jesse. "Those piercing eyes." He pressed his blade down hard and slit the lamb's belly. Entrails glistened. Talia watched, breathing hard.

"You do that well," she murmured.

Devorah and Shira brought bunches of hyssop leaves and dipped them into the blood. "Come," said Devorah. "We'll paint the doorposts, as Moses instructed. Then the angel of death will not come in."

From the doorway Nathan stood watching. He smiled slowly. "You don't really believe all that, do you?"

"What?" Devorah whirled around. "You would argue with me still? After what you have heard?"

"I heard a man making threats," said Nathan, "telling people to do strange things. Blood on a doorpost! Everyone eating their young lambs — the people have gone crazy."

"But you have seen the plagues," cried Devorah. "You have felt the power of Adonai."

"Woman, you are without sense. Everything that happened here was a natural thing. There has been red clay in the river before, and fish have died. Frogs inhabit Egypt and always will. Vermin are a curse everywhere. As for sandstorms and locusts, we are used to those, the swarming pestilence that destroys crops."

"And hail?" Devorah demanded. "Hail in Egypt?"

Devorah turned back to Jesse. She watched him work, then said, "Jesse, speak to your father. I saw the way you looked at Moses. There was fire in his eyes — you saw it, too."

"When the fire dies," said Nathan, "the heat disappears. So it is with Moses. He's a good talker — but afterward, it is all nonsense."

Jesse looked from one to the other. His head pounded with confusion. He did not know whom to believe. Moses looked and spoke like a true leader, but they had been deceived before.

"Jesse," his mother said, "I want you to come with me. Talia, too. We can all go." She took Shosha from her basket and wrapped the baby in a shawl at her hip.

Jesse wiped his brow with his sleeve. Dressing the lamb was hard work, and he was drenched with sweat. "Where are we going?"

"To the Egyptians," she said. "Moses said we must go to them, to demand jewels, gold, and silver. Now you have a chance to show me this fine house of In-hop-tep."

"He is not going," said Nathan, hands crossed over his chest. "My son is not going to make an enemy of one of the most powerful men in Egypt. When all this nonsense blows over — "

"It will not blow over!" Devorah shouted. "It is our due for all these years of torment." She whirled around. Jesse saw the look in her eyes, fierce as the eyes of a wild dog. How could his mother be so transformed?

"Mother . . ." He stretched out his hand. She would never understand his anguish and shame at going to his masters, making demands. Jennat would view him as a common beggar or a thief. "We can go tomorrow," he muttered. "It is nearly dark. We must prepare the lamb; we must make bread — everything that Moses told us to do. We should do it, just in case."

His father picked up a hoe, and with the sharp point he struck the ground, splitting a stone in half. "Very well, you two," he said. "You leave me no peace. We'll roast the lamb and make the bread and sit in our houses holding our breath, and in the morning everything will be the same as before, and we will have eaten a fine supper — that's all."

That night Jesse scarcely tasted the meat that on any other day would have comprised a feast. Succulent lamb, a dish of festival and celebration, was tonight a meal of dread and foreboding. Their Egyptian captors worshipped the lamb and sacrificed to it; now the lowly slave nation had flaunted this slaughter, preparing the meat out in the open for all to know. Terrible punishment might fall upon them at any moment.

They ate the unleavened bread and drank the wine, as Moses had prescribed. They ate bitter herbs, to signify the bitterness of their labors all these years. The bitter taste remained in Jesse's mouth, and he nearly retched from it and from fear. Outside a strange wind howled, and debris was pitched all about, as if this whirlwind were but the beginning of a headlong attack.

Shira, Efrem, and Talia remained for the night. Talia sat close between her parents on the earthen floor; Devorah brought a blanket for them, and they pulled it up to their throats, their eyes wide and terrified.

"They will come and kill us," said Nathan. He lunged out to uncover a hidden jug, and he drank from it, passing it now and then to Efrem, who took just a sip, then sat back, pale and watchful.

Nobody could sleep; death lurked outside as surely as the wind. Jesse stared at the lintel, upon which the women had painted the lamb's blood, the dry red streaks reminding him of the terrible plague that had fallen over the Nile. Tonight was the night for retribution, theirs or the Egyptians'. Jesse sat motionless and numb, expecting at any moment the trampling of Egyptian feet, the flash of a sword.

Shosha fussed and squirmed; Devorah pinched her nose to keep her from crying, as mothers have always done in times of crisis. The baby gasped, grew red, then pale, and Jesse took her close to his chest, rocking, until at last she slept.

In the morning, as the sun rose, a strange distant wailing sounded over the land. Everyone awakened. They rubbed their eyes, dazed. "What is it? What's that sound?"

"It is the Egyptians," said Devorah, with a knowing look. "They are in mourning."

Pharaoh rose up in the night, he, and all his servants, and all the Egyptians; and there was a great cry in Egypt, for there was not a house where one was not dead. And Pharaoh summoned Moses by night, and said, "Rise up, and go forth from among my people; and go, serve the Lord, as you have said. Take your flocks and your herds, as you have said, and be gone; and bless me also!"

CHAPTER 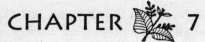 7

Jennat's first awareness that morning was the soft sound of a woman weeping, a woman who, not daring to give full vent to her feelings, muffles her sobs behind hands and cloth, yet cannot completely still the anguish in her soul.

Jennat tiptoed from her bed. Outside, nature was still; the air held neither wind nor clouds nor the usual sounds of activity. There was only this nearby weeping, and a ceaseless distant sound, like the hum of a thousand bees.

Jennat pulled on her robe, stepped into the small room where her maid, Ipuia, slept, and beheld a scene so strange and stark that she stood motionless, unable to organize her thoughts. Upon the reed mat lay Ipuia, stiff and still, like a sleeping figure sculpted from stone. Crouched beside Ipuia was Ahouri, the Nubian nurse, sobbing, beating her head against the floor. "Child! Child! Wake and look at me. Child, it is your mother. Oh, Heqat, how have I offended thee? I begged you for this child, and you have taken her from me. Oh, Buto, why did you not protect her? Oh, Thoth, she is yours now — be kind to her, take her gently, grant her peace and plenty in the world beyond!"

Rhythmically the woman beat her head upon the floor, her sobs renewed with each phrase, which she now repeated, "Oh, Heqat, how have I offended thee?"

Jennat went over to the woman and laid a hand on her shoulder. "Ahouri, Ahouri," she called, scarcely able to penetrate the woman's grief. "What happened? What tragedy?"

"She's dead. My firstborn and only child. Oh, Heqat! Yesterday I heard them whispering at the gate, but I thought it was only gossip and nonsense."

"What?" Jennat demanded. "What did they say at the gate?"

"That the Hebrew God would cause the first" — Ahouri sobbed — "the firstborn of every household in Egypt to die!"

A chill wrapped itself from Jennat's spine to her fingertips, and she shivered uncontrollably. "Then — oh, then — ," she stammered. It seemed her legs would collapse beneath her. Her teeth chattered. She stumbled through the maze of hallways and rooms, dreading to find out, needing to know.

She ran to the bedroom of her mistress and found it empty. She ran to Seti's room, then to the storerooms. At last, in the great room where Memnet had entertained over one hundred guests to celebrate Seti's birthday, Memnet sat, entranced. She swayed softly to and fro, her eyes vacant.

Before her on his couch, dressed in a simple gown of fine white linen, lay Seti, dead.

Several people stood in the doorway. Their shapes cast blue shadows into the room where Memnet still sat, mute.

Ahouri, ever mindful of her duties, went to them, hands clasped before her chest and inquired, "Yes? What is it you wish?"

A slender, careworn Hebrew woman with a child in a sling

at her hip took a step forward. "We have come," she said, "for valuables. Gold. Gems. Clothing. Things of value."

Her voice was cold, emotionless, but the tight clasp of her hands showed her tension, and she cast her eyes restlessly about the room.

"You — want jewels? Now?" The nurse glanced at her mistress, then at Jennat. She twisted her hands and implored Jennat, "What shall we do?"

Jennat stood staring at the Israelites. She was speechless with rage and astonishment.

"To compensate us," the woman went on, "for all these years we — generations of us — were slaves, working for nothing. These are to be our wages."

Jennat strode to the far corner, where a basket stood, filled with the objects she and Jesse had made. Another lidded basket contained woven shawls and several pairs of sandals. "Ahouri!" Jennat cried. "Give them these clothes." Jennat herself took the basket of gold and silver trinkets and put it into the woman's hands. "Take them and be gone," she said bitterly. "Be gone!"

But the woman stepped forth, drawn as if spellbound to the cot where Seti slept his final sleep. "Is this . . . ?" She moved nearer, peered at the child, and her face crumpled. "Oh — a beautiful boy! Oh, wretched mother!"

Weeping, she covered her face with her apron and turned away, grasping the arms of the two other women, one young and staring, the other averting her eyes in a posture of modesty or shame.

Another figure emerged from the shadows. Jennat's breath caught in her throat. It was Jesse. She murmured his name in disbelief. Still the women waited, and the awareness dawned on Jennat that they wanted more, that they would not leave until they were satisfied. Swiftly she tore off her necklace, her bracelets, and her earrings and gave them to the women, and the Nubian nurse likewise took off her large silver earrings, gold-and-silver pectoral, and the rings from her fingers and nose.

Then the Hebrew women, without a word, turned to go. But Jesse remained. He stood before Jennat. "I didn't want to come here, Jennat," he said beseechingly. "We have been commanded to do this. We are leaving, all of us. We will go through the wilderness, to our own land, which our God has promised us. He commanded us to come to the Egyptians and ask them for gold and silver and gems, for we will have need — "

"Go, then," Jennat said without expression. "Take everything. What good is it to us now?"

And suddenly Jesse wept, his face contorted with soundless sobs. His shoulders shook, and he covered his face with his hands.

"Don't weep," Jennat said, her voice firm and without feeling. "We cannot take blame for what the gods do — they are capricious. They play with us, with our destinies. It has always been so. There is no hope."

"Jennat, listen." Jesse held out his hands. "Come with us. You say yourself, there is nothing left for you here, only death and destruction. Come with us. Many others — our neighbors, Pharaoh's other slaves — are going with us, and even some free Egyptians who now see the might of our God."

"No." Jennat lifted her head. She fixed her gaze upon Memnet, who sat unseeing, still swaying to and fro. "I have to stay here. It is my duty. My mistress took me in as a babe. Now she has nobody. She is" — Jennat gestured to Memnet — "she is sick now. How can I leave her?"

"But she has been cruel to you," Jesse objected.

"In her way," Jennat said, "she has also been kind. No, I

must stay. But listen, Jesse, there is someone who will go with you. Take my friend Shepset. She has been hiding in the granary since four days ago, homeless and without friends except for me. Take her, if you care for me at all."

"I care for you," Jesse whispered, his eyes filled again with tears. "Oh, how I care for you!"

"Then do this thing, for our friendship."

"Surely more than friendship!" Jesse exclaimed, taking her hands in his. "Oh, how can I leave you?" He leaned toward her, and Jennat remembered the one time they had kissed, and how she had dreamed afterward of lying in his arms. Now she stepped away from him, still numb with grief and shock.

"Go to Shepset, Jesse. Tell her I sent you. And — when you are in this new land of yours — remember me."

Jesse found Shepset in the granary, huddled in her shawl, sitting amid the sacks of grain.

"I've come to take you away," he whispered loudly. "I am Jesse, Jennat's friend. She told me you need help. Come with us to Canaan, the land — "

"How can I go? Everyone looks upon me with loathing," the girl murmured in a low voice. "The only answer is for me to kill myself, but I have no blade, and no courage."

"Nonsense," said Jesse, feeling somehow like a parent or an older brother, for the girl shivered and looked piteously frail. "It makes no sense to kill oneself. Besides, it is against God's will."

The girl shuddered. "I heard wailing and thought surely I would die. I have already made my peace with the gods."

"Are you a firstborn?" Jesse asked.

"No. I have older brothers."

"You will not die of this plague," Jesse told her. "Come.

92

No more talk about dying." Jesse reached out his hand and drew her up, out of the shadows. He brought her out to the light, and now he saw the ridges and scabs on her cheeks and brow. One eye was half closed and oozing with pus.

"Aiii," he murmured. "Are you in pain?"

"No. Itching, sometimes."

"My mother will have some balm for that. She is wonderful with medicines."

"For me?" Shepset gave a bitter laugh. "She would only scorn me — I have heard about your people and this God of yours, who maims and kills."

"When my mother sees you," Jesse said, taking Shepset's arm, "her face will be set like marble. But inside, her heart will break, and she will treat you tenderly."

Hordes ran through the streets. Jesse heard them shouting, "Here! Take these. Take everything — only leave. Leave Egypt, you and your God, leave us!"

The Israelites gathered their bundles — blankets and utensils, tools and rope and hunks of dried meat, sacks of dates, mats and clothing and hastily beaten bread dough that had not had time to rise. They piled as much as they could upon their beasts, the mules and cattle, and the rest they flung upon their own backs. Little children were saddled with implements and extra garments. Dogs barked hysterically; other animals were wild-eyed, pawing the ground, bellowing.

Amid the commotion, Jesse's parents battled fiercely. He screamed, "Hurry! Hurry!" but they seethed with their own passions. Nathan grasped Devorah's arm. "Listen to me! Not everyone is leaving — some of us have the sense to stay where we know we can live. Devorah, please, stop for a moment and think. We'll die of starvation out there in the wilderness. Isn't it clear to you that if they thought we would leave, none of the Egyptians would have parted with their treasure? They'll follow us."

Devorah retorted, "They will *not* follow us — they are bowed down with grief."

"They'll strip our bodies when we are dead — they have the power. What if Pharaoh changes his mind and brings his army to massacre us? We are without arms, without protection."

"We have protection," said Devorah. "Now, leave me alone!"

"You go. Only let me keep Jesse here with me."

"You will keep no child of mine!"

"You can take the baby."

"No!"

"Woman, I am not letting you go. I am not letting you take these children!" He grasped her arm so hard that she winced, but she twisted from him and braced herself, fist raised.

"If you say one more word," Devorah gasped, "I will tell Jesse the truth. Everything. Now, you can come with us, or you can stay here alone and rue it all the rest of your days, you stubborn fool of a man! You choose! *We are going.*"

The Israelites moved out, no columns in orderly formation, no standards or leaders except for the two old men whose gray heads bobbed before them, Moses, and Aaron, carrying upon his shoulders a small stone ossuary that held the bones of their beloved patriarch, Joseph. Through the years Joseph's dying plea had been preserved: "When God remembers you and brings you up from this land to the land He swore to our fathers, then bring up my bones from here with you."

94

The Israelites moved out, disbelieving, shocked, too burdened to rejoice.

Occasionally, through the dust and the debris of thousands of fleeing persons and animals, Moses' head, with his long, waving hair, was visible. Moses held his staff aloft, pointing east.

Tribal leaders tried to keep their members together; all was chaos. Some people had flatly refused to leave Egypt. They sat behind their locked doors or fled to Egyptian masters, looking for refuge — from what? Nobody knew what might follow. They knew only that there had been a cataclysm in the land, an uprising of greater than human force, for when had slaves ever wreaked such vengeance upon masters? In the last moments, Jesse's father, unwilling to be left behind, had gathered his belongings into a large bag and slung it upon his back.

Jesse remembered his mother's strange threat: "I will tell Jesse the truth — everything!" and he wondered what she had meant.

Jesse brought up the animals, struggling to keep his flock together. Almost every family had several sheep, a dozen goats, and maybe cattle. Chickens, quickly thrust into cages, were brought along but swiftly abandoned. The foolish birds, once let loose, ran off into the wilderness, and to carry them was hardly worth the effort.

Jesse and Avi found each other and quickly embraced, and Jesse cried, "My God, Avi, has it really come true?"

Avi shook his head, dazed, but grinning. "I never really believed it possible." He seized one of the lambs about to be trampled by the surging herds. "Come, come, we must keep moving — time for talk later."

Jesse had sat Shepset upon a donkey, despite her cries — she had never ridden before. He held the animal's halter, trotting alongside. "What's this?" Avi demanded, then roared out, "A woman of Egypt? Have you lost your senses?"

"This is Shepset, friend of Jennat. She is coming with us."

"Your mother will kill you," said Avi flatly.

"He is right," said Shepset, her voice muffled from behind her shawl, which covered her face entirely; only her eyes peered out. "Let me go back. You said there are others, a mixed multitude also fleeing — I shall walk with them."

"No. You are weak from sickness and lack of food." The donkey tore up a clump of grass in its teeth, attempting to pause, but Jesse was adamant. "Come! Come!" he called, and he beat its hindquarters with a stick.

Heads of clans pushed their way to the front, some dragging their possessions. They argued loudly. "What is this? We are marching south. This way is long, and roundabout. We should head due east!"

In panic, the men ran to Moses, shouting, "The shortest way to Canaan is due east. Everyone knows that. It was told us by our fathers and their fathers' fathers."

"To the east dwell our old enemies, the Philistines," came Moses' harsh reply. "Do you want to do battle? You would quickly lose heart and run back to Egypt!"

Chastised, the leaders retreated, but their anger still smoldered.

Rimon came to find his son. He nodded to Jesse.

"What is it, Uncle?" Jesse asked, hurrying beside Rimon. "Is Moses taking us afar, as they say?"

"I don't know," Rimon said brusquely. "Supposedly he speaks with God."

Cousin Seth came back to check on his flock. He carried his two young girls, one on his back, the other in his arms. "We'll have to rest soon," he panted. "With all these animals and little ones ... This man of eighty runs like a wild ox! Pharaoh said we could go. Why the hurry?"

"Best to keep moving," Rimon said with a nod. "Who knows whether Pharaoh will keep his word this time?"

"You mean he might come after us?" Avi asked nervously.

"I don't know, son," Rimon said, and Jesse looked about, anxious and distracted, trying to keep the animals together. He had never heard Rimon so doubtful before; it was unsettling.

"Look!" Avi said, pointing.

Jesse followed Avi's direction. Now he could see a glimpse of Moses' staff, pointed straight ahead, and farther on, a strange cloud formation, like a pillar.

"What's that, Uncle?" Jesse asked.

"I don't know, Jesse." Rimon's mouth was set in a hard line.

Jesse squinted ahead. The pillar seemed to bob forward, then to retreat. Such visions, Jesse had heard, were common in the desert, where wind and dust and vast granite mountains soon wearied the eyes and blurred the senses. The pillar looked gray, then brilliant white; then it was touched with pale rose, like a sunset.

Rimon shrugged. "A cloud," he said. "Moses is following a cloud."

Korach, one of the tribal heads, rushed by, holding several bundles protected by goatskin and tied with rope. A man of learning, he had gathered up his manuscripts, carefully etched on parchment, stories of the fathers and of ancient days.

He walked swiftly, as if he must lead an entire army, and indeed, many of the sons of Levi formed a column and marched behind him, some singing the old songs.

As Korach passed, he waved to Rimon and called, "Think we made a mistake following such a leader?"

"I hope not," said Rimon, shaking his head. "Truly I am surprised," he added, "to see you following anyone."

Korach was known for his surly independence. He and Rimon had been friends since boyhood. As such, they were always in competition.

Korach grimaced. "Moses says that cloud pillar is the essence of the Lord. He says that Adonai speaks directly with him, face to face, and leads us by way of this cloud."

Both men fell into dubious silence. Jesse could see they were struggling to hold back judgment. God in a cloud? The idea was too strange. But then, their very presence here in the wilderness was stranger still.

They journeyed all day and all night without rest, until they came to the sea. They stopped and stared at the water in disbelief. A few fell into panic. "What shall we do now? Walk upon the water?" At last, exhausted, they made camp.

Then Devorah, gathering her possessions around her, told Nathan to stretch out a tent so that she could recline and care for Shosha. The baby cried weakly and lay at Devorah's breast. "Come, come," she murmured, stroking the child's silken head. "Poor little one, you must be starved!"

The baby began to nurse, gulping hungrily.

Jesse helped Shepset down from the donkey, and he bound the beast's hind legs, so it would not stray. Shepset rubbed her back, groaning. "This mule," she said, "has bones like iron, and sharp. Will I ever walk erect again?"

Jesse laughed. "Of course. It is new to you."

"I would rather walk forever," stated Shepset, "than mount that beast again." But her eyes were shining, and she added gratefully, "I thank you, Jesse, for saving me. Someday I will repay you."

"Not necessary," said Jesse brusquely. "Look, I must bring you to my mother. Come."

Slowly Jesse approached, with Shepset reluctantly following. "Mother, I ask your indulgence," he said humbly. "Here is a young woman called Shepset, suffering greatly. She was abandoned by the temple priests when she most needed them. I told her you could help."

Jesse drew Shepset forward.

Shepset let the veil drop from her face.

Devorah looked from Jesse to Shepset. She stood motionless, then shook her head and, still clasping the baby to her breast, extended her hand to Shepset and drew her into the tent.

Later, when the baby slept, and Shepset, too, lay with her head propped on the saddle bags in the shelter of the tent, Devorah came to Jesse.

"You have a good heart, my son," she said softly. "I know matters have not been good between us of late. If I have been harsh — "

"I have been stubborn, Mother," Jesse said, ducking his head. In return for his respect, Jesse knew, his mother would be lenient.

"We were always so close, you and I," she murmured. "Look, I want you to swear to me, if anything should happen to me here, that you will always take care of Shosha."

"Of course!" Jesse exclaimed. "She is my sister."

"Swear to me," she breathed, her hand on his arm. "Swear it, Jesse — give me your word."

"I swear I shall always take care of Shosha. I will protect her with my very life."

"When this young woman's face is healed," Devorah said, "she must not remain among us, but she can dwell with the others, with that mixed rabble that ran after us."

Jesse stiffened at the words "mixed rabble," but he held his tongue and nodded. "I thank you, Mother, for tending her wounds."

"I do it in gratitude for our freedom," she said. "But you must keep yourself separate, Jesse, from all these others, from their ways and their influences, do you hear me?"

"I hear you, Mother." He made his tone and expression pliable, but, in truth, Jesse had no intention of abandoning Shepset. He owed this much to Jennat.

"Besides, it does not look well, since you are promised to your cousin Talia. And Talia and her parents would take offense — "

Jesse sighed. "I understand perfectly, Mother. Shepset means nothing to me; I hardly know her. I was asked by a friend to take her. She was ready to kill herself. I only did that which Adonai would have wished, and as you have always taught me, to heed the cry of the sufferer."

"Yes, yes," Devorah said faintly. "Leave me now, I must rest. Have you anything to eat? Take some bread dough; toss it upon the pan over the coals. There is meat in the bag — "

"Don't trouble yourself for me, Mother," Jesse murmured, and he softly kissed her brow.

The first light lifted itself up from the horizon, setting a luminous sheen over the sea.

The people were spread out, their animals foraging, families sleeping where they had dropped, their fires left to smolder or die. And even before the people were fully awake, they heard a roaring from behind them. Even as they still slumbered, they could hear the heavy thrusts of horses' hooves, the clash of speeding chariots, the horses being whipped and driven so that their screams pierced the desert and rang out before them. The spearmen mingled their shouts of conquest among the screams of the beasts, so that the Israelites knew, to a man, exactly what had transpired: Pharaoh had repented of his decision to let his Israelite slaves go. He needed them. And if the Hebrews should rebel and be successful, how could he keep his other slaves in tow? How could he prove to his people, who called him Lord, that he was truly chosen by the gods, if he could not manage to keep control of his kingdom?

Pharaoh was on the march. Everyone knew his might — six hundred chariots. Horses, hot-blooded steeds from which bowmen shot their arrows and hurled sharp, deadly spears, an army of men who were the most vicious and the least afraid to die — these he would set against the arrogant Israelites, to show that none could rebel against Pharaoh and live.

Trapped against the sea, in terror, the Israelites heard the advancing army.

They tore their hair and screamed at Moses and Aaron, "Are there no graves in Egypt, that you led us out here to die? What have you done to us? We told you, back in Egypt, we told you, 'Let us alone! It's better to serve the Egyptians than to die in the wilderness!' "

Jesse's father, standing on the sidelines, took up the cry. "We told you! We told you!"

And he lashed out at Devorah. "I told you! I told you we'd be killed. You wouldn't listen. Now see, you will live to watch your children slaughtered, your husband hacked into pieces! I told you! I told you!"

"Coward!" screamed Devorah. "Have you no pride? Have you no manly instinct to fight for us?"

He struck her once, then twice more as she lay crouched on the ground.

Jesse ran to thrust himself between them. His heart pounded in his ears as he lunged toward his father. But Devorah grasped Jesse by the edge of his robe, sobbing. "Take the baby!" she pleaded. "For the love of God, take her — keep her safe!"

Moses said to the people: "Do not be afraid! God will fight for you, but you must remain silent."

And God said to Moses, "Why do you cry out to Me? Speak to the sons of Israel that they go forward. And lift up your staff and stretch out your hand over the sea and split it, so that the sons of Israel shall go into the midst of the sea on dry ground."

CHAPTER  8

A deafening sound rose, and an east wind so powerful that Jesse could hardly brace himself against its might. The water grew dark as it churned and roiled and turned into a rising mass, obliterating light and air.

Dimly before him Jesse saw his Uncle Rimon, hands raised in command, mouth wide open. Rimon moved forward, his head flung back and arms wide, to embrace the raging waters, even to embrace death if it were the will of his God.

Jesse followed, and as he watched, the raging green-and-gray waters were pulled back and back as if by invisible hands. The sea was raised up into two walls. Now the seafloor lay exposed. Pebbles and shells rolled underfoot. Small crabs leapt in fright. Wind and icy water whipped at Jesse's head.

Shosha screamed. Jesse shielded the baby under his robe, pressing her tight against his skin, and she clung to him, her little hands gripping his chest like pincers.

Where was his mother? Shepset? Avi?

In the blinding fury of the waves and the wind, Jesse could only stumble forward. The cries, both of his companions and of nature unleashed, overwhelmed his senses, blurred his vision. He moved on, following the others. His legs were mired in mud. Strange leeches clung to his skin. Things whirled above him, bits of wood and stone, sand and leaf, blown from distances he could not fathom.

Everything was transformed into darkness and wind, deeper and colder than that night in Egypt when Jesse had lain with his friends, braced against the storm. This was depth and darkness unimaginable, with utter confusion of direction. Which way was up? Which way was down? The very sea had been lifted and its depths displayed. And as Jesse moved on, he lost awareness of his own body, and his fear disappeared.

Jesse walked, as if on a path of light. He felt a quiet joy. Now his feet lifted easily, and although he heard horses and chariots approaching from the rear, still he proceeded — and all the Israelites with him, as one.

Time, it seemed, did not move. Darkness and fury combined and held while the Israelites came in a steady stream with their beasts and their burdens, crossing on the floor of the sea. It was almost silent within the center of the clashing forces. It felt, indeed, that nothing unnatural had occurred, for there was this core of quietness and complete understanding in the midst of the unfathomable.

At last Jesse stumbled out on the opposite shore, and people all about him were drenched and shaking, bewildered, amazed. They looked back from whence they had come. Jesse, too, stared at the walls of water between which the Israelites continued to walk; he saw people he knew — relatives, friends — all dazed as if they had been to the land of the dead and back again.

People stood or lay on the beach, dumbfounded, and before there was time to assemble, a new sound came roaring even over the force of the wind — the shouts and curses of the

Egyptian chariot drivers, the shrieking of beasts that, under the fury of whips, struggled to free themselves from the mud. In their frenzy, some of the charioteers leapt from their carts and threw their weight behind the rear wheels, trying to free their vehicles from the mire. But straining muscles and whips and cries were insufficient against the power of the sea.

In that last moment, the Egyptians turned their faces and saw certain doom. They cried or they cowered, understanding in that split second that this was the end. The mountain of water closed over them.

As the Israelites watched in disbelief, the charging pursuers became corpses floating on the sea.

Helmets and spears and richly decorated shields were tossed about in the foam. Dead horses and pieces of chariots washed up on the shore. Bodies drifted out and back, out and back, a testament to total and devastating defeat.

Without a single encounter or a single spear finding its mark, the battle had been resolved. This was not the hand of man; in their hearts the Israelites knew the name of this power, and they shivered both in joy and in terror.

Slowly the Israelites recovered. They swayed and staggered, as if drunk. The men lay on the sand, each listening to the hammering of his own heart.

But the women raised themselves up, and as Jesse lay gasping, he saw the women moving almost like phantoms upon the sand. Shira and Talia were among them. Devorah came for the baby, and with the other women, began to dance.

Miriam, sister of Moses, her white hair glowing in fresh sunlight, held a tambourine up high. She shook the tambourine with the bright vigor of a young woman, exuberant and ecstatic. The women followed, all eyes upon Miriam, united in movements of hands and body, swaying and singing in a glorious harmony of voices:

Sing to God for His great victory;
Horse and rider He has cast into the sea!

On and on the women danced and sang their refrain. From the youngest, barely steady, to the oldest, white-headed and bent, they threw off their sandals and pushed their shawls aside. They brought up instruments — drums and lutes. Tambourines cascaded with sound, and their song rose in spirit and in fullness:

Sing to God for His great victory;
Horse and rider He has cast into the sea!

And Jesse watched, amazed at the strength of these women, for they continued for an hour or more, until they dropped, exhausted, onto the sand.

"No more songs," Miriam called out. She laid down her tambourine and covered her head. "Mothers in Egypt are weeping for their sons."

At the edge of the crowd of Israelite women stood the women of the multitudes, distinguished by their clothes and their jewels and some by their color, for there were black Nubians, too.

And Jesse saw that Shepset had joined these women.

Jesse looked again, disbelieving at first, then shocked. Beside Shepset stood Jennat.

Through the years Jennat had, of course, witnessed grand festivals to Hathor or Osiris, or to Apis the bull. Parades always followed the figure of the god as it was borne through the streets. There would be music, dancing, and feasting. Barges, decked with flowers and ribbons, accompanied by musicians and merrymakers and dancers, would move down the Nile following the boat on which the god, dressed in splendid garments and covered with jewels, would proceed back to the home temple. All night the merrymaking would continue, with wine and beer overflowing, and lovemaking and the complete abandonment of work.

As for the Israelites, they had no such festivals, none that Jennat knew. She only knew the dissonant Hebrew chants that were sometimes heard in passing. They had no brave legends of wars between gods and goddesses. They possessed no figured deities, some in human shape, some part animal, bird, or crocodile. The Egyptians had tales of their gods forever clashing and cavorting. The Israelites' tales were of ordinary people with common names — Abraham, Noah, Lot — who somehow gave shape to this strange religion. And their festivals, if they had any, were a mystery to Jennat.

Clustered in their walled villages, the Hebrews had kept their peculiar faith to themselves. But suddenly, here in the wilderness, abandonment seemed to have seized them, one and all. How had they caused their God to send that tempest? How had they persuaded Him to split the sea? Jennat had always prayed for simple things, like love or a new jewel or an afternoon of peace, to go to the Nile and dream.

Was it possible, she thought, that she had never asked for enough? Was it possible that gods answer extreme prayers with extreme demonstrations of power?

She had run, that last day, from the house of Memnet. She had flung herself into the fleeing crowd and was swiftly borne up in the crush, with sharp kicks and jabs and cries, all part of the chaos.

The Israelites were tough, ready to abandon their homes, their fields. They did not look back. All night they had marched, and Jennat, moving with them, at last had fallen to the rear along with the other peoples — Syrians and Libyans,

Nubians and some Egyptian serfs, discouraged and desperate. All these multitudes simply could not share the passion that seemed, in the Israelites, inbred. It was as if the Israelites had been preparing themselves silently and secretly for this escape for generations. How else could they have moved so swiftly and with such purpose?

Of course, when they had come to the sea, a terrible cry had arisen, and a tearing of hair and menacing movements toward the leader, Moses, who silenced them with his fury. He raised both arms. His eyes seemed aflame, and he hurled himself into the raging water, his staff held high — and then the waters parted.

They had all crossed, entranced by the summons of their invisible God; Jennat had never seen such a display of faith or of power. Then came the Egyptians' chariots. Jennat had watched in wonder as the waves rushed back, covering the splendid horses, the gilded chariots, the surging warriors — until everything was silent and death grinned hideously from every face.

Then Jennat had stood, trembling. For she realized that she, too, was a stranger among these people. The same might that had crushed Pharaoh's best warriors could also crush her.

In awe she had crept toward the sparse rocks littering the shore, trying to hide behind the wispy growth of shrubs. The dance of the Hebrew women, the passion in their faces, made Jennat truly afraid.

She bent, making of her body a closed circle, and sickness washed over her. Alone amid this rabble! How could she endure it? Where was Jesse? She had searched for his face among the thousands, and had seen only hostile looks. People were busy finding their own kin; nobody wanted to share even a glance with a lone young woman.

It was then that the other miracle had occurred. A voice,

familiar and eager, had called her name. Jennat looked up. Shepset ran to her, and they clung to each other.

The two young women embraced, weeping for joy. Afterward, when they had quieted from the shock of reunion and everything preceding, Jennat and Shepset drew apart from the crowds, and they sat in the cleft of a boulder and spoke eagerly, Jennat telling of her escape.

"After Jesse left the house of In-hop-tep, and his mother and her relatives took our jewels" — Jennat turned to spit onto the sand, then wiped her mouth as if to wipe off the taste of hatred — "we looked for In-hop-tep. He had gone to the ships. Some men at the docks said he had sailed away. Abandoned us. Still my mistress said nothing, only stared.

"Later, Memnet seemed to come to herself," Jennat continued. "She moved about, ordered food to be brought, and she set a table. She offered me cakes and meat. She had beer brought to drink. And I thought, How strange that she can be so strong — to make herself calm now that everything is lost.

"But I was wrong, Shepset," Jennat said. She pressed her knuckles to her lips, frowning deeply. "No sooner were we seated than Memnet got a look of wrath on her face — worse than any I had ever seen. She set her eyes upon me, and she picked up a knife and began to pursue me. She spat and cursed. I leapt onto a small table. She jerked the table out from under me, and I fell and split my chin." Jennat pointed to the cut on her chin, which was still raw. "And she shouted, raving that I had killed her baby, that I had caused this terrible catastrophe. She screamed that we must bury him, that I must be embalmed along with him to serve him. She babbled and caught me once, held me by the hair, raising her blade in front of my face."

Shepset gasped. "How were you saved?"

"The nurse. Ahouri placed herself between us, then

brought Memnet to rest for a few moments, and crooned to her as one would to a baby. Ahouri clasped Memnet in her arms, all the while speaking to her softly and gently, and then with her eyes she motioned to me, and with her lips made the words 'Run. She will kill you, child. Run!' "

"And so" — Jennat sighed and shook her head — "I ran. Where could I go? I saw the clouds of dust and the animals and people leaving. So now . . ." Jennat lifted her eyes, and she forced herself to smile. "I have always wanted to travel, to leave Egypt and see the world."

"The world?" Shepset gave a deprecating laugh. "How silly! Why would anybody want to leave Egypt? Surely no land is as rich or as beautiful."

"Well, you were born in Egypt," Jennat said. "You have memories that tie you there. As for me" — she shrugged — "I have only empty spaces behind me."

"What a strange girl you are!" Shepset objected. "You could still go back, you know. You could find yourself another place. Where have we come? This is a wasteland!" Shepset shuddered. "I hate the smell of those cattle, the bleating of the sheep. Doesn't it make you sick?"

In truth, the smell of the animals was sickening. Their odor clung to tents and inhabitants alike, to their clothing and beards and hair. For an instant Jennat felt ill with longing; each year, immediately after the Nile receded and the planting was begun, Memnet had her servants clean and fumigate the entire house; then they scattered sweet incense of terebinth, resin, and balsam. Jennat thought of the cool water in its shining basin, the couches where they lounged in the heat of midday, drinking fresh beer and eating pomegranates.

Jennat looked at her robe, concealing her disgust at the filth. She stood up and confronted Shepset squarely, saying, "Well, I'm going to find myself a caravan and go with traders.

What better way to see the world? There are many seas and rivers in the world. I have heard In-hop-tep speak of them. I wish to see them."

"You are dreaming, Jennat," said Shepset, dusting off her robe and hurrying beside her. They began to walk back toward the Israelites, now preparing to move on.

Then Shepset asked, "How could Memnet think you had anything to do with Seti's death? You loved that boy."

Jennat nodded. Suddenly tears started in her eyes. "I always took care of him. Since he was a baby. When Memnet gave me to In-hop-tep, I hoped that at least I would have a child."

"By the gods!" Shepset shuddered. "You're not serious. Who'd want that burden?"

Jennat only walked faster, and Shepset hurried after her.

"As for me," Shepset went on, "I will certainly go back to Egypt when my scars are healed. I would not have come even this far if it hadn't been for Jesse. These people are coarse and crude, but Jesse is different. He sat me upon a donkey and he led me out. He told his mother to give me medicine. You were right," she said, her eyes skipping about. "He is very kind, very gentle."

Sudden, quick anger gripped Jennat. Then she looked at her friend, saw the disfigurement, and was aghast at herself. Why could she not be generous?

"He is engaged, you know," Shepset said readily. "To his cousin Talia — that girl with the shining long hair and fair skin — do you think she's beautiful?" A strange high tone leapt into Shepset's voice.

Jennat tossed her head and said irritably, "What do I care? After Jesse and his relatives stole my jewels, they can all go to the netherworld! I came away not to be with him, but to save myself."

A horn sounded, echoing from the hills.

"What now?" Jennat turned, squinting into the distance, where the Israelites were already rushing to the call of the ram's horn. They assembled at the foot of a low mountain, their leaders — Aaron, Joshua, Hur, and Moses — preceding. The setting sun shone upon their white garments. The sheer mass of people assembled, gazing heavenward, provided an awesome spectacle. In spite of herself, Jennat began slowly to walk toward the Israelites, as if she were indeed one of them.

"Another meeting," Shepset scoffed, following her. "They love their meetings." She turned, and Jennat saw that the scars were fading slightly. They drew strange designs on her face, patterns like the masks of the gods.

And Jennat thought, "She is ugly now — no man will ever want her," and she felt ashamed.

"Another meeting!" Nathan grumbled. He wound up the lengths of rope that had been fastened to the tent pegs and tossed them into a pile. "He is going to wear us out with words — never have I had to listen to so many!"

"Let's not go, then," Jesse muttered. He dragged the several goatskins together and heaped them upon the mule. The beast balked, then hung its head down, depressed.

Jesse squinted against the sand that suddenly blasted into his face. Sand left its residue even between his teeth. It was not the slippery, silken sand of Egypt, but a sand that caked into mud and bristled with sharp edges.

"Maybe he'll tell us how long we have to stay in this cursed wilderness," Nathan said.

"On the other hand," grumbled Jesse, "maybe it will just be more orders. Instructions. Remember this, do that, not only today, but forever. Curse 'forever'! All I care about is getting something to eat before nightfall."

Guiltily Jesse glanced over his shoulder. If his mother heard him, she would accuse him bitterly: "How can you forget so quickly the miracle Adonai made for us? He split the sea for us. He slew our enemies."

Indeed, Jesse couldn't explain his own grumbling, except that he was hungry and tired. Yesterday's miracle gave no help today.

Nathan grunted. "Maybe Moses will at least get us water. The skins are nearly dry, and there isn't a well in sight."

Jesse nodded and pressed his hand to his stomach. "Oh, what I'd give for a slice of melon!"

The wilderness, with its harshness, had brought father and son closer. Before, they were seldom in the house at the same time. Now, at nightfall, they pitched their tent, and the family lay in it all together, listening to the unfamiliar howls that swept over the desert. By day, there was fuel to be sought; food to forage for; and protection to be provided against the wind, the sudden, harsh bursts of rain, and the plundering men among them, who, in this new burst of freedom, had become ruthless.

"I miss the bread," Nathan complained, "even when we had no fat to spread on it. Well, a number of us will be going back to Egypt, you can be sure. In the meantime, we obey when we are summoned."

"Like cattle?" Jesse cried. His stomach rumbled with hunger. He said nothing about Egypt — that was the fight his parents waged. As for him, he had no desire to return, but only to move forward, finally to claim the reward that Devorah and Uncle Rimon had been talking about for years, and that Moses echoed nearly every day. Let me plant my feet in Canaan, he thought; then I will believe all their stories.

Nathan placed his hand on Jesse's back. "Look, it does no good to complain. Think your own thoughts, but don't let them know. Make your face soft, Jesse. Learn to smile and look down."

"I thought that's what we left behind in Egypt," Jesse muttered. He kicked the ground where a goat foraged near his foot; he did not like the life of a herder, or the stink of the goats. He hated the way they butted up against his legs.

His father shook his head. "No. We only traded one Pharaoh for another, one name for another. Learn this, Jesse! Learn to be what they want you to be. Say yes or no, depending on their whim. There are still favors to be handed out — do you understand me?"

"You want me to bow down to Moses?"

"Why not? What's a bow more or less? Nod and smile and agree. Let him see you as a good follower. Nothing changes, Jesse. A smile is always rewarded."

"I thought we left Egypt so we could be free," Jesse burst out.

"Free?" Nathan gave a snort. "Look, son, when you are married you won't be so restless." He winked. "Talia is well favored, and she adores you."

Jesse kept silent. He was promised to Talia, yet he could not keep Jennat out of his thoughts. He had seen Jennat once more since the crossing — only a mere glance. She had squinted at him, hand on her hip, then whirled around, busying herself by picking some twigs from a bush, perhaps to burn for kindling. She looked unkempt and worn; her hair must have caught in brambles, and it was whipped by the wind, giving her a wild look.

And in her wildness, Jesse realized, she was even more beautiful. He felt a turmoil, as always in the past when he was with her. He had thought that once out of Egypt, he would be done with these cravings and the guilt they brought.

In the assembly, surrounded by his people, Jesse felt

calmer. Maybe his father was right; he needed love. It was lonely here in the wilderness, without houses or roads or any standing thing made by human hands. Such loneliness could bring one to the verge of panic.

But now they stood together — Talia and her parents, Uncle Rimon, Aunt Channa, Avi, Seth, all the other relatives — and Jesse forgot his turmoil. The wilderness bonded them more closely than ever before, tribe by tribe, clan by clan. It felt good to be united, faces turned toward their leader, Moses.

Moses stood on a low hill, with his brother Aaron beside him, and several others of the Levite tribe.

The Levites clustered near, some touching the hem of Moses' garment. They reveled in their kinship with the leader, following close behind him, waiting outside his tent.

Now Moses spoke, and his voice seemed to draw strength from the very clouds above him, though it was not loudness that spread, but rather a resonance. There was authority in his voice, and also love.

And Jesse, listening, knew that this man might claim him utterly, as a master claims a slave, body and soul. He struggled to hold himself away. Never again would he give himself completely! Never would he allow anyone to own him.

Moses' eyes burned with divine fire, and his uplifted hands seemed to twist the very air round about, drawing down currents of power, as when nature explodes with hail or thunder. "He is only a man, like any other," Jesse reminded himself as he stood listening, nearly overcome by the sound of Moses' voice. "Only a man, not a god, no different from the rest of us."

But he was different, Jesse had to admit. In Moses' bearing, in his face and voice, there lay not a trace of arrogance or anger or pride. This man was aflame with some inner fire that had nothing to do with himself; Moses was utterly humble.

Moses spoke. "Remember this day, when Adonai led you

out of Egypt, with signs and wonders and with a mighty hand. And when God brings you to the land of Canaan, to a land flowing with milk and honey, you shall observe this service in this month. You shall eat unleavened bread seven days, and there shall be a festival consecrated to God. And then you shall tell your child on this day, it is because of what God did for me when I came out of Egypt. . . ."

When he had finished speaking, and the people began to disperse, there came a sudden commotion at the fringe of the gathering. Voices clashed. Dust rose. Someone yelled an epithet.

Several angry Hebrew women and men had surrounded a small group of non-Israelites. The "strangers," as they were called, had been separated out, the way a shepherd isolates the lambs destined for slaughter.

"Heathen!" shouted a woman, bent over with hatred.

"Go back to Egypt — we did not ask you to come here!"

"We are hearing the words of our God — how dare you stand before Him with your filthy ways?"

"Look! Look! They deck themselves with bracelets and earrings, which should be ours."

"They show their arms and shoulders — shameless harlots!"

Pebbles flew. Then stones.

"They are only girls! Have you no shame? They came to us for succor!" One of the Levites rushed over to disperse the crowd, waving his staff like a weapon.

The crowd still seethed and yelled. And Jesse could not understand their hatred. As he watched, his heart pounded with anger at the injustice, and he felt himself about to rush in, even before he saw Jennat.

Jesse turned to Avi. They exchanged a look, the will to act. Avi flexed his hands. Jesse was ready for a fight.

"Disperse!" shouted one of the Levites, raising his staff menacingly. "What mean you, to torment these people?"

"Come, boys," said Nathan, taking each of them by the shoulder. "It doesn't do to mix into these things — we have our own households to manage. Come away."

CHAPTER 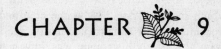 9

A few days of peace: they camped at the oasis of Elim, with twelve gushing wells and seventy palm trees and countless small tamarisk shrubs. These they used for shade and shelter, for fuel, and for the bark that provided an antidote to the poisonous wasps and scorpions that bedeviled the Israelites day and night.

Elim reminded them of Egypt. While they drank the cool water, the Israelites reminisced: "Remember the free-flowing Nile? The good waters? Sometimes at midnight, I'd take a dip in the river — ah, yes." Efrem, Talia's father, filled his goatskins and sealed them with pitch. Shira, his wife, added, "Remember the fruits we picked from the trees? The harvests we gathered in twice a year?"

"If we could only stay here, in this place." Cousin Seth picked his teeth and looked longingly at a cluster of dates. He was too lazy or too stiff to climb for them. "Avi, my boy, how about taking down some dates for all of us?"

Avi readily obliged, throwing off his sandals to climb up the slim trunk of a bowed palm tree. Jesse watched from below, and Talia spread a cloth to catch the dates, laughing as the tree shook and dates and debris tumbled down.

Baby Shosha, just beginning to stand, held her mother's hands and raised her knees high, squealing with delight. She was starting to speak, her favorite words being "Ma" and "Ahsi," which meant "Jesse." Now she charmed everyone with her vocabulary, and Talia picked her up and kissed her, and Jesse saw how lovely his cousin was, how gentle.

An understanding had been reached between the parents. Jesse and Talia would become officially betrothed as soon as they reached Canaan. There was time, Jesse thought, to nurture the idea. Time, perhaps, would dim his desire for Jennat.

The encampment at Elim lifted their spirits, especially after the experience at Marrah. There they had come upon a much-longed-for water hole. They had dipped in their cups and pails, tongues hanging out from thirst after three days without a drop. Jesse had filled his hand with water and given some to Shosha to drink, but the baby spat and wailed, "No! No!"

The water was bitter. Disappointment turned swiftly to rage. The people surged, as one, toward Moses and Aaron. Jesse and Avi were swept up by the angry crowd. Even in the midst of the chaos, Jesse was shocked by the people's swift, ugly rage. He saw the glint of a knife blade, the handful of stones that one man held. Women spat and screamed out horrible epithets. Someone hurled a mass of animal dung toward Moses' tent.

Jesse had never feared his own people before. Only the Egyptians, with their whips and their horses had made him cower. Pushed and punched by the surging crowd, he felt drowned in the Israelites' cries, chanted in roaring unison: "What shall we drink? *What? What?*"

Moses had gone into the wilderness then, staggering to and fro, and returned at last with a tree limb, huge and twisted.

This he flung into the water hole, while the Israelites watched, gaping in astonishment. Foam appeared upon the water. Then it sparkled, clear.

"See!" Moses cried. "If you will only listen to the voice of God!"

Aaron's eldest son, Nadab, went to dip in his cup, and he found the water sweet, proclaiming it all around and shouting, "See what the Lord has done?"

Once the people had drunk their fill and had eaten the dried, salted meat that, without water, had been utterly unpalatable, they were content.

"There was no need to confront Moses," Devorah said one evening at Elim. She was making sandals — chewing the leather to soften it, then stitching the straps with a stout needle. While she worked, Shosha sat on a blanket beside her, playing with a pile of seed pods that Jesse had found for her. "Moses knows what we need. He has only to ask Adonai; we will be maintained."

"Moses lived in the wilderness for years," said Rimon. He tugged at the tip of his long beard. "He should know what plants are useful, without having to ask anyone."

"You change from day to day, brother," Devorah said sharply. "Only a short time ago you urged us all to follow Moses. Now you say he is a mere man — "

"Of course he is a man!" Rimon shot back. "What else can you be thinking?"

"My wife longs for a savior," said Nathan, grinning, "since she found herself so poorly married."

Devorah flushed and bit her lip, twisting the leather straps around her fingers. "I say, let's look with our eyes and trust what we see. You all saw how Moses made the bitter water turn to sweet. Is this not a wonder?"

Jesse thought of the magicians of Egypt and the strange

feats they performed. Truly, he did not know whether Moses was a magician or a prophet.

"Well, we want to believe it," said Talia's mother, Shira. She had become thinner since the escape; folds of skin hung loosely around her chin. "But how do we really know that Moses is the one chosen by Adonai? We already have our leaders — like Rimon."

"I'm not asking to be the leader," Rimon objected, thrusting out his chest. "I only say we must use our heads. We have been gone now for a month. We should have gotten to Canaan long ago if we had followed the right route."

"Well, we went roundabout," said Efrem, "but still — I've heard the journey from Egypt should take no longer than two or three weeks."

"I am sure Moses wishes to get to Canaan as much as any of us," said Devorah tartly, "especially with all the murmuring and complaining he has to endure. Anybody would think the bitter water was his fault."

They moved on from Elim, thankful at least to be getting closer to their goal. Home. Canaan. Egypt was never really home, Jesse thought. Since his early childhood, his mother had taught him that their sojourn in Egypt was only temporary, until God's promise was to be fulfilled. Whenever Jesse enjoyed himself at the canals or in the fields, fishing, hunting, or playing, he was later made to feel wicked, somehow, by his mother, who cursed and resented every moment spent in Egypt.

He used to come upon her at prayer. Her face would be transformed, almost glowing, and Jesse would envy her connection to this distant God who had no face, no body. Then, too, he resented her purity. Sometimes it seemed that his mother was the only one who really believed in this redemption. How could Canaan be their home? Nobody alive had

122

any memory of it. Their great-grandfathers had labored in Egypt. Canaan was less than a myth, and this God who was supposed to protect them had been utterly silent and invisible for hundreds of years.

Now, suddenly, Adonai had appeared, like a long-absent father returned to demand fidelity and love. True, He had shown them His might and miracles, but in the long, dreary days between, it seemed that He had hidden His face again, perhaps forever.

Now the words "land of milk and honey" urged them onward, filled them with hope and longing — but when would they get there? For the wanderer, the only time that matters is tomorrow and tomorrow; today is only a means of getting there, something to be endured.

Gone from the oasis of Elim, they confronted the wilderness of Sinai, harsh and uncompromising, worse than anything before. Where before the earth had been tamed and leveled, here huge granite peaks suddenly loomed ahead. Deep canyons promised disaster; even the shrubs along the side of the road were deadly, as they soon discovered. One man chewed on an innocent-looking leaf for breakfast and was buried late that afternoon.

They were hungry. Hunger made them weak and desolate, and finally, furious.

"Moses!" Women's voices rose sharply among men's. "Why didn't you leave us in Egypt? Better to die there with meat in our bellies than to starve to death in this desert!"

Word came down, for Moses had walked again to the hills, and he called out to the people: "Bread shall rain down from heaven!"

They jeered, disbelieving.

Moses told them: "In the evenings you shall have meat, and in the morning you shall have your fill of bread, and you will recognize that Adonai is your God, the same one who brought you out of Egypt, and who now has heard all your complaints."

Jesse stood with the young people, his cousins. He heard a strange sound, a humming, and he smelled a pungent odor in the air, like moist hide or feathers. The sky darkened, as if a purple shadow had been laid over it. Talia clutched Jesse's arm, pointing to the sky.

"Look!" she breathed. "Birds."

"Quail," said Jesse. "Avi, quick! The nets. Omar, help us," he yelled. "It takes four to hold the net."

Omar came running, ready for the hunt.

Jesse ran to his pack, where among the bundles and bags were several large nets for fowling and trapping. He got a net, and each took a corner, stretching it out between them. The four fanned out, then braced themselves as the birds, screeching and diving, were caught in midflight.

The struggle, the chase, the joy went on for hours. The migrating birds, exhausted and stunned, were bagged by the thousands, plucked, roasted, and consumed.

Jesse and Talia sat together, sated for the first time in weeks. They rested in a small clearing, their backs to a natural wall carved by the wind out of a granite hill. A small pile of quail bones, picked clean of meat, lay between them, and there were still plenty of roasted birds for tomorrow. They had shared their fire with a dozen others, who had by now drifted off, and Talia and Jesse were alone.

"In Canaan, when we are married," Talia proposed, smiling slightly and looking away, "you won't have to herd the goats and sheep anymore. I know you hate it."

Jesse looked up at her, surprised. "How do you know?"

She laughed. "Your face, whenever you have to bring them

round. Maybe we will grow our food — corn and beans and wheat."

"Who will provide our meat, then?"

"Oh, I will keep a few animals and tend them myself — until our children are old enough to do it."

Jesse started. Children. He saw the flush on Talia's cheeks and realized she knew all that was implied by the thought of their having children. "You want many children?" he asked.

"Many," she said. "The first boy, I will name Nissim. Because it will be like a miracle that you love me, and we are finally married." Talia's breast heaved, and her eyes darkened with passion.

Jesse reached out and touched her hair, thick and glossy. The soft strands clung to his fingers. Her cheek was near his, her mouth parted, her breath sweet and warm. He placed his fingertips to her lips, gently touching; then he traced her cheek and her throat, and then his lips were upon hers.

He had seldom kissed anyone, never on the mouth this way. The Egyptians kissed with their noses, a sorry substitute for this warmth and joy. Jennat had offered him her nose, and she had turned her face away when his lips sought hers.

Not Talia. She seemed to have waited for this kiss all her life. Sounds enveloped him, such as he had never heard from a woman. And then, suddenly, he heard laughter.

Jesse drew away from Talia. His heart pounded and leapt when he saw the group of young people, all foreigners, strangers, watching them. Jennat and Shepset were with them, and Jesse called out a curse, shocked by the interruption and painfully embarrassed.

"Look how they mate!" one of the boys jeered, laughing. "Even dogs know better!"

"Come," said Jesse, taking Talia's hand. "Let's go."

But Talia's eyes blazed, and she stiffened her body as she stared at Jennat. "I know who you are," she said with a viciousness in her tone that struck Jesse like a blow.

"Of course you know," Jennat responded, unmoved. "You came to our house. You stole our jewels."

Talia bristled; she raised herself to full height. "Your house?" she scoffed. "I thought it belonged to an Egyptian man and that you were his — what were you in that house?"

"I was a slave," said Jennat. "Like you. But at least I wasn't a thief." She pointed to a chain around Talia's neck, gold with small turquoise beads. "That was mine," she said. "How does it feel to wear stolen ornaments?"

"We only did what we were commanded," Talia retorted, angry. "I stole nothing. I asked you for them, and you willingly gave —"

"You can have it," said Jennat. She spoke to Talia, but her gaze was directed at Jesse. "It's nothing to me." Jennat tossed her hair over her shoulder. "I have everything I need."

"Then why do you come begging at our camp?" Talia asked.

"Begging?" Jennat's eyes narrowed. "What did I ever take from you?"

"Come, Talia," Jesse said. "Come away." He pulled her arm, but she remained firm.

"The quail, for one thing," said Talia, pointing to the string of birds that hung at Jennat's side.

"The quail? Yours? I hear the gods provide, not you!"

"Not *gods*, only our God, Adonai. Who do you think parted the sea for us? Who do you think sent the quail? Have you no shame?"

"Talia, *please!*" Jesse stared from one to the other; in a moment they would come to blows. Talia was trembling, and Jennat's entire bearing predicted assault.

Jesse turned and began to walk away. His heart hammered with dread, embarrassment, and a surge of desire. The two of them were ridiculous. And wonderful. They were fighting, he knew, not over jewels or quail or deities, but over him!

On he went, loping back to camp to find Avi. He had things to talk about that one could share only with a best friend.

As he went, he heard one last taunt from Talia. "Why don't you ask your little wooden gods for food? Then you don't have to take ours."

And Jennat shouted back, "Don't worry about me — I'm leaving you and your kind the moment I can!"

It lay on the ground in the morning. It glistened from the hollows of trees. Manna, it was called, said Moses. It had fallen in the night, God's gift, to be gathered, baked, eaten.

It was soft and powdery and sweet. When baked, it was crisp. Mixed with grain, it became chewy, highly satisfying.

Jennat and Shepset went out early to gather it.

Shepset complained that it tasted bland, like clay. Jennat, on the other hand, loved the manna and ate hungrily. She baked it into cakes and chewed it while she walked. She had heard Moses instruct everyone that it must be gathered fresh each day except the Sabbath. Only on the Sabbath would the manna collected the previous day stay fresh. Shepset, unbelieving, picked a quantity and put it into a jar for the next morning. Upon opening the lid, Shepset discovered to her horror that the jar was filled with writhing worms.

"Their God, Adonai," Shepset said hotly, "does deliver fine food!" She shuddered in disgust.

"You did not listen," said Jennat. "So the worms are your reward."

"Are you coming under their spell, then?" Shepset inquired.

127

"Do you really believe that this is sent by their God? I hear from the shepherds who have known this land that the stuff is given out by an insect. It is nothing new, neither magic nor miracle."

"Well, I like it," said Jennat. She had formed the habit, upon gathering her portion, of swiftly whispering her thanks to the unseen God. Shepset would have been aghast; she kept her daily rituals to the various gods of Egypt.

"Primitive," Shepset called the Israelites. "They know nothing of ceremony, of beauty. Do you remember the gorgeous temples and shrines of Egypt? Abodes of the gods — ah, this cursed wilderness."

"And yet we are able to live in this wilderness," murmured Jennat. "Their God provides."

"Look," argued Shepset, "if this God of theirs were really to provide food, why the same fare every day? Why not fishes and melons and onions and grapes — the sort we used to eat in Egypt?"

"I don't know, Shepset," Jennat said between clenched teeth. "I really don't know."

Jesse came to her and Shepset early one morning as they gathered the manna. He held out a small clay pot to Shepset.

"My mother prepared some more salve for you," he said. "You have not been about much," he added, looking not at Shepset but at Jennat.

Jennat spoke. "We know when we are not wanted," she said.

"Pay no heed to Talia — she's just a girl," said Jesse.

"Woman enough to consider herself your bride!" Jennat snapped.

Jesse sighed. He moved nearer to Jennat, and Shepset, pretending full attention to gathering manna, walked on.

"You know how these things are, Jennat," Jesse said, extending both hands to her. But she ignored the gesture.

"She is a rude person, as well as a thief," Jennat retorted.

"Well, *I* am no thief," Jesse said evenly. "I took nothing." He added, "I heard you say you are leaving. How can you leave? Where would you go?"

"What business is it of yours? I go where I please. Did you think I escaped from In-hop-tep to be tied to another master?"

He glanced at her jar full of manna. "You'd better gather enough for tomorrow, too," he said. "Tomorrow is the Sabbath. None will appear."

"So I heard," snapped Jennat. Then, after a pause, "Your Adonai does perform some unusual wonders," she admitted, "even to setting aside a day of rest."

"The manna is a miracle," Jesse said earnestly. "Everyone has what he needs, no more and no less."

"So it should be," said Jennat. "What do you want from me?" she asked, suddenly brusque again.

"Nothing! Only to talk to you."

"Your people don't want you near me. I can feel that. Your mother hates me. I see it in her face. Why do you come after me this way?" She turned aside, her posture rigid. "As soon as we meet other travelers, I am leaving you and all this trouble behind me. I will live with people who know how to talk to each other."

"I know how to talk," Jesse said softly. "Let me talk to you. Let me tell you — I regret the things Talia said to you. They were untrue. She is hasty and — very young. She is frightened out here in the wilderness. She is —"

"She, she, she!" Jennat clapped her hands over her ears. "Go and talk to *her*. I don't need to hear your words. I am not frightened, not of anything! Listen, I am going to see strange lands, wonderful sights, cedar trees, copper mines and turquoise . . ."

She turned her back to him, and Jesse, standing behind her,

spoke softly, his tone half amused. "How are you going to do that?" he asked.

"I'm going to join a caravan, work hard, soon become the owner of my own wagon. Maybe I'll own a camel! Listen, I know how to barter — I've known it since I was three years old. And I know gems and spices and fabrics and things — it's not for nothing that I lived and worked in the home of In-hop-tep all those years."

"Hush, hush," Jesse said, trying to soothe her, his hand on her arm, but Jennat pushed his hand away.

"Caravan lady!" she cried, filled with the power of it now, with the idea of wealth and independence. "That's what they'll call me, and I'll be rich, and I'll go wherever I please, to the copper mines and the cedar trees and the bazaars where merchants gather —"

Then Jesse's arms came around her, soft, and he whispered, his mouth at her neck, "Will you go alone? Or will you take a friend?"

She tried to hold herself stiff, but she felt herself warming to his touch and his breath.

Jesse's hands were on her back now, slowly caressing, and he murmured, "Why did you laugh that day you saw me with Talia?"

She turned to face him. "I didn't laugh," she said.

Then his lips were upon hers. The touch surprised her, almost tickled, and she nearly did laugh out loud. But then, as Jesse's mouth pressed hers, lips parting, every other thought was blotted out, and she thought his name, *Jesse*, over and over, and she held him close in her arms, feeling the strength and the warmth of him, and when at last he released her, she could not speak for confusion.

"Oh, Jennat," said Jesse, his voice husky, "don't leave. Stay with us."

"With you? Why?" she whispered. Then her voice rose as she demanded, "Aren't you promised to your cousin, Talia? What do you want with me?"

"I — we are friends," Jesse said. "Aren't we friends?"

"Was that the kiss of a friend?" she asked, turning away, her heart pounding with a wild mix of feelings.

"Jennat," Jesse said, hands outstretched, "I think of you constantly. Is it so terrible of me? Everything is in confusion, this cursed wilderness, the promise of a land —"

"What has this to do with us?" Jennat asked.

Jesse shook his head. "We need time to know each other. Time to be settled. Things could change for us —"

She faced him, chin thrust forward, features set. "Will you take me to your people, then? Tell them to treat me like their own?"

"Nobody has treated you badly."

"Ha!" Jennat cried, whipping her cloak tight around her body. "What do you think will change, unless you, yourself, change it? You're a coward, Jesse, and a fool. You think you can come and kiss me whenever you like, and that I will come to you. I'm going to the Midianites. I know that your Moses lived among them once, that his father-in-law, Jethro, is returning with his servants to Midian."

"What has that to do with you?" Jesse asked.

"Perhaps they will let me go with them, for protection," Jennat said, forming the plan even as she spoke.

"Stay here," Jesse repeated, his voice filled with longing. "I will protect you. I promise."

"How?" Jennat demanded.

Jesse gave no answer, except to pull her close again. She resisted, pulling away. And then she surrendered to his kiss. And she thought, I will stay a little longer, for Shepset's sake — knowing it was only part of the truth.

* * *

Again, water gave out. There were no wells, no natural springs to be found.

The people marched upon Moses, shouting and threatening to return to Egypt. Moses lifted his head and his voice in loud agony: "Lord, what shall I do with these people? Before long they will stone me!"

Then Moses grew silent, and he meditated. At last he summoned the elders. He led them to a place where a large rock dominated the barren landscape, and the dry rustling of sand and the skittering of lizards held out little hope of any water.

And here he told them that they would find water, for thus had Adonai instructed him. Moses drew up his staff. With one swift blow he struck the rock. Water gushed out, spilled down into gullies, rippled over the stones, bubbled into a pond, and all the elders rushed back to the people, shouting and rejoicing:

"Moses has brought forth water for us! He brought forth water from the rock!"

The people gazed at Moses in wonder, and they bowed their heads, and for a time, they were trusting.

The tribe of Benjamin, to which Jesse belonged, brought up the rear. It meant that they did not have to break a trail, but it also meant having to be on guard for marauding desert bands, wild men who rode horses and preyed on travelers. The Israelites, unused to fighting after their years of servitude, struggled to learn to defend themselves.

Nathan, uneasy in close combat, fortified himself with a full quiver of arrows, which he kept at his back. Jesse, according to his cousin Avi's instruction, had learned to wield a long, sharp blade. He was not of age to be a soldier, but Nathan had told him firmly, "You must be vigilant, Jesse. Our enemies won't look to your age. Besides, you have the size and strength of a grown man."

At the start of each day's march, tribes kept together in formation. Avi moved out with his people, all the Reubenites, and Jesse with his, the Benjaminites. Later, Avi and Jesse would always meet. They moved their small flocks out together, they talked and joked, and they made plans.

"When we get to Canaan," said Avi one day, "I'm going to build things."

"I didn't know you were interested in anything but wrestling," Jesse teased. Then he added seriously, "What will you build?"

"Well, we have to build ourselves a city, with thick walls and storehouses, with roads and granaries. Everything we build — every wall, every rooftop — will be ours. Imagine it, Jesse! Not to labor for somebody else's sake, but our own. Imagine it!"

Avi's passion transported Jesse into his own dream. "I would make fine and beautiful things," he said. "There must be gold and gems in this new land, if Adonai promised it to us. I shall make gilded vessels, necklaces, rings."

"We'll all plant our vegetables," Avi went on. "And they will be watered from heaven. It is a land of milk and honey, my father says. I'll find a wife and settle down —"

"Where will you get a wife?" teased Jesse. "You are too rough for a woman."

"Several have wanted me," Avi objected, giving Jesse a punch on the arm. "That Egyptian, Shepset, casts her eye on me constantly."

"But you can't marry an Egyptian," Jesse said.

"Why not?" Avi responded.

"A heathen? Your father would stop you."

Avi hurled a small stone out to the shrubbery, making it skip and spin. He said, "Moses himself married a Midianite woman. The woman has let go of her gods. His sons follow Adonai. They are even circumcised.

"How do you know this?"

"When your father is an elder," said Avi with pride, "you learn such things."

"Do you like Shepset?" Jesse asked.

"She is — interesting to me," said Avi.

"But her face . . ."

"It interests me," Avi said shortly, and he took to skipping pebbles along the ground, whistling as he did so. He glanced at Jesse. "What about you and that girl, Jennat?"

"What about her?" Jesse snapped. "We are friends — that's all."

Avi laughed and threw a pebble high and far.

"Besides, she isn't the type to settle down," Jesse added. He felt the flush on his face. "She wants to join a caravan."

Avi shrugged. "That's what she says. I've seen the way she trots after you — like a young pup."

Jesse shrugged, then sighed. "She also trots after her little wooden gods. She is not the type to change. Shepset is different, accustomed to being pleasing. Jennat is . . ." He cleared his throat, thinking the words *stubborn! wild!* And he let the thought trail away.

The long, endless march took its toll on the old, the women, the little ones.

Devorah came to Jesse and urged him, "Take the baby for me, Jesse. Let her ride the mule for a few minutes. She loves it so, and I'm getting weary."

"Of course," said Jesse. He took the baby and held her atop the mule with its pack, and Shosha giggled and kicked her little legs. The day was mild, and they had eaten plenty, both manna and meat, and had drunk their fill of fresh water, so that travel was easy and even pleasant.

A few men took up a chant. It was one of the songs they had sung in Egypt, while toiling in the quarries and the mines, a song of entreaty to Adonai, which of course the Egyptians did not understand. It had given them some small satisfaction to be praying under the very noses of their taskmasters, cursing them to heaven in their very sight.

> *Hear our prayer, O Lord!*
> *See Thy children, how they groan,*
> *Sorely afflicted by evil masters,*
> *Weary and sick, sorely oppressed,*
> *Hear our prayer, O Lord!*
> *Lead us home!*

The laboring song gave way to another song, one of merriment and thanksgiving, the same song the women had sung at the sea. One after the other the people took up the refrain:

> *Sing to God for His great victory;*
> *Horse and rider He has cast into the sea!*

The attack came without warning. "Amalekites! Amalekites!" cried the scouts. There was no time to think; Jesse saw the dust of the marauders rising behind them. He heard the hooves of their horses and the clash of metal as swords were drawn and ready.

A single word screamed in his brain: *Shosha! Shosha!*

Suddenly they were surrounded, and the very ground seemed to leap with the force of the attack, and it brought its own stench and steaming air. Their bodies were thick, their bare chests broad and hairy. Their faces were indistinguishable, eyes glinting with joyful lust. Spears, arrows, stones flew about, piercing and smashing. The crush of bone, the thud of a body, the ear-splitting shriek of a horse, and the huge groaning of fallen men all mingled in an unreal tableau. What had been, moments before, a gentle passage, turned to mayhem.

Limbs were torn from living bodies. The belly of a woman was split wide open; her hands clutched at the gap. A child was crushed under a horse; its skull became, in an instant, as flat as a plate, with ooze all around. One man, hobbling on a crutch, was instantly beheaded as a horseman streaked past. Head and body lay apart, joined by a thin trail of blood.

Shosha! Shosha! She had simply vanished when the Amalekites came.

Evil Amalek had watched the Israelites' slow progress, had waited until this turning point to attack from the rear, to plunder and murder and spill out his glee at the bloodshed.

Awareness of the catastrophe swept along the lines. Trumpets rang out, and the shofar's call to battle. Moses, with Joshua and Hur beside him, commanded the fighting from a hilltop.

Later Jesse would know that the battle had raged all day. While he was caught in the middle of its ferocious noise and pitched assault, it seemed everlasting and yet a mere flash of time. And later, too, he would remember hearing a single scream as Shosha fell to the ground, and in an instant, she seemed to have disappeared.

A warrior fell upon him, huge of chest and arm; blood spurted into Jesse's eyes as he plunged his knife into taut flesh and felt it give way, like the flesh of cattle being quartered. Jesse felt no emotion, only surprise that it was easy, so easy, to kill, to sense the warm rush of blood on his face and arms, then to whirl about looking for another, another, to discover his own voracious appetite for it, a need that grew stronger with each thrust of his dagger.

Jesse heard no clear commands. He reacted only to his thoughts — to live, to kill, to thrust, to run. He was hardly aware of his own screams, but heard them as from a distance, and felt the contortions of his face and body much later, when the battle was done.

The odds were impossible. The surprise attack should have left the Israelites decimated. But the Amalekites were beaten. Their corpses littered the desert floor.

In the aftermath of the battle, Jesse lay slumped against a dead horse, hardly aware of the flies and the smells around him. His eyes felt glassy, his vision blurred. A hand fell upon his chest, and he heard a faint sob.

He opened his eyes, and to his amazement, there was Nathan, crouched before him, fist raised and shouting to the heavens, "Curse You! Now You have killed him!"

"I'm — all right," Jesse managed to say through parched lips.

"Get up, then!" Nathan shouted. "Get up or they'll bury you, you fool!"

Jesse got up. He stared at his father. Nathan was unscathed, while Jesse ached in every bone and felt as if his ribs were broken.

People like my father, he thought bitterly, bear no marks, experience no pain. They slide through life like serpents, creeping on their bellies, never meeting anyone eye to eye, unless it were in preview to striking them dead.

Only moments later Jesse realized, when he heard his mother's voice raised in terrible anguish, that Shosha was dead. In the melee, she had been crushed.

And the Lord said to Moses, "Write this as a reminder in the Book, and repeat it carefully to Joshua. I will utterly blot out the memory of Amalek from under the heavens."

Moses built an altar and named it "God Is My Banner." And he said, "The Lord will make war with the descendants of Amalek forever."

CHAPTER  10

To wake up in the morning, still innocent from sleep, was the worst punishment, for then came the blow of realization, repeated: she's dead. Gone. Shosha is dead, and it's my fault.

Sister. Baby. Child of his mother's lost hope. Jesse had promised Devorah to care for Shosha always. And now she was dead. Shosha had been in his care. Now she was dead.

Amalek, the evil one, killer of babies — hatred filled Jesse with a strange new power. He was glad he had killed; he wished he had drawn more blood to drench the earth in revenge for his sister. Over and over Jesse replayed the battle in his mind, the rushing hordes, the swift butchery. How quickly they had all become embroiled in this killing, and Jesse knew that his lust for blood had been no less than that of Amalek and his battalions.

"What courage! By heaven, Jesse," Avi had exclaimed, eyes wide in admiration. "You were ferocious! How many did you get? I saw you fell two of them, at least. You should have a trophy. Since when did you become a warrior?"

It was not courage, Jesse knew, but naked fear. And more: savagery, the lust for revenge. Sometimes, especially when he awakened in the night and heard the desert wind slamming into the granite hills and whistling through the steep, cold canyons, Jesse trembled at his own savagery. His mother had taught him, since childhood, to be merciful, to kill even an animal in the spirit of grace.

At other times, when he thought of his baby sister, how she clung to him, how she laughed and clapped her little hands in joy at her discoveries, he was glad for his fury; he had avenged his little sister. He was a man.

The women prepared the tiny body for burial. They wrapped Shosha's broken limbs in white linen, and Seth, who was skilled in carpentry, patched a small coffin from bits of acacia wood brought from Egypt. And all the while Devorah only stared out from her hood, eyes wide and dry, a woman entranced with grief.

Nathan disappeared for a day and a night, and returned reeking of liquor, heaving and swaying.

Uncle Rimon, come to bury Shosha with ritual and prayers, took a look at Nathan, and led him away to the edge of a stone bluff. Jesse saw their shapes from afar, outlined against the sunlight, Rimon gesturing, his body and limbs jerking with the force of his words. When the two men returned, Nathan was chastened — red-faced and weak.

Then Uncle Rimon lifted his arms and his voice in prayer, so rich, so resounding, and so filled with heartbreak and trust that even strangers wept, and the lamentations rang across the wilderness for hours and hours. "Oh, God, we trust in Your wisdom and in Your power, in Your merciful, ineffable ways. We cannot know Your design or Your justice, but we abide with perfect faith . . ."

Even Nathan's back quivered, and Jesse shuddered with sobs. Only Devorah remained dry-eyed, her face set like granite, the features sharp, as if chiseled by a blade.

She had not eaten in days, Jesse knew. She had not wept, even in the night, for her eyes remained wide and clear, though deeply sunken into the sharp ridges of her cheeks.

"Bow your heads," intoned Rimon, arms extended and hands spread, to bless them. "The Lord will bless you; darkness and weeping may tarry for the moment, but He will change your mourning into joy —"

"Liar!" screamed Devorah. "Liar!"

A gasp fell over the assembly. Hands reached toward Devorah, but no one would touch her; she seemed demonic in her grief.

"Hush, sister," Rimon flung at her, his eyes still blazing with the intensity of his prayers "Submit, Devorah — it is His will —"

"Killer of babies!" Devorah screamed, her fists clenched so tight that the knuckles glowed white as stone, and her face a mask of hatred. "He loves us, you say? Liar! Liar! What is this love, that kills babies, that tears a little one from her mother's breast, that asks for sacrifice and more sacrifice — I have nothing left to give. Nothing!" she screamed. Jesse ran to his mother and caught her in his arms, but she pushed him away violently.

"Never speak to me again of Adonai," she said, her voice a rasping whisper now. "I do not submit. I did not give Him my baby. He stole her from me, just as He has stolen all my love, my labor, my heart, so that I am only a stone. What can a stone give? Nothing."

One by one the mourners came, each tossing a handful of earth upon the little coffin. All except for the mother, who stood aloof under a wispy branch, sunk into silence again.

Afterward, when they moved out with their beasts and their belongings, Jesse's mother became a shadowy, silent shape, her body enclosed in her black robe, her steps measured and tireless. Where before Devorah had known fatigue and soreness, like everyone else, now she seemed void of feelings, her body nothing more than a tumbleweed, pushed by the wind.

Jesse felt like a shadow in her presence. To look at her face, with those luminous, unforgiving eyes, was painful.

Jesse's father rattled off remedies. Tragedy had loosened his tongue. Jesse felt the keen edge of his parents' estrangement. They were opposite even now, in their grief. Their bitterness turned toward each other, not in words, but in the set of their heads, a flick of the hand. And Jesse thought, How terrible marriage is, that it twists two people together forever in bonds of iron, inseparable, unbending.

"Look forward, Devorah," Nathan said loudly. "Go mingle with the people. You'll make yourself sick with this silence. What's to be done? Nothing. Life is what it is. You must go forward, wife, think of tomorrow. Don't look back. There can be other babies. . . ."

Devorah only stared ahead. She had lost even the will to oppose him.

Uncle Rimon and Aunt Channa came every evening, when they were settled into camp for the night. Then they sat round the small dung fire, the dull smoke stinging their eyes, and Rimon led them in prayer. He stood swaying as he prayed, and was soon lost in his meditation.

But Jesse could not concentrate for all the questions that afflicted him, like the stinging insects that lit on his ears, his mouth. If God knows all things, Jesse thought one evening by the fire, why did He allow us to be prey to Amalek? Why didn't He warn us? If God knew of our agony in Egypt, why didn't He lead us out sooner?

"Praise Adonai for all His works," prayed Rimon.

Praise! For what? For suffering? If God were infinitely good,

Jesse raged, would He allow a baby to be trampled to death? Would He allow a mother to lose not one child, but three? Jesse thought back to the two sons that had preceded him. They were like dim shadows in his own past, conceived and killed long before his birth, yet they were also part of him. They were part of his mother's intensity for him, the way she looked into his face or touched his cheek. It was in the words she didn't say to him — even in her harshness.

While Rimon prayed and swayed, Talia and Shira listened. Their faces shone with commitment. But Devorah sat empty, sagging, and Jesse's mind was aflame with his burdens.

Afterward, when the others had gone, Talia remained with Devorah by the dung fire, and Jesse saw clearly the contrast between the two women — one young and full of vitality, the other empty.

Talia stayed with Devorah in her tent and slept beside her at night. Talia seemed to soothe Devorah, so that she did not cry out so often in the night.

"When Jesse and I are married," she murmured to Devorah, "you will have babies again. Grandchildren. You will be happy again — you'll see, Ima. If our firstborn is a girl, we will name her Shosha. I will be your daughter. I will tend you and care for you always, and when you are old . . ."

It was true, Jesse thought. Talia would bond herself to Devorah in duty and in love. She would be a true daughter to her. Watching Talia with his mother added to Jesse's guilt over his impossible desire for Jennat.

On three separate nights, he dreamed the same dream. There was a steep road, littered with rocks that, when he set down his foot, skittered down past him, leaving him bruised, forcing him to proceed on all fours, like an animal. Ahead, blinding sunlight accosted him. He became aware, then, of two paths, one steep and treacherous, the other obliterated by a strange whirling fog. Each time it was the same; he set his foot upon the steep path, and he was plunged down into an abyss.

All day as Jesse walked, bringing along the sheep and goats, he could see Talia and Devorah ahead, walking without speaking. Occasionally Talia took Devorah's hand or adjusted Devorah's shawl. Jesse resented Talia's growing strength against Devorah's growing weakness, and then he cursed himself again for his meanness. Talia also mourned Shosha. She was the only one who could speak of the baby to Devorah, somehow bringing back the living memory.

"She was the sweetest, dearest baby," Talia said. "I loved her. Those bright eyes! And she was starting to talk. Adonai wanted her with Him," she said to Jesse. "I believe that."

Jesse bit his lips, biting back sharp words.

He hated the daily trek, the alternating heat and cold, the monotony. His feet became numb. Pebbles cut into his flesh. Scabs and painful ridges formed on his feet. His back ached from the constant climb and from lifting the lambs out of danger. He had to pull and whip the donkey. That damnable beast would lie down, rolling on its pack, and once it bit Jesse on the arm. At home in Egypt, the animals had been pastured on the green hills. Now they had to be tended, herded, kept from falling down the cliffs.

Late each afternoon, all eyes would be upon Moses, waiting for his staff to point to the resting place. Then came the tedious rounding up of beasts, the setting up of tents, making dung fires, rummaging through one's gear for a bit of flour or dried meat, or fortuitous bounties — dates, nuts, berries — harvested along the way. There was never really enough to eat, but neither was there energy enough to cook and consume much.

It had become a ritual to sit at night and talk about food.

"Remember the flesh pots of Egypt?" Efrem would begin, chewing on a small bit of dried lamb.

His wife snorted. "What flesh pots — when did we eat meat? Once a month, perhaps."

"Ah, but that once was succulent, superb! Remember the corn, juicy and ripe?" He turned to the others — Devorah, Nathan, Jesse. "My wife knew a hundred ways to prepare the corn — cakes, puddings, biscuits, stew."

"Lucky man, whose wife likes to cook," said Nathan congenially. "Now, Devorah is a storyteller. I have said it often: if only we could eat your words!" He laughed.

Jesse, glancing at his mother, tensed. She seemed not to have heard, though her lips moved silently.

"Aunt Devorah is a good cook," Talia murmured, patting Devorah's arm. "But actually, I think I would rather hear a story than eat."

"Tell us a story, Devorah," Shira urged.

Devorah looked up, startled. She gathered her shawl around her shoulders, shivering against the night chill.

She shook her head. Then, oddly, she began to laugh, her voice rising dangerously and her shoulders shaking, as if she were struck with fits and might die from her own laughter. Jesse ran to hold her.

"What is it?" Nathan called, uncomprehending. "She laughs! Tell us, what is so funny?"

"Hush, Nathan," said Shira in a low voice, and Jesse saw tears in Shira's eyes. "She is not to be consoled."

Early one morning, Jennat came to the tents. Under her arm she carried an extra shawl, which she had carefully washed at a small trickling spring. In her hand was a leather pouch filled with coins. She looked for Jesse, but saw nobody. She heard the sound of women's voices from a distance. Perhaps they had gone to gather the morning's manna.

Jennat stood aside, watching the animals nuzzling about for fodder. The sheep brayed comically, sounding almost like children. A baby goat dashed out from the fold, kicking up its hooves. The sand rose in a cloud. Its mother, turning, gave a sharp bleat. The kid rushed to her side, eager to drink. The mother delivered a sharp kick. The kid cried out, then loped off to do more mischief. And as she watched the animals, for the first time closely observant, Jennat wondered, Were they really gods incarnate, as Shepset said?

The Apis bull, Shepset said, was the god Osiris come to earth. When the bull died, another was born, reincarnated; thus the gods lived continually among humans, taking forms of animals.

The Israelites slaughtered and killed their sheep. They harnessed their cattle and also consumed them when they were old. Jennat shuddered.

She was about to leave when Avi appeared, his hair wet from washing, holding a jar of manna into which he dipped again and again. He nodded, laughing, for his cheeks were full.

" 'Morning," he said at last. "You are looking for Jesse."

"I heard about his little sister's death," Jennat said, looking down. Avi's muscular legs and chest were fully revealed, as he wore only a loincloth and sandals. The Hebrew men usually dressed more modestly. It was strange to see a man so exposed again, and Jennat realized with surprise that already, in these few weeks, her ideas were changing.

"Jesse's mother is desolate," said Avi with a sigh. "She won't speak, hardly eats. She used to pray in the morning, always. Now she is silent. Or she laughs."

"Laughs?"

Avi touched the side of his head. "Grief makes her laugh.

Who knows why? What is her laughter for? We don't know. Even my father, Rimon, her brother, can't break into her melancholy."

"I'm sorry," sighed Jennat. "I came to —"

"Shepset isn't with you?" Avi glanced about, as if to discover her.

"No. She is —" Jennat kept silent, unwilling to explain Shepset's revulsion — "she is resting."

"Ah." Avi crossed his arms over his chest. "She has no relations here. She is quite alone." They were statements, but also questions. Jennat knew immediately where this would lead but was unable to seize control.

"Yes. She is alone, except for me, her friend."

"She is a fine-looking girl," Avi said.

Jennat started. How could Avi say this? Scars crisscrossed Shepset's face, never to be obliterated. As she aged, the skin would pucker, like cloth.

"She used to be a temple dancer," Jennat said.

"I know. I have inquired about her. She was supposed to become a priestess. Well, my father says there is a reason for all things. My father says that God makes plans for us. In time, they are revealed."

"A plan for every person?" Jennat smiled, and she quickly covered her mouth with her hand.

"I would like to marry Shepset," said Avi without further preamble. "I would like you to speak to her for me, as you are her friend. She needn't bring anything to the marriage. Since she has no parents, of course, we wouldn't expect it. Only herself."

Jennat stared at Avi, and she swallowed hard, her throat suddenly invaded by the dryness and the constant wind. "But — is it what your family wants? Can you marry anybody, even —"

"Look," Avi said, "even Moses has a heathen wife. My father and I will teach Shepset about Adonai. We'll bring her into our midst."

"But your aunt — Jesse's mother," Jennat stammered, "she always — she looks at me as if I were an evil spirit. I feel her hatred. She doesn't even want Jesse to speak to me."

"Well, Aunt Devorah is different," Avi said. He traced a circle in the sand with his big toe, staring down at it. "Devorah has always loved Talia and wanted her for Jesse. She says there is grief enough in marriage, without taking a foreigner." He stopped, coughed, then muttered, "Your pardon."

"Foreigner — who was the foreigner in Egypt?" Jennat demanded. "What makes her think I want anything from her precious son? I never even spoke to him until he forced himself upon me, came to my window.... Well, it's nothing to me what she thinks." Jennat tossed her hair over her shoulder. Then she said, "If you want me to talk to Shepset, I will."

"Tell her I will provide for her."

"All right."

"And if she is willing, my father will come to speak with her, and then —"

"Yes, yes," said Jennat, brushing her hair back from her face, for the wind had risen, whipping things about in sudden gusts.

"Avi! Avi!" Jesse approached, looking for his cousin, stopping short when he saw Jennat.

"Hello!" he exclaimed.

Jennat scanned his face, found the sorrow there. Softly she said, "I heard about your baby sister, how she died. I came to bring you my — to tell you —" Tears choked back her words. She held out the shawl and the leather pouch with coins. "I have brought this shawl. For the baby. You can wrap her in it, and some coins for the afterlife —"

Jesse glanced at Avi, then said brusquely, "We buried my sister two days ago."

"Already?" Jennat bit her lip, glanced about uneasily. "I'm sorry. I didn't know. I thought . . ." In Eygpt, a funeral was a spectacular event lasting for weeks, with mourners chanting, sobbing, gashing their cheeks, bringing gifts for the dead, to ease the long journey to the next life.

"We don't send things with our dead," Jesse said coldly. "We offer prayers, not money and clothing. Don't you know that the body rots in the grave? The body is nothing. Only the spirit rises —"

"Jesse!" Avi interrupted loudly. "Jennat only meant to be kind. She came with gifts. Now, you are sounding like —"

"Like what?" Jesse glared at his cousin.

"Like my father, when he is at his worst!"

Jesse whirled around, and in the next moment he was gone.

Jennat tried to blink away her tears of rage. "What's the matter with you?" she cried. "You are hateful!" she screamed after Jesse, despising her own shrieking voice, her inability to reach him. She ached with the need to soothe and heal, and he had damned all her best intentions. Curse him!

"Your cousin is rude and arrogant," she burst out at Avi, who stood before her, chewing his lip.

"I'm sorry," Avi murmured. "You'll still speak to Shepset, won't you?"

She glared at Avi, ready to scream. Then she nodded. "Yes. I said I would."

"Thank you."

Jennat turned away, breathing deep, remembering the accusations from Shepset and In-hop-tep, of Hebrew arrogance and apartness. Yes, they separated themselves, peculiar people with peculiar ways. How, Jennat asked herself, could she

149

have found Jesse attractive? How could she have lain awake nights, wanting him?

She bundled the shawl tightly under her arm and flung back at Avi, "I will never bring gifts to your people again. I will never speak to Jesse again, and you can tell him so."

With his cousin Avi, Jesse could be truthful. He told him of his dream. "The two roads, of course, are the two women," he said wearily, his head in his hands. "I know I should go to Talia's parents and tell them I will be their son, gladly and willingly. It is all arranged."

Avi nodded slowly. His brow was furrowed, his lips pursed. "The whole family would be pleased," he murmured.

"But I feel as if I'm cutting myself off, falling into a canyon with high, steep sides."

"I thought you loved Talia," Avi said.

"Everyone loves Talia," Jesse said. "She is like a sister to everyone."

"I see. There is no — passion."

"Not for me. Not with her." Jesse's face burned. He remembered the pleasantness of Talia's kiss, but Jennat's kisses touched him like flames. "Jennat is — different," he said.

Avi nodded. "My father says passion is not necessary in marriage."

"Ha!" Jesse scoffed. "Then what do you feel for Shepset? I've seen how you look at her. That is no brotherly love."

"Shepset will mold herself to our family if we marry," said Avi. "You are right about Jennat being different. She does not try to make herself pleasing." He gave Jesse a sidelong look. "She told me she will never speak to you again."

"Well, she gets angry," Jesse said. "She speaks her mind,

not like those soft women without sense or opinions. Jennat has opinions. Jennat knows what she wants. Jennat —"

"Jennat is stubborn and wild," said Avi.

"Stubborn and wild, but I love her!" cried Jesse.

"So you were cruel to her," said Avi, "because you want her but you can't admit it. Poor cousin! Maybe she has bewitched you, using some Egyptian sorcery, perfumes, enchantments. . . ."

"You see for yourself how beautiful she is," Jesse said, his voice very low. "She is no sorceress. She is just a girl making me lose my mind, making me confused and evil."

"What's evil about love?"

"My mother loves Talia. Talia has promised her babies, a namesake for Shosha. The two of them are already like mother and daughter."

"Have you told your mother how you feel?"

"What? After losing Shosha, now you want me to tell her she is losing Talia, too? And me? She has given everything for me. And this is how I would repay her?"

"Your mother will understand. She loves you."

"My mother," Jesse said bitterly, "is in her own world. She doesn't talk to me now."

"She is still grieving," said Avi. "Give her time." He smiled slightly. "We have to learn to get by without our mothers, I suppose. My mother still tells me when to wash my hair!"

Jesse frowned. "While my mother worshipped Adonai, she was always hounding me to change, to pray, to make sacrifices. Now she says nothing. Avi, how can we believe in a God who makes us suffer so?"

"My father says it's not God who causes suffering, but other people. I have trouble, too, believing it. If we thank God for all the good things, why can't we blame Him for the bad?"

"At least your father talks to you about it. I have nobody."

"You have me," said Avi, looking hurt.

"You know what I mean. Your father is a leader, a holy man."

"You think it's so easy to be the son of a leader?" asked Avi. "My father watches me constantly, forces me —"

"Your father is wise, admired, and respected. What do I have? A father everyone despises, and now my mother has slipped away into her silence, and I am so tired of carrying my mother's burden."

"What burden?" asked Avi.

"The burden of loving Adonai."

Moses had gone up toward God, and God called to him from the mountain: "Speak to the children of Israel and tell them, 'You have seen what I have done to the Egyptians, while I have lifted you on eagle's wings and brought you to Myself. And now if you will listen to My voice and keep My covenant, you shall be My special treasure. You shall be to Me a kingdom of priests, a holy nation. . . .

"Go to the people. Have them wash their garments. Let them be ready for the third day, for on the third day God will descend before the eyes of all the people upon Mount Sinai."

CHAPTER  11

For three days, an eternity, it seemed, Jesse had to wash himself thoroughly, to clean his clothes, to clean underneath his fingernails, to scrape his teeth clean, and above all, as Uncle Rimon had commanded, repeating the order from Moses, to cleanse his mind and his heart.

The people scurried to obey, with no less haste than when they had obeyed their Egyptian taskmasters. Moses and Aaron, with Joshua and Miriam, gave out the commands. "In three days Adonai will appear to us. Three days! Make yourselves ready."

Nathan cleaned his garments and washed himself; he combed his ragged beard. During the three days of waiting, he laughed and smiled a great deal, eager for the spectacle promised by Moses.

Jesse watched his father, baffled, then amused. He knew that his father didn't believe a word of Moses' claim, that Adonai would actually appear to them. No, he wanted to be among the crowd, to be filled with the drama of expectation, for who knew what manner of tricks and magic Moses might employ? It was bound to be a good show, something to talk about.

When the appointed morning came, Nathan leapt up to the blast of the ram's horn. "Hurry! Hurry, up to the front!" he prodded Jesse.

His mother, moving silently, clasped a long white shawl around her body and over her head. She was bent. She looked like an angel, somehow, her eyes glowing not with love, but with infinite grief.

It was early. The sky was the color of deep lapis lazuli, with a few lazy stars still shining faintly. The air held a heavy desert chill. People stumbled in the darkness, hungry, for they had been told to fast. Cold, still sleep-stunned, they dragged themselves across the wide, empty plain where they had encamped these last three nights; they followed Moses, whose tread was heavy and resolute, his arms lifted high, never falling, as he strode toward the mountain.

Each person drew close into himself, hands bundled under armpits, head down, wary and expectant and afraid.

The mountain loomed ahead. It seemed to recede as they approached. The mountain was shrouded by fog and mist. Yet Moses remained visible, his cloak billowing before them. Where at the outset there had been rumbling and talking, now the people were silent. Footsteps sounded upon the soil. Feet shuffled almost in rhythm. The swish of cloth and the movement of air traced a path behind Moses.

Nathan's walk was casual, almost careless; he looked around at his compatriots like an overseer, above the rest. Devorah's steps were slow and reluctant. She clasped her arms tightly across her breasts, as if the baby still lay there to be consoled.

Jesse went ahead, his eyes fastened upon the shape of Moses and the mountain beyond.

Small things became signs to be remembered; a flicker of light, a momentary puff of wind, slight as a breath, barely disturbing the air round about. The world scarcely moved; it might have hung suspended on thread, swept by the slight and constant breeze. A bird sang. A lizard crept. A leaf fluttered from a branch. But silence among the people was complete. No baby cried. No man, woman, or child murmured a single word.

Silence reigned deep in Jesse's being. The climb became harder, the path steeper. Jesse's breath forced its way in and out of his lungs, as he followed the mist and Moses. Then, suddenly, the air came clear and unencumbering, so that he seemed to float, feet gliding above the treacherous path, the rocks no longer forcing their way into his flesh, nothing touching him, only at the distant horizon, a faint dawning light.

The piercing sound of a ram's horn shattered the stillness. It reddened the atmosphere, ringing out, a deafening blast.

And then the sky went wild — crimson flashes, streaks of thunder, a hail of starry light, blinding against the sudden blackness of sky, then thunder rang from hill to hill, blazing ever louder; a thousand anvils of thunder crashed at once, so that all ears were stopped with it, and Jesse hung suspended, tormented beyond feeling, his heart a thing of iron beating in his breast so hard that he thought it would surely shatter him completely. His eyes were crowned with a glare that rang into his skull, sound becoming vision — gold and smoke. Smoke filled every space, and the mountain skipped and shook and rumbled, cracking deep in its core. Jesse covered his face against the flames, and he became aware of his own voice raised in a cry so long and deep that it filled the very earth. His scream mingled with all the others, screams of anguish and dread, longing and exultation. It lasted; it reached down to the beginnings and up to the endings of time. Jesse, no longer anchored to the earth, trembled violently, caught in the grip of sound that filled every space around him and every pore in his body.

"I . . ."

Jesse fell down upon his face, threw his arms over his head.

"AM . . ."

Jesse clung to the ground, feeling its tumult.

"THE LORD YOUR GOD . . ."

Jesse opened his eyes a slit; the hills around reverberated with motion; they skipped like wild sheep.

"WHO BROUGHT YOU OUT OF EGYPT, FROM THE PLACE OF SLAVERY."

The breath was sucked out of Jesse's body. Words became leaping shapes. Light blinded him and made him tremble from head to toe. His teeth clattered, his tongue beat against the roof of his mouth, and his nostrils were filled with the heat of this dreaded radiance.

"YOU SHALL HAVE NO OTHER GODS BE-FORE ME!"

Tears poured from Jesse's eyes, obliterating sight, except for the prisms of light that still flashed at the edges.

"DO NOT BOW DOWN TO SUCH GODS TO WOR-SHIP THEM. I AM GOD YOUR LORD, A GOD WHO DEMANDS EXCLUSIVE WORSHIP."

A deafening cry arose from the people, a unity of anguish and fear. "Go. Go from us, Moses! Go!" Jesse heard the voices of his parents and all the others, intermingled with his own pleading: "All that God says, we will do and we will harken. But don't let us hear any more the voice of God. We'll die! Go up to the mountain and let God speak with you, lest we die."

"Don't be afraid!" Moses shouted, his arms raised, as if to hold his people and give them the courage to stay. "God came only to raise you up! His fear will then be upon your faces, and you will not sin."

Jesse felt a heavy hand upon his neck, pulling him back. He glimpsed his father's face. Nathan's hair seemed to stand on end, as if he had been hit by lightning, and his eyes were hard coals of determination. "Come away, come away," he whispered urgently.

"Father — did you see?" Jesse could not say more; words were locked within him.

Nathan's face was blank, his body stiff. He shook his head again and again, stunned and amazed, like a man who has seen a corpse get up and walk.

Devorah moved slowly backward, her hand now braced against her heart, eyes downcast.

"Ima!" Jesse called.

She glanced at him, mouth set tight. The expression in her eyes, veiled and unforgiving, spoke more than words.

And now Jesse's heart pounded all the more. He was alone and utterly forsaken, despite the crowd. He stood a moment longer, eyes straining to pierce the mist and the smoke, ears poised for one more sound, even a whisper. But the heavens had closed, and all that remained was the wailing and the dread of the people.

The people walked or crawled backward, dragging their little ones, hands braced against the vision. They distanced themselves from Moses and the mist and the mountain.

Sleep, when it came, was a total annihilation. Jesse dreamed no dreams, stirred not at all, nor did he feel the hardness of the ground beneath him.

Awake, he felt shocked into new alertness. Every small peeping of a bird accosted his ears. The sight of a scorpion creeping over the cleft in a rock held him entranced; the creature's pincers waved and beckoned, now in curiosity, now in prayer. As far as he could see, hills followed hills, each one different in its magnificent composition of rock and sand, tinged with colors borne up from within the earth itself, traces of red, blue, green, tan, brown, rust, purple, black — why had he not seen before? Infinite variety lay exposed now, clear and startling.

Plants beneath his feet twisted their leaves out of every crevice, longing for life and health. Tiny leaves were tipped with buds of white, yellow, pink; flowers burst out upon the land, violent crimson speckled with dots of yellow. It was more than the mind could absorb. Again and again Jesse blinked, covered his eyes, breathed deep of the air that filled his body with a new sustenance. He felt keenly the tips of his fingers, the ends of his hair, the soles of his feet. His skin absorbed every nuance of light, the feeling of cloth, leather, sand, water, wind.

Early morning, as he went with the animals to a lonely mound, Jesse sat down on the knob of earth, his head in his hands. And suddenly he felt drowned in desire. His entire body flamed and reeled from it. And he cried out, "Oh, God! Why have You given me this body, these feelings? Do You know my agony? The eye of the lamb fills me with tenderness. Its bleating stabs at my heart. How then can I look at Jennat and not be moved to terrible desire? Will it ever end?

"I want her. You set her before me to taunt me. Why do You torment me this way? What is it You want from me — to see me suffer? You made me as I am. You created me with all the hungers of my body. And yet You don't let them be satisfied.

"And I talk about this while my mother grieves. I gloried in killing — I tasted the blood of two humans! How evil I am! But You made me. See! You made me selfish and evil. My little sister is dead, oh, so newly dead. I loved her. But am I grieving? No! I am sunk in lust." Jennat's face and Jennat's body, her hands, her eyes, the arch of her brows, all swam before him.

Images poured into Jesse's mind, and the more he tried to erase them, the more they persisted, images so real that his breath came rushing, and his hands began to sweat. He ached with desires; he replayed every scene he had ever heard or contemplated, of bodies entwined, mouths wide and warm, all the textures of the human form revealed, giving and receiving.

Jesse sat, unmoving, while waves of unresolved passion flooded over him. Then he began to moan, and he spoke again.

"If You are my creator, why didn't You make me good? If You are almighty, why can't You make my mother love You as she did before? Why won't she love me as she did before?" Jesse began to sob. And now all the slights and evils and frustrations of his life came rushing to the surface.

"You gave me a harsh and scornful father. Everyone mocks and despises him. Why couldn't I have a father who is wise and good, like Uncle Rimon? My father never held me. He never loved me. Why did Mother marry him? People scorn him. I've seen it since I was small. But it was as if I didn't really see it — now You have torn the blinders off from before my eyes, and what do I see? Agony everywhere. Misery. Longings. Why? Why? Why isn't there something better?"

And Jesse sat, numb and empty of words. At the edge of his vision came a slight fluttering. A dragonfly, pale green with shimmering, nearly transparent wings, landed for a moment on a long, dry blade of grass. Then it rose aloft, and Jesse saw its wings whirring against the blueness of the sky. The sight overwhelmed Jesse, and he stared, speechless, at the strange beauty all around him.

* * *

A brilliance lay over everything. It was as if a shining rain had washed the world.

Jennat had no doubts as to the cause. The morning Adonai appeared, she had gone with the others, keeping herself at the fringe with most of the other "mixed" or "foreign" peoples. But the voice and the vision had reached into her soul; it had found her and drawn her into its midst, and into the midst of all of them.

No longer apart — never again! — she moved now in complete harmony with the rising and setting of the sun, the heavenward climb of the moon, and the spreading of stars. For the first time in her life, Jennat felt entirely contented.

She had slept afterward, like all the others, overcome by the vision. She and Shepset had lain entwined; they must have clutched each other first in retreat, then in sheer exhaustion, holding on to each other for fear of being borne away entirely into that spiritual state from which they might never return.

Awake, Jennat became intensely aware of her own body. She looked down at her leg, her foot, her hand. And she found them perfect.

She remembered how she used to look at herself in the mirror at Memnet's house, thinking, If only my chin were slightly narrower, my eyes larger, shoulders smoother . . . She would frown and dab color onto her eyelids to make her eyes appear brighter. Now she felt completely clean and glowing. Her face was perfect, her body lacking nothing.

Jennat stood up. She spread her arms wide and opened her fingers. Her movements spoke of grace that she had never before known she possessed.

"You saw me," she declared, smiling with happiness. "You

knew me. Jennat," she whispered. "I am Jennat, the one You saw and spoke to. Thanks to You, a multitude of thanks, for all these blessings, for the manna You provide daily, for the quail and the green things, for the water, for the hills and the flowers and for Jesse. For Jesse. Oh, Adonai, thank you for Jesse, my beloved!"

"What makes you think he loves you?" Shepset asked, scowling. She rubbed her back. "My body aches, down to my very bones. You? You don't feel exhausted?"

"I feel splendid. And I know Jesse loves me."

"Because the last time he was so rude to you?" Shepset sneered. "Because he treats you like a slave?"

"Men can be like that," Jennat said soothingly, "when they are upset. And he was grieving. He wants me. That's why he speaks so harshly. He can't help himself. He means one thing, says another—I know how that is. The truth is in his eyes. The way he looks at me."

"He lusts for you, the way men always lust for women." Shepset shuddered. "They are all alike. They only want to own you, keep you in their bed all night, and in the morning—"

"Avi has asked me to speak to you about him."

Shepset gasped. "Avi! That burly cousin?" She gave a laugh. "And what does he say he wants with me? He won't be the first Hebrew to suddenly decide there's merit in paying homage to Osiris—by making love to a young temple dancer! What liars they all are. Well, tell him I'd rather go off with the nomads and end up milking their filthy goats all my life than get involved with him. A Hebrew! What does he think I would want with him? Babies? They breed like spiders, dozens at a time. . . ."

Jennat listened, watching Shepset's every expression, seeing the hurt behind the scorn. "Avi wants to marry you," she said simply.

Shepset sank onto the ground, her legs folded under her, her garment spread all about. There was grace in her movements, a beauty that her scarred face could not disguise. Was this, Jennat wondered, what Avi had seen all along? The yearning in Shepset's tone, the reluctant tenderness revealed in the movements of her hands, that depth of pain in her dark eyes, the way the shadows fell upon her throat — had Avi seen all this long ago?

Suddenly Jennat felt overwhelmed. Stepping toward Shepset, she opened her arms and drew her close, and Jennat felt her friend's pain and yearning. They wept together, close as sisters.

Everything about the day seemed ordained — the calm weather, their meeting just where the two palm trees stood entwined, providing a haven of shade and soft underbrush. She was picking dates. He had come to look for water, following the slim line of trees and sturdy grasses. He was learning to heed the signs of the wilderness.

Jennat and Jesse saw each other as if for the first time. The moment Jennat saw Jesse's face, she knew that he had felt the same sweeping fire and gladness and inner power. They had both heard and seen wonders, and it had changed them.

Jesse moved with a new awareness of his body. He smiled at Jennat, a brilliant smile.

"Jennat!" Joy rang in his voice. "It's you!"

She laughed slightly. "Of course, me. Jesse, now I understand the things you were trying to tell me about your God — I heard Him, and He spoke to me, down to my very being. I felt Him there, and now — I have buried the other gods. Deep in the ground. Adonai brought us out of Egypt. He saved us from Pharaoh. Maybe He even brought me here to meet Him."

Jennat stood still. Jesse stepped toward her. She looked into his eyes and saw everything there, every feeling she had ever had, magnified. Then Jesse came to her, arms wide and eager, and he held her close, and they kissed.

They walked. They talked. They ate the dates and sat under the palm trees. She told him about her childhood, her fear of Memnet, the swift changes of mood and temper, and how she had longed for a mother.

He told her of his dead brothers, unknown to him, but always a shadow over his life, and how he felt responsible to provide double and triple goodness to make it up to his mother.

He talked about Talia, the expectations they had for him and her. And he blushed and sighed and raged and said, "I don't know what to do." And Jennat held his hands and looked at him calmly and replied, "It will come clear to you. Don't worry." They talked about all the people they knew. Jennat felt close to them all, connected.

"I think Shepset would grow to love Avi," Jennat told him, "but she is afraid. Always, she has only been kept for a night or two, then cast aside."

"Avi loves her," Jesse said. "He would be faithful."

"I told her. She said" — Jennat glanced at Jesse hesitantly, then decided there must be only truth between them — "Shepset said she will marry Avi. She needs a home."

"Does she love Avi?"

Jennat shrugged. "I don't know. I do know that she won't change. I hope Avi doesn't expect it."

"How could she not change?" Jesse exclaimed. "She heard

the same things we heard, and she saw . . . and yet, my father also saw and heard, and he has convinced himself that it was all a hoax, magic, to make us submissive."

Jennat frowned. "Shepset trusts only the priests and things of the past — the temples of the gods, the pageants. She would never give up her idols. Avi should know this."

"Well, Avi has his father's faith to cling to. It makes him strong. He only has to follow in his father's strength."

"But you," Jennat said softly, "who helps you?"

"I guess I, myself," Jesse said.

She reached out and touched Jesse's hair. She loved the feel of his curls, the thick strands in her fingers. He lay down, his head in her lap, and she touched his forehead, brows, and eyelids. Never had her fingertips explored another human this way; even when little Seti was a baby and she held him in her arms, Jennat had never dared to stroke him or kiss him. Seti was not hers.

"Have you prayed to Adonai?" Jesse asked softly.

"Yes," Jennat breathed. "I thanked Him."

"I blamed Him," Jesse said, a low rumbling. "I blamed Him for making me want you so much — for tormenting me with you."

"Blame? He allows it?" Jennat exclaimed. "Weren't you terrified He would strike you dead?"

Jesse sat up, facing her. "I suppose I was afraid, but I couldn't stop myself. I didn't think about fear or being struck dead — I just had to speak to Him, heart to heart."

"Did He answer?" Jennat asked. She smiled.

"No. Yes. He answers in strange ways. There was a dragonfly . . ."

"I have seen a nest with a tiny egg in it!" she exclaimed.

"I saw the mountains, all the colors . . ."

"Did you see the little flowers, the buds?"

"Oh, more than anything," Jesse said, "I wish Shosha were alive. I wish my mother could laugh again, be happy, take the gift that Adonai has given us. All her life she waited for this. Now He has redeemed us, He has spoken to us, and my mother closes her ears. She has turned her face away even from Him."

Jennat sighed. "Your mother just couldn't give any more. She loves too much. Suffers too much. I saw it in my mistress. How Memnet loved that child! When Seti died, she went mad. Maybe some people are wise not to go too far in love, if it ends in madness."

"And you?" Jesse reached out to touch her cheek. "How far will you go in love?"

"Forever," Jennat said, and she bent to him and gloried in his kisses.

It was different for everyone, but yet it was the same. The Israelites had followed Moses and gathered together to listen. They had expected something extraordinary, but the sounds they heard and the feelings that reverberated in their bodies were so magnified, the joy went so far beyond any earthly joy they had known before, that none would ever be able to describe it adequately.

They had been lifted up higher than anyone might imagine, lifted up so high that their hearts sang and their bodies were aflame. They had been singed by the very fire of the living God, and when He was done, they felt the echoes of that energy and the brilliance and the sheer exhilaration, and they wanted it again.

They remembered it in their dreams. It hovered at the edge of everything they did, while they ate or slept or turned or talked, they remembered the essence of that feeling, the sheer physical radiance of it, and they needed to get it back.

As the weeks went by, they forgot the cause and remembered the effect, and they would do anything to get back that feeling.

Moses listened to the voice of Adonai. He heard the commandments as to what man must do for man and what man must do for God, and these he gave to the people, and they answered, "All you have told us we will do." And this was the covenant: Adonai would be their God, and they would be His willing servants.

And God called Moses up to the mountain, where He would give Moses tablets of stone, on which He would write the commandments. Moses went up into the mist onto the mountain.

The people began to realize that Moses was taking a long time to come down from the mountain. They gathered around Aaron and said to him, "Make us a god to lead us, for we know not what happened to Moses, the man who brought us out of Egypt."

CHAPTER 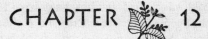 12

The revelry went on and on. Smoke ascended from the blazing coals over which the people roasted succulent ribs and legs of lamb. Kegs were broken out, of wine saved from Egypt, and of new spirits, quickly fermented from dates and pomegranate.

The dancing and drinking and singing continued day and night. Jewels flashed, faces glowed from oils and cosmetics brought from Egypt. They got out their drums, horns, lutes, and tambourines; sounds of jubilation filled the air. Little children raced about, shrieking and clapping their hands. Men and women whirled together, gasping and laughing, dancing the lewd dances they had seen before. They leapt and lunged, tore their clothing. Flesh glistened by the fires. Hair tumbled down loose; women laughed and lolled while the men came after them, panting like dogs and inventing new ways to enhance their glee.

The people had come to Aaron, at first requesting, then threatening. They had come with stones in their hands and fury in their eyes. "Make us a god," they had said, "to lead us, now that Moses is gone. Make us a god! We hunger; we are abandoned. Make us a god!"

At last, overcome by their incessant demands and by the fear in his heart, Aaron had relented. "Give me your jewels, nose rings, earrings, bracelets, necklaces of gold."

The people ran to bring Aaron the gold. They prepared an immense cauldron, and Aaron had the gold thrown into it. When the gold was melted and hot, he ordered it cast into a shape that the people remembered, the shape of Apis the bull, revered in Egypt, a small, immature bull, no bigger than a calf.

"Here is your god!" Aaron thundered, standing above them, the small golden calf lifted high above his head. "Here, oh, Israel, is your god that brought you out of Egypt!"

But they didn't hear the irony in Aaron's tone, or see the looks he threw them. They tore the calf from his hands. Men carried it on their shoulders, taking turns, and they danced with it. Women circled around, laughing and singing. Their piercing noise drowned out the cries of those who begged the people not to profane the holy name.

Rimon pleaded with the idolaters. "How can you do this? We promised to obey Adonai, to keep His covenant." Rimon wept and swayed in grief. "He told us to have no other gods. He commanded us to make no images, yet you make yourselves this abomination — He will punish you. Beware!"

Korach, cousin of Moses, had his own following, and his people were bitter. "What sort of a leader leaves his flock?" they cried. "Moses isn't ever coming back. Off he goes! What about us?"

Korach, Rimon, and the other leaders conferred and argued. In Egypt, they had inspired the people. Now Moses held sway, and he was gone. Korach rallied against Moses. "This rabble needs a strong leader to keep them in line. Moses should have known it and appointed someone in his place. Someone worthy."

"Moses did appoint Aaron and Hur," Rimon said. "They

have served him all this time — or would you say Moses is in *your* debt?"

"What sort of a leader is Aaron?" Korach flung back. "It's he who made them the calf!"

Jesse stayed beside his uncle, praying with him, as Avi on the other side joined in his father's ritual. And Jesse knew, by the look on Rimon's face and the tears in his eyes, and by the way he prayed, that his uncle's heart was full of longing. Rimon yearned to be chosen in the manner of Moses, to lead the people and speak with God.

Rimon prayed. "Forgive them, Lord! They don't understand. They are used to seeing other gods — be patient with them."

Rimon gathered his male relatives — Efrem, Nathan, Seth, Jesse, and Avi. "We must try to pull them away. We must not stand by while they sin — come!"

Rimon had them link arms, forming a human chain as they approached the dancers and the flames. One man reeled drunkenly toward them; another showed a knife.

"Save your breath," Nathan told Rimon. "Why waste your time on these stupid animals?" He coughed, then spat. "They think that little piece of trash can lead them? Man leads himself. Man makes his own luck and plans his own destiny. When will they learn it?"

Jesse's breath caught in his throat. "Father, you say we don't need Adonai? Who saved us from Pharaoh? Why can't you believe the miracles you saw with your own eyes?"

"I heard things, and I saw things," said Nathan, chin raised in a look of superiority. "Don't trust everything you hear. Trust this," he said, pointing to his own forehead, "and this," he said, making a fist.

"Nathan!" shouted Rimon, his eyes flashing. "At least let your son find his way."

"Why don't you keep your own son?" Nathan growled.

"It's the heathen — they set us against each other," shouted Rimon.

"Oh, Father," Avi broke in, "you blame everything on them. Look at your precious Israelites. They couldn't wait for Moses to leave so they could make themselves a party."

Jesse had never seen his uncle so fierce as now. His beard trembled and his eyes flashed. "Silence, silence!"

Talia came running. Frantic, her hair flying loose, she ran to Jesse, and she took his hand, even for everybody to see. In spite of himself, Jesse felt his cheeks flaming, his emotions teetering, almost as if the music and the fires and the screams of ecstasy were reaching him, too.

"I had to find you." Talia gasped. "I was afraid that you might — I know you have friends among the heathens," she said. "Thank God you are with us!"

"Of course I am with you!" Jesse cried angrily. "Where else?"

"You're hurting my hand." Talia pulled away and stood confronting him. "You say you are with us, but whenever something happens, you are gone, off into the wilderness, God knows where and with whom."

"I have animals to tend!" shouted Jesse. "I have to go out to find fodder for them. You are already jealous, Talia, and we aren't even betrothed yet."

"That's not my fault," she retorted. "You act like a child, never sticking to your responsibility."

"How can you say such things?" Jesse cried. "I take care of my family, the animals . . . How can you say such things to me?" Amid the din Jesse shouted at Talia, frustrated, for even as he denied it, his heart leapt and his feet tapped, and he found himself looking for Jennat.

"Oh, Jesse, let's not fight!"

Talia trembled and started to cry. He felt worthless and mean. Why did she love him? he wondered. And why couldn't he conform? The drums beat in his mind, the dancers swayed, and the golden calf glittered. "Go back, Talia," he said sternly. "Go back to the tents with the women. I'll come as soon as I can, and we'll talk."

Contemptuously Talia stared at the dancers. "Animals," she said. "They are animals."

"Talia, some people try, but they find it difficult — "

"They should try harder," she replied, and turned away.

Suddenly her father, Efrem, broke away from Seth and Rimon and leapt into the circle of dancers.

"Father! Father!" Talia screamed.

Jesse lunged toward Efrem and tried to block him, but Efrem knocked the wind out of Jesse's chest.

Jesse fell flat and had to drag himself clear of the revelers.

Talia ran to Rimon, screaming. "Stop him, Uncle, please!"

"How can I?" Rimon flung back. "Who listens to me? Oh, God, God, have they all gone mad? Efrem, Efrem, come away."

But the circle widened, and Efrem, now swept into the center, began to dance.

Tirelessly, Efrem leapt and swayed. He bent his knees to the ground. He tossed his head and rolled his hips. Four men swooped down upon him; they lifted him and swung him in an arc, and then they set him down, and Efrem danced like a wild man. His face was puffed from heat. His eyes were shut, his mouth wide open. And he bellowed out words that nobody knew or ever had heard before. Spit and foam flew from his mouth.

"Father! Father!" Talia screamed, sobbing in terror. "You will die for this — Father!"

But Efrem, always weak of spirit and hesitant, having once

felt the glory of God, lusted for it again. Feelings surged through him, both agony and joy, plain on his face. He tore his clothes into shreds; his naked flesh gleamed with sweat.

"Efrem! Efrem!" Shira, his wife, came running, and she implored him and wrung her hands, but Efrem seemed transported, crazed. Seth and Rimon tried to grab his arms. Efrem beat them back. He bit and snarled like a dog gone mad.

Talia rushed in. "Father! Father!"

He vanquished her with a single blow. Rimon carried Talia out from the circle and set her down, shouting, "Go! Go from here to the tents." Talia and the women fled, covering their faces with their hands.

"Come. Come!" Rimon called the men back into line — Jesse, Avi, Nathan, and Seth — a ridiculous army, Jesse thought, but he dared not disobey. They followed Rimon into the melee, as if their presence might deter the madness. But of course, nobody heeded. Fires broke out everywhere. Wine ran from people's mouths and stained their bodies red. Some had brought pocket gods, and they played and paraded with them and sang the old songs.

Jesse found Jennat standing aside, watching, her hands clasped to her face. She glanced at Jesse only briefly, still absorbed, and as he drew close, he heard her say, "It's like Egypt, just like Egypt."

"Thank God," he exclaimed, "you are only watching."

But Shepset was with the idolaters, once again in her element. Her body was wrapped in layers of filmy cloth, and her bare feet were encircled with bangles. As the sounds of tambourines and drums filled the air, Shepset pulled the first veil from her body. Alluringly she swayed her shoulders and hips. The revelers clapped and shouted and whistled and groaned. A man leapt out opposite Shepset, matching movement for movement, his eyes hungrily upon her.

Jesse put his hand on his cousin Avi's shoulder, felt the knotted muscles. Avi's face was lathered in sweat. "How could she?" Avi moaned.

Another man took the first one's place. He twisted his body like a serpent. He tore a veil from Shepset's waist.

Avi sprang, clutched the man by the hair, and kicked at his groin. It excited the onlookers. They roared and clapped. They found full wineskins and poured red wine over the two men as they writhed in the dust. Avi tore himself loose from the other man's grasp, wrestled him down, and beat his head upon the ground; Shepset, screaming, ran into the crowd.

From behind him Jesse heard Korach. "See the preacher who cannot control his own son!"

Rimon's beard and brows quivered with wrath. With the strength of a giant, Rimon took Avi and lifted him as if he were a mere twig. Rimon shook him, plunged him down to the ground, and, his foot upon the boy's back, commenced to beat him with his staff until blood ran and Avi's screams merged into the madness.

Jesse's family had withdrawn to their cluster of tents, defeated and filled with dread. Throughout the night and all the next day they sat, afraid and paralyzed. "God will punish all of us. He will wipe us out," Rimon said again and again. He prayed throughout the night, and in the morning, when he saw that his son had not even awakened and still writhed in pain, Rimon beat himself on the chest with his fists and went to sit alone.

Shira moaned and wept and tore her clothes, already in mourning for Efrem. Talia sat with her. "Mama, Mama, it's all right. Father will come back. You'll see — God will forgive him."

"No," said her mother. "Not this. Never."

Devorah and Channa, Avi's mother, soothed Avi's back with a plaster Devorah had prepared from herbs and plant oils. Jesse brought him water, but Avi would not drink.

"Rimon has changed," Channa said, her mouth pinched, frightened. "I don't know how to talk to him anymore. Everything I do, he examines. He tests me continually. Is this what it means to love God?"

"Rimon is frightened, Channa," Devorah said wearily. "It is a terrible thing to confront the living God."

Devorah sat on a mat; she was wrapped in a thick shawl but was still shivering. She looked pale, her eyes sunken. "For me," Devorah went on, "it doesn't matter. Adonai and I finished our arguments long ago." She laughed, a strange and bitter sound.

"Hush, Auntie," said Talia, moving nearer to Devorah. "Please don't. . . ."

Avi groaned and writhed, then slept again. Rimon went to his side and looked down at him, then moved again into solitude.

"You see what has become of us," Shira said bitterly. "My husband has gone mad, dancing and cavorting — and Rimon beats his own son half to death."

Devorah nodded. "What difference has it made that Adonai came to us? Nothing has changed."

"Hush, Auntie," Talia pleaded. "Don't say such things. He may punish you."

Devorah gazed at Talia. She smiled wryly.

Jesse stood beside his mother, looking down at her sagging shape. "When the people began to stray, why didn't you go out?" Jesse demanded. "You used to inspire the people. They always listened to you. Why didn't you even try?"

His mother sighed. "I'm tired. Tired of telling lies."

"What's a lie? What is truth? You used to tell me to have faith. 'Think with your heart,' you used to tell me. Don't you remember?"

"I lied!" she shouted, for the first time energetic again; then she sank back. "Leave me alone, Jesse. If you care so much, why don't you go and fight for Adonai?"

Jesse stared at her. "Maybe I will!" he shouted. "And maybe I won't. Maybe I've had enough of all this."

"Jesse!" Talia rushed to bring him back. "She didn't mean that. Your mother is still grieving and weak — "

"Please don't tell me about my mother," he said coldly, and then he pulled away from her grasp.

He looked to the horizon, where the haze hung heavy from the fires and the rising sun painted crimson and purple stains in the sky, the same sky that had turned into a wilderness of sound and light, bringing both terror and exultation that morning at Mount Sinai. Maybe it had been only a dream, a shared dream.

Or was it a miracle? Well, if it had been a true miracle, wouldn't everyone agree? Wouldn't they all have seen it and felt it the same way, and finally been moved to oneness?

No — his father still sneered at miracles. His mother still blamed God for the loss of Shosha and her other children. Devorah was right: nothing had changed.

Except — he had changed. He felt different, somehow. Vulnerable, but also strong, he was aware of his body, of the space he took, the way the air parted when he moved his hands, the way the earth itself seemed to open up and listen when he spoke or even when he breathed. *He* was different. In the night, he slept a deep and deathly sleep. In the morning, he awakened to sheer joy or deepest pain, nothing in the middle. Everything affected him — the taste of food, the touch of cool water, his feet on the ground, steady and solid. Beneath and above his

177

daily toil, bringing in the lambs and the goats, gathering food, shaking out the tent skins, finding fuel, there seemed to be another plane of life. It made a faint hum in his ears; it suggested a shadow flitting across the sun. Was this the presence of God? Maybe this was what Moses meant when he told the people that Adonai lived among them, filling every space?

But what did Adonai want of him? He thought of Jennat. If Adonai had not wished him to love Jennat, why did He present her to him? Or was she sent to tempt him, like the serpent tempting Adam? Was he supposed to prove his love for God by rejecting Jennat?

He walked and walked, first toward the fires where some people still danced and roared, though most were spent, sleeping entwined, like snakes.

Shepset was nowhere among them. Perhaps, Jesse thought, Jennat had led her away. He walked past the rows of tents that sheltered the Levites, then farther, past the other encampments, until he came to the ragged tents of the "others," those who had willingly fled Egypt, joining the Israelites. Now for the first time Jesse asked himself why they had come. Was it for fear of drudgery in Egypt? Or was it for the promise of a better life, under the protection of Adonai? Why had Jennat come?

She could have stayed in Egypt, run off to some other man's house. She could have worked as an artisan or a nursemaid. She could have been pampered and protected — yet she had come out to the wilderness.

Jesse found her with Shepset and several other young people. All were sleeping, except for Jennat. She sat cross-legged, fanning herself with a small papyrus.

She looked up, saw Jesse, and quickly slipped something into her pocket.

"Come," he said. "Let's walk."

He took her arm, leading her to a rocky outcrop, high and elaborate as a pharaoh's tomb, but belonging to nature, intricately carved out by wind and sand. Shapes in the rocks tantalized Jesse. Each one was different, each one a work of art. And suddenly he knew for certain that the power that had accomplished this had also created him. And to him, his creator had spoken! He felt now like a king, kindly and wise, able to solve anything.

He asked Jennat, "Why did you come with us into the wilderness?"

She hesitated, then smiled. "I came to find Shepset."

"Is that all?"

"I told you. I had to escape from Memnet."

"You could have gone south."

"What is it you want, Jesse? What words?"

"Words of love," he murmured ardently, taking her hands in his.

She only smiled and looked down, reached into her pocket. "Are you hungry?"

He gazed at her. "Very."

She handed him several dates, soft from the heat of her body. He ate them greedily.

With a dull sound, something slid from Jennat's pocket out onto the rocks.

"What's that?"

"Nothing." Swiftly Jennat grasped the small wooden object, half concealing it in her hand, but Jesse saw the crude features and stiff limbs.

Jesse was aghast. "Jennat, I thought you told me you buried your gods." The figure had a round belly and a strange, solemn face.

"I did," Jennat said. She clasped the figure tightly in her fingers.

"You didn't!" he cried in great alarm. "You said you buried them, and you didn't. You lied to me, Jennat."

"I didn't lie. I did bury them. Except for this one, Hathor, my favorite. I can't give her up. She has been with me since I was a baby. She has loved me and helped me — "

"She has loved you? I told you, Jennat, I love you! And yet you need this wooden thing?"

"How can you compare your love to that of the goddess?" Jennat exclaimed. "It's completely different."

"Yes! I am here. I am flesh and blood and this — this thing is wood and paint, don't you see?"

"No, I don't see. This is a figure, not the real goddess. I know that. But she inhabits this sometimes, and it reminds me and soothes me. Everybody needs something to hold and to see. Why can't you understand that, Jesse?"

"Gods that one can hold have no power," Jesse said, grappling for the right words. "The power has to be outside us, something we can't touch or even fathom."

"Then what good is it? How can we speak to a god without a face?"

"Oh, Jennat, I don't know. Why do you always have to talk about this?"

"Because you are so stubborn and demanding, that's why!" Jennat glared at him. "Why do I have to give up everything? Why don't you give up something, too?"

"I have! I am. I'm giving up — "

"What? That little cousin of yours? She's always with you, looking at you and touching you — does she sleep in your tent?"

"Jennat!"

"How can you say you love me," she cried, "and then you hate my goddess, Hathor? She is part of me."

"But you heard Adonai with your own ears. He made it plain: 'No other gods before Me.' "

"I never said that Hathor comes before Him. Never! See how you twist my words. I only said I will not bury her. Why should I? I am willing to worship Adonai, even to make Him the first, the chief of all gods. So, if Hathor doesn't mind, why would you?

" 'No other gods' means none at all, only Him, exclusive and — "

"What right do you have to tell me how to worship? I am not an Israelite!"

"But you heard — "

"So did all the Israelites, and even many of them don't see why your God has to be so jealous. What's the harm of honoring others, too? Look around you, Jesse. One god couldn't be in charge of this entire world, responsible for life and death and harvest and rain and — "

"Jennat, I wanted to take you to our camp, to tell my parents — "

"Am I not good enough as I am? Do I have to change for you?" she cried. "Shepset is right. You only want me as a servant, a slave."

"How can you say such things?" Jesse cried. "I let you be free, come and go as you please — what do you want?"

"I want to be myself!"

"You are yourself!"

They paused, each breathing heavily, flushed with anger. Then Jesse went to her, and he made his voice tender.

"Jennat, put Hathor away for a while, and you will see you don't need her."

She replied sternly, "That's good for you, Jesse. Your parents and your ancestors have known Adonai for a very long time. For me, He is new. How can you expect me to trust Him?"

She shook her head. "Maybe when we are in the land of Canaan, when we are safe, when you and I . . ." She tossed her hair over her shoulder. "What about your little cousin? I've seen her — how pious she is! I suppose you love her, because she would never touch Hathor, she keeps herself so pure and clean — "

"Stop it, Jennat," he said warningly.

"Go to her!" Jennat cried. "She understands you. She has your mother's love. She is exactly what you always wanted, with those eyes of hers and her — "

"Stop it! Stop it!" He grasped Jennat by the shoulders and shook her, and when she began to cry, he pulled her close and murmured over and over, "I love you, I love you, Jennat. I'm not asking you to change. I like you the way you are. I'm just worried about you, what people will think, what might happen — "

"Well, I'm keeping the goddess," she said, muffled.

"Do what you will," Jesse said. "But don't cry."

*God declared to Moses, "Go down, for the peo-
ple whom you brought out of Egypt have become
corrupt. They have been quick to leave the ways
that I ordered them to follow, and they have made
themselves a cast-metal calf. They have bowed
down and sacrificed to it. Now, do not try to stop
Me when I unleash My wrath against them to destroy them. I will then make you into a great nation."*

*Moses began to plead before God for the people:
"Remember your servants, Abraham, Isaac, and
Jacob. You swore to them that you would make
their descendants as numerous as the stars in the
sky, giving them the land You promised, so they
could occupy it forever. Withdraw Your anger, and
refrain from doing evil to Your people."*

CHAPTER 13

It was midday, hot and dry, and smoke lay over the valley, the ash descending and making the air acrid. Some of the people had gotten new energy and renewed their jubilation and feasting.

These Israelites, Jennat thought, were strange and excitable people. They talked about allegiance to a single invisible deity, yet they loved idols as well as anyone. Why didn't they admit it? If it was indeed so terrible to sing and dance around an idol, why had their priest, Aaron, made it for them? She had watched the feasting from afar, feeling strangely apart from Shepset and the others. Part of her had wanted to leap into the celebration; another part stood away. Something about the merrymaking seemed perverse, as if the people were trying too hard to summon a passion they didn't really feel. She saw people doing things that she used to take for granted in Egypt. Here, in the barren desert, swept clean by the continual blowing of wind and sand, the singing was obscene, the dancing too violent. So she had watched, fascinated, not so much by the revelers but by the feelings that pulled her first one way, then another.

Jennat ran her comb through her hair. It was the only part of her morning ritual that had survived here in the desert. Her hair was knotted and long; she pulled it back and tied it with a narrow thong. She had no cosmetics, no bathing stool and worst of all, no calendar. Without her calendar, Jennat was helpless against evil days, ignorant of opportune, lucky days. It made her feel desolate and vulnerable, like living on an island. She shuddered. What were her choices? Some of the "mixed multitude" had already gone over to the Israelites, prostrating themselves before the priests, the men begging for circumcision, so that they might truly belong, the women begging to be taken in marriage.

Well, Jesse talked about love. How typical of a man! Talk was easy. As for marriage — she couldn't say that she'd marry him, even if Jesse asked her. Because belonging to Jesse meant belonging exclusively to his God, and that was something too extreme to imagine.

This invisible God of theirs delved into every aspect of one's life, prying into one's very soul. Moses lectured to the people constantly. How could anyone remember all those commandments, let alone keep them? No wonder the Israelites had rebelled and enjoyed themselves with their golden calf.

After the night's dancing, Shepset slept until noon, while Jennat sat quietly, thinking. She watched her friend awaken, stretching, smiling.

"Mmm," Shepset sighed, stretching luxuriantly, "what a night! Wasn't it grand?" She laughed slightly. "Avi was magnificent, a warrior. He fought for me!"

"Don't you care at all how he suffered?" Jennat exclaimed. "He was trying to save you from those others."

Shepset laughed. "It was sweet of him, I'm sure."

"For love of you," Jennat said heatedly, "he let himself be beaten and humiliated in front of everyone."

Shepset reached for Jennat's comb. She began to dress her hair. "Nobody ever fought for me before," she murmured. "Nobody ever took a risk for me. I will go to him," she said, smiling.

"I think it's too late," Jennat told her. "Now you want him, but his father won't allow it."

Shepset's eyes narrowed, like a cat's. "You don't know men very well," she said. "Avi will come to me, despite his father."

"You would compete even against this God of theirs?" Jennat exclaimed. "Rimon follows every commandment, down to the smallest point. He will force Avi to do the same. We weren't supposed to make that calf—"

"I made no calf," said Shepset haughtily. "I only danced, as I always did."

"You danced to the gods of Egypt."

"No, I danced for the men. Listen, Jennat, you are a child when it comes to such things. I heard all those commandments that the Hebrews got from their God. They will never keep them. Our gods have the good sense not to ask people to do the impossible. They know how men lust and what they need—"

"We need these wild nights?"

"Yes," said Shepset with a smile. "We need these wild nights."

"And what about those who are hurt? The children put through the fire, the young girls who are given, as virgins—"

Shepset waved her aside. "Every faith has sacrifice. If a person is pious, then the sacrifice is a privilege."

Jennat felt her cheeks grow hot, and her heart pounded, as if she were doing battle. "Adonai doesn't ask for sacrifices like that," she argued. "He asks them just to love Him, and to do justice for each other. Didn't you hear His voice?"

"What did we hear?" Shepset tossed her head. "How do you know what it was? I say it was a trick. It's not hard for a magician to fill a mountaintop with smoke, and to throw his voice so that it seems the words come from the heavens. I heard only a few words —"

"They say everybody heard it differently," said Jennat, still feeling the flush on her face, "depending on what they were ready to receive."

"Ah, you always elevate yourself over me," cried Shepset, angrily. "You pretend to know mysteries — I tell you, they have caught you in their net like a quail. That voice, those commandments — all things that Moses wants, because Moses wants to be their master. Wait, soon he will gather all the gold they took from Egypt. You'll see."

Jennat stood opposite her friend, her enemy. They had been locked in dispute, it seemed, from the beginning, alternating the role of student and teacher, wise one and fool.

Jennat stood ready to fling out arguments, but she could not summon her thoughts. And maybe Shepset was right. What could one trust? One's own eyes? Feelings? Deceivers lurked everywhere, in nature as in man. Look at a twig, and at times it turns into a living insect. Stick your finger into a blossom, beautiful and tame, only to be stung with its poison.

An outcry rang over the valley. Jennat and Shepset ran with the others toward the mountain, everyone shouting and straining to see. It was Moses, descending from the mountain at last.

High against his chest Moses carried two enormous flat stones. He leaned back against their weight as he walked. It had been forty days since Moses had ascended. Now he came down, and the people called out to him, "Moses! Moses! We thought you were dead." Some covered their faces, trying to hide their guilt.

Moses looked upon the sacrificial fires, at the idols raised onto platforms, and the remains of a full feast. He strode from one place to the other, his mighty arms swinging, his wild mane of hair flowing from his face, accentuating the fury that beamed from his countenance.

"You!" Moses shouted. "Idolaters!"

Straining, his face and arms crimson from the weight, Moses lifted the sacred tablets high above his head. He held them aloft for a moment; then, with a mighty groan, he threw them down. The tablets shattered into pieces. For a time there was utter silence. The fragments rolled, then came to rest. The demolished pieces of the tablets lay at their feet, jagged and broken, just as their covenant had been broken.

Moses sprang to action, running to and fro, fists waving in agitation. The people scattered like a startled flock of birds, first fleeing, then again assembling to coo and croon and cry to their leader. "Moses! Moses! We were wrong, we are sorry, we sinned, what can we do?"

From the entrance of the camp, Moses answered them, calling out with a mighty voice, in an ominous tone, "Whoever is for God, join me!"

Shouting and pushing, the Levite tribe gathered round Moses. "Put on your swords!" he commanded. "Go from one gate to the other in the camp. Let each one kill those involved in the idolatry, even his own brother, friend, or relative."

Jennat and Shepset stared at each other. The sentence was not meant for them, was it? Weren't they called "strangers" and unbound by the laws of Israelites?

"Let's go." Jennat pulled Shepset away. "Let's go!" and they ran, and then they heard the chase and the outcries and all the sounds of slaughter.

* * *

Lamentations rang out all night long. In the morning the people walked about pale as ghosts and still trembling. They had barely the strength to bury the corpses. There were three thousand dead.

They followed Moses to the base of the mountain, weeping and chastised, watching Moses ascend once more to try to gain pardon for their crimes. And this time while Moses was gone they sat and waited, weeping or telling stories of their dead.

The men argued, but softly, as if even from the top of the mountain Moses might hear them. Dissenters were afraid of Moses now; he had the power to have his own people slain. Though they had tears in their eyes, the Levites had gone about their task with vigor. The elders from the other clans sat together and muttered that they would never have killed their own kinsmen, never, not for Moses, not even for Adonai.

Jesse sat with Nathan, Avi, Rimon, and the women at the entrance to the tent, unable to focus on anything except the fact that Efrem had been butchered like an animal, and by his own people.

Talia had thrown herself upon the corpse of her father, screaming, and had to be torn away by Rimon and Channa. Her clothes were blood-soaked.

Later, Jesse tried to talk to her, but she was listless and cold, as if something in her, too, had died.

"My father, oh, my father," she cried, weeping. "I loved him. I never really knew him at the end ... he changed. He was never a leader, never one to act — just sat and listened. Suddenly, he had to dance! How could he dance round that calf, that idol?"

"He went mad," said his wife, Shira, shaking with grief. "Since that morning at the mountain, Efrem was never the same." She shuddered. "It is not good for mortals to hear God's voice."

They all gathered to bury Efrem, and they sat together, raw and wounded.

"Look, Talia, you will be happy again," Jesse told her softly. "Soon we'll be out of this desert, in our own land."

"My father will never see Canaan," said Talia, weeping and clinging to Jesse's arm.

"We'll name our firstborn son for him," Jesse whispered.

Talia looked up at him, her face puffy and stained with tears. "I hate this wilderness," she moaned. "Sometimes I think we will never get to Canaan. Sometimes I think we'll all die here — and then I think of the promise, and I try to believe —"

"Don't stop believing, Talia," Jesse said ardently. "Don't ever stop believing. I need you to believe."

It was true, and Jesse was suddenly struck with it. He needed Talia.

"I'll make you a house, a fine house," he said, the words gushing out as if his destiny were now clear.

"A house?" she whispered. "How will we have a house?"

"I shall make it with my own hands," said Jesse grandly, spreading his fingers so that she could see his strength. "Avi will help me. Look, this will be a lesson for us. We must follow all His ways, all His commandments."

"You mean it, Jesse?"

"Yes, yes," said Jesse, though his heart ached and he knew that the words were only an effort to bring his feelings into line. Maybe if he said them often enough, he would be sure. "We must obey. I see that. It means our life — the difference between life and death."

Some of the elders wanted to make permanent camp in the desert. They would build homes, set out their animals, trade with the Midianites and other tribes that wandered these sandy plains and hills. They might cultivate a few plants, dig wells, concentrate on breeding their livestock — why not? They could live here, at the base of the mountain where God had appeared to them. They would be a holy people, doing His will, their lives uncluttered by the attractions of other peoples, their idols, their ideas. They had been cleansed of the sinners among them. Now they could rededicate themselves and remain pure.

Purity became a matter of constant concern. For all the weeks that Moses remained on the mountain this time, the people waited quietly on the broad plain that lay within its shadow. Early in the mornings, when the sun rose, they stood and faced the glowing clouds and knew that Moses was there, as high as any individual could climb, to meet Adonai face to face. They left off their jewelry and cosmetics, and they bathed themselves, and they prayed morning and night, sometimes prostrating themselves, and then rising, tear-stained and trembling.

And when at last Moses came down from the mountain, holding another set of tablets, the people fell on their knees. Moses raised up the tablets in his hands, and the Israelites saw the writing on them. They saw that Moses' face glowed strangely, and they were frightened.

Moses covered his face with a veil while he stood with them, and he told the people to sit down and listen while he told them everything he had learned during those days and nights on the mountain.

Moses taught them what they might eat and which foods

were forbidden to them, "because you are a special people to Adonai, and your ways must be His ways, and different from the ways of other nations." Moses taught them how to worship with prayer and sacrifice and festival; he taught them how to care for the widow, the orphan, the stranger, the poor. He taught them with whom they could lie and how to rear up their children. He taught them what is clean and what is unclean. He taught them how to execute justice for every crime, when to forgive, and when to punish, and he taught them how to pray.

The elders sat at Moses' feet, Rimon among them, drinking in Moses' words.

And Moses told the people, "Look, you will make fringes to wear on your garments, because you are a nation of priests."

The people were surprised and proud; in Egypt only princes were allowed to wear a fringe.

Afterward, Rimon gathered his people. He motioned Avi to sit close beside him, and he repeated the instructions over and over again, even though everyone became weary. Far into the night they sat, trying to stay awake; Jesse and Avi usually fell asleep long before Rimon was finished with teaching.

Avi, accustomed to being active, suffered his father's demands. Prayer each morning, noon, and night. Learning and memorizing the commandments, understanding their meanings. While his father spoke, Avi's eyes were downcast, his mouth sullen.

Bitterly Avi told Jesse, "My father humiliated me in front of the entire world. I will never forgive him."

Jesse, pained at the rift, argued. "Your father was afraid you would die if you got involved. He saved your life."

"So did Nathan save yours," Avi snapped, "and you've never loved him."

"What are you talking about?"

"All fathers save their children," muttered Avi, biting his lip. "My father is more interested in saving himself than anything in the world. He uses me, to show people how pious he is. He wants to make me an example. I'm sick of it!"

"You are just angry with him because of Shepset," Jesse accused.

"I don't want Shepset. She's a harlot."

"You do want her! You reek of wanting her."

"Damn the lie! I don't want her, after the way she behaved that night. No decent man would take such a woman as a wife."

"She was always a dancer — you knew it," Jesse replied. "And you knew very well what temple dancers are expected to do for the gods they serve."

In the next moment Jesse felt himself tight in his cousin's grip, so that he thought his neck would snap if he moved but a muscle.

"Avi!" he cried through clenched teeth. "For God's sake! Let me go."

"Never, never talk about Shepset to me again," Avi raged. "Never say her name to me. As far as I'm concerned, she is dead." With a shove, he released Jesse.

"Your father," Jesse said, gasping, "is a saint. He has always kept you with him. He protects you. He loves you. He is a great leader, and Shepset would be a curse to you — I don't care if you strangle me. It's the truth. How I wish I had a father like Rimon. What I wouldn't give!"

"You ass," Avi said, his lip curled in disgust. "You think you have everything arranged and figured out. You know nothing about my father — or yours."

They fought, biting and punching and wrestling like two dogs in the dust, until suddenly it was over, and the two drew apart, dazed, noses bloody, eyes blackened. Avi sat up first. He pointed to Jesse. "You look terrible. Your eye . . . yellow and purple . . ." And he started to laugh.

"Your hair is white," sputtered Jesse, pointing at the dust that coated Avi's head. "You've become a hoary old man all at once." Jesse reeled back, letting the laughter claim him utterly, and the two of them clasped each other about the shoulders now, laughing and swaying as they walked together to find water for their bruises.

Talia met them at the edge of the camp. "Avi, Jesse," she called, wringing her hands. "Devorah is sick with plague — it has struck the camp."

Jesse and Avi ran with Talia to the tent, where Devorah lay on her mat, her face beaded with sweat, her breath quick and shallow.

Jesse knelt beside her. His mother's hands were cold and damp. "What is it?" he whispered, gazing up at Talia.

"A plague sent by Adonai, they say. Punishment for the golden calf." Talia bit her lips. "They writhe with cramps and fever. Some have already died."

"Where is my father?" Jesse asked angrily.

"Gone," said Talia.

"Gone? Where? Why is he always gone when there is trouble?" He looked at Avi, full of fury. "You see?"

Avi said nothing, but nodded heavily. "I'll go and fetch my mother. Maybe she can help."

Through the night Jesse sat by his mother's side. She lay on the goatskin mat, turning and panting, fighting some invisible foe.

"Don't take him!" she screamed out. "Don't take my only one!"

Jesse's heart ached; she was thinking of her two lost boys, those murdered by the Egyptians. Oh, God! Why had he never

194

been able to make it up to her? Why hadn't he loved her well enough to make her forget?

In the morning Rimon came to see Devorah. He stood looking down at his sister, his beard quivering, his hands clasped into fists.

Then he stood at the entrance to Devorah's tent and raised his voice in prayer. He motioned Jesse to join him, and for a few minutes Jesse did. Then Rimon's entreaties became unbearable, and Jesse stumbled out into the merciless bright sunshine and flat, dry desert.

Rimon followed him, breathing heavily. "You walk away," he accused. "Haven't you time enough or interest enough to seek His forgiveness?" Rimon shook his head and gritted his teeth. "Young people," he spat. "Even if you had only one thousandth of the blessings you enjoy every single day, you should fall on your knees in gratitude."

"Gratitude, for what?" Jesse demanded. "My mother is dying."

Rimon breathed heavily, as if he had climbed a mountain. "You see," he rasped, "the consequences of sin."

"How has she sinned?" Jesse cried. "My mother kept hope alive for years — she preached to everyone — she never lost courage until Shosha died, and who can blame her for that? How could a merciful God blame her?"

"What is faith if it dries up the moment there is grief?" demanded Rimon, unmoved. "Look, we are being tested. We are the only people in the world who have ever heard the voice of God. Whatever else happens to us, this is enough to last for a thousand generations, and we must never ask for more."

"I ask for more," retorted Jesse. "I want my mother to live. I want her to love me again. She's like a shadow, a shell. Don't you feel her anguish? What happened to you, Uncle? You used to feel our pain and comfort us —"

"How can I comfort a sinner who does not want to change?" Rimon retorted. He moved toward Jesse, his steps heavy, his look almost menacing as he reached out and grasped Jesse by the shoulders. "I am not talking about your mother's sin. Your mother is crazed with grief. Adonai understands, and she will return to Him, and she will be forgiven for her doubts. But you" — Rimon pointed a finger at Jesse, leveled his eyes at Jesse — "you are unrepentant."

"For what shall I repent?" Jesse stormed. "I've done nothing wrong."

"You see the pride of the young!" Rimon exclaimed, furious. "You lust after strange women. You question Adonai's judgments."

"I do not lust!" But Jesse's own lie stopped him short. He was shocked and embarrassed that his uncle knew his secret desires. "My mother is sick. And now you say it's my fault. Why is it me? What about my father? He's the one who scoffs and swaggers about."

Rimon gave him a fierce look. "Honor your father!" he declared, fist raised. "Honor your mother! Listen and heed these commandments, Jesse, or you will surely die."

"Must I honor a man I hate?" Jesse cried.

"Who makes you judge of your parents?" Rimon demanded. "True, Nathan is an unbeliever. He has never pretended to be pious. But you — you are worse, half in and half out. One moment you are for God and our people. The next moment you are for yourself, and for the idolaters. At least Nathan knows where he stands."

"Why are you for my father, and never on my side?"

"I am on your side. I want you to live."

"You want me to be a slave again. A slave to God, if not to Pharaoh."

His uncle stood back, regarding Jesse as he would a serpent.

"What a horrible thing to say," he gasped. "If I were your father, I would beat you black and blue."

"As you beat Avi? What good did it do you?" Jesse cried.

"I saved Avi's life!" Rimon shouted, his voice ringing out like a thunderclap. "Don't you think I feel the fires of hell when I remember what I did to Avi? But what if I had let him go in the midst of the idolaters, and he had been put to the sword, like our other kinsmen? What do you know about life and pain? Nothing!"

"Well, I'm learning," replied Jesse, steely-eyed, his face set. "And you are certainly teaching me, Uncle."

Rimon looked at him, his arms thrust forward, about to spring. Then he turned on his heel and left Jesse alone in the wilderness.

Jesse sat on a rock, feeling the dry heat baking his body, his bones. His heart ached with dread and pain.

Rimon, in his search for God, was losing his touch with the people he loved. If this is what happens to men when God seizes them, Jesse thought, I want none of it.

He felt sickened, empty. Oh, if he could only go and leave them all. Now Jesse counted every grief of his life, so that they all came together within his breast, heavy as stones, hurting.

He thought of the two infant brothers he had never known, and he mourned them. He remember Shosha, her brightness, her smile, and he wept for her. He thought of Efrem, gone, and his mother, sick unto death, and he beat his fists against his chest, and he opened his mouth to cry out loud, like a wild animal, and none of it brought him any help.

That night Jesse watched over his mother again. She was delirious, and even then, while Jesse knelt beside her, wishing and praying for her strength, he knew she would slip away.

"Nathan never told him," she murmured. "Never will."

"What, Ima? Who?"

"He needs to know it, my son."

"Hush, hush, don't worry, you'll be all right."

"I love you, Jesse!" Devorah sat upright and clutched Jesse by the sleeve. "Oh, Jesse, I've made terrible mistakes. I thought I could live it well, do the right thing. I wanted it all to be so perfect ... It ended without ... Why couldn't I love him?" she cried. "Jesse, you must love him. You must *love him*. Promise me!"

"I promise," Jesse whispered, without the slightest sense of reason, for his heart leapt in anguish as he held his mother in his arms. She tensed, and he felt the frail bones of her back and heard her swift, rasping breath.

"Oh! Oh! Oh!" she cried out, her eyes wild and her arms flailing.

"Ima," Jesse called out, "I will live for you!"

Her breath stopped. He thought she was gone. A long shudder seized her, a sharp intake of breath seemed to open her up. And then came the final silence.

CHAPTER 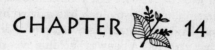 14

"If you continue to lie there like a sick toad," rasped Nathan, prodding Jesse with his toe, "I'm just going to let you starve to death. You have chores to do. Don't think I intend to gather fuel for a fire. Don't think I'm going to set up that stinking tent all by myself."

"Yes, Father." Jesse looked past his father, repulsed by the sight of him. Nathan's hair was matted. His body gave off a deep, offensive odor; without a woman around, he implied, why bother?

Since his mother's death over a week ago, Jesse had seen no one. Nathan had stayed for the burial, then, typically, disappeared, and Jesse sat in his tent, flap drawn down, signal that he wanted no visitors. Twice he had heard Talia calling.

"Jesse! You have to eat something. Come out. I've cooked a nice broth of lamb. Pieces of meat, onions. Come on, Jesse. We're worried about you."

Jesse sat without moving. His silence at last discouraged Talia. It was what he wanted.

But now Nathan came to prod him, as if he were some lazy

animal. Slowly Jesse rose, feeling the stiffness in his limbs, the hoarse thickness of his throat. There was a sour taste in his mouth.

"Get yourself to the water buckets," Nathan grumbled, seeing that Jesse had risen. "Cut your hair. Clean your nails. Make yourself human — you look like a dying hyena."

"Thanks," said Jesse, stepping over a pile of dry dung that his father had gathered. A pot was bubbling over some stones. "What's that?"

"Some stew Talia brought over. You'll clean yourself up, groom your hair — get that stink off your skin. We'll eat, and then we'll go and present ourselves."

Jesse gave a laugh. "Oh? We're going to some nobleman's house? Are you planning to hire me out, then, as some woman's lover? I'm surprised it took you so long, in this wilderness, to find employment for me."

Nathan reached back as if to strike Jesse. Then he grumbled, "Don't be fresh."

Jesse stripped to the waist and began to wash his chest and arms, using a handful of sand and a few leaves for the scrubbing. Devorah, in the last weeks, had not provided soap or food, or any necessary things, not even a smile.

Jesse felt his chin. Coarse hair sprouted there. So, nature had finally decided to give him the look of a man. Fine time, he thought sardonically; he had never felt less like a man or more like a stupid child. Now, with his mother gone, he faltered over the oddest things — what to eat, where to sit, when to sleep, how to feel. It was strange, for he hadn't been going to her for guidance lately, or even for conversation. Somehow they had merely coexisted in this wilderness with its trials. But her presence had given him comfort. Now he could neither work nor rest without feeling displaced.

"Where are we going?" Jesse asked his father after he had washed himself and slipped on a clean robe.

Nathan snapped out his reply. "We are going to Betzalel, to offer your services. We are going to set you up with the powers that move this community. Moses."

"What are you talking about?"

"Have you been asleep all these days?" Nathan coughed and spat in disgust. "Have you got mud in your ears? Moses has been holding forth for days about the holy ark, the meeting tent, all the furniture, vestments, sacrificial vessels, curtains, objects of gold and silver — "

"What are you talking about?" Jesse repeated, leaning forward now, his interest aroused.

"Adonai has ordered Moses to have us get busy and make a place where the tablets will be stored. A fancy ark, covered with gold and designs — everything is given in detail. When we travel, the ark will be borne on poles by priests, specially chosen for the honor. They will be members of the precious Levite family, of course." Nathan snorted. "You see, there are always honors to be given out, and it doesn't hurt to be related to Moses." He scratched his side vigorously, then continued. "When we are camped, the ark will rest in the middle of a tent, a tent of meeting. Everything in the tent will be of the finest materials by the best craftsmen — objects of gold, copper, silver, woven curtains. Aaron and his sons will wear special jeweled garments."

"Jeweled?"

Nathan nodded. "Moses has asked every man and woman of skill to appear before Betzalel, overseer of this project."

"I understand," said Jesse.

"I don't think you do," said his father. He ladled stew into two cracked clay bowls, handed one to Jesse, and motioned for him to eat.

The smell of meat stirred Jesse's senses. He ate quickly, using his fingers and his spoon, wishing for bread, licking out the last bits with his tongue.

"You are going to work on this," Nathan continued, chewing as he spoke, "and you are going to show them what you can do. Honors will come to those who make these holy objects, you can be sure. You," Nathan said, pointing, "will volunteer. You will be the first at the workplace each morning and the last to leave at night. They will say of you later, 'Jesse, Jesse, the son of Nathan, worked harder than anyone, faithfully, tirelessly. Jesse, the son of Nathan — ' "

"And what will you do, Father?" Jesse asked, his bitterness unconcealed.

"I will see to it that you work hard and well," said Nathan. "I will make sure they know your name. And I'm going to bring offerings to this venture. I will be repaid a hundredfold."

"What offerings?" Jesse asked.

"I have resources," said Nathan vaguely. "Rest assured, my son, you will be guaranteed a place in this community. They will know your name."

"Who? Who will know my name?" Jesse grumbled. "And why should I care?" Jesse stood up, kicking sand into the ashes, and Nathan rose with a jolt, ready for a fight. Then he retreated, grunting, shaking his head.

"Come with me," he said. Ducking, he moved into the shadows at the far end of the tent. He bent over, picked up a small goatskin sack tied to a saddle, and then gestured, whispering, "Come."

Jesse followed. Here in the dim light, and in the oppressive closeness of the tent, Jesse felt the vast chasm between him and his father. His father's breath came in swift gusts, and his eyes bore a greedy gleam.

Nathan reached into the sack. A glittering array of gold and jewels lay in his hand. There were gold chains, silver amulets, beaded necklaces, and bracelets and rings of turquoise, garnet, emerald, and onyx.

"Where did you get this, Father?" Jesse gasped.

"From my life's work," whispered Nathan, and his eyes gleamed up at Jesse. "What do you think now, lad? What do you think of your old father now?"

Never in her life had Jennat seen people work with such eagerness and devotion. Jennat herself came early each morning, to bring water to the artisans and to prepare huge pots of stew and a constant supply of flat bread, tasks that many of the non-Israelites assumed.

It went on for months, a frenzy of work, and as they worked, the separate families and tribes became fused into one being, one nation. They had a goal.

Perfumers created aromatic incense and anointing oils. Their presses gave off heavenly fragrances. Artisans had brought dyes from Egypt, the highly prized crimson, purple, and sky blue. These they prepared in huge vats, dyeing the cloths created by the weavers, who sat with their looms beside the dozens of women spinning thread to make draperies for the tent.

Two gorgeous, intricate figures of angels were carved and gilded, then mounted on top of the ark, in which the tablets of the law would lie.

Skilled carpenters, Avi among them, fashioned the posts and sockets from acacia wood brought from Egypt. Others made furniture — washstands and tables and utensils, to be

203

covered with pure gold, silver, and copper from materials melted down in huge kilns.

Jennat bartered her work for necessities; a bit of cloth, a goatskin, leather for sandals. Food was at least handy; a cook can always eat. From morning until dusk, Jennat trudged back and forth between groups of workers, listening to their banter, their camaraderie, their joyous pride. They called to one another, laughed and sang, talked about the future.

"When we come to Canaan, we will make a house for the holy ark; Adonai will meet with us there."

"Ah, look at this gorgeous basin, all of gold! Look at these linens, white as snow, soft as down!"

She saw Jesse sometimes, for he was apprenticed to Betzalel, the great teacher. Talia remained beside Jesse nearly all day, gazing at him in admiration, handing him tools, being beautiful. Jennat's hatred of Talia grew into a thing she could almost see, with a shape and a smell to it.

Well, he has to do it, Jennat told herself; his father probably made him do it. He loves me! He said so. Talia is probably assigned to him as an apprentice.

But why did Jesse seem so completely immersed, so happy?

Voices flew back and forth in her thoughts. She hated herself for staying close by, to be tormented. Yet somehow, she could not stay away. Every moment was a conflict. To go, to stay, to see Jesse, or to avoid him, to speak to him or to scorn him . . .

She saw him standing at a workbench beside Betzalel himself, nodding intently as the master instructed him. "Yes, yes," she heard Jesse murmuring, "I see. I'll be very careful — and the gold mounting — I know how to do that, for I worked in the home of In-hop-tep with Sinuhe, the Egyptian."

The teacher smiled at Jesse and clapped him on the back, and Jennat felt smothered with anger. Who worked beside him with Sinuhe? Who shared every new technique? Who saved him from punishment when he stole that buckle?

Jesse seemed transported, blind. Several times Jennat waved to him, and once even called his name. He turned and nodded, and in the next moment Talia distracted him, and Jennat burned. She decided not to return to the work site. Yet she found it impossible to stay away. Each day, it seemed, the work became more intense and the workers more exhilarated. Each night Jennat found it harder to sleep, and she played and replayed possible conversations, proposals, arguments.

"I want to help," she would say, presenting herself to the one in charge, to Betzalel or his assistant, Oholiav. "I have skills — I will work for nothing, eagerly. Just let me take part! I love to work with gold and jewels. I'm a good artisan. In Egypt everyone admired my work."

Retorts raged in her mind. "No. You are a woman, you cannot."

"Other women are working! Let me help. I'll be so careful — I'll do exactly as I'm told."

"Others have contributed materials, their own jewels."

"I'll contribute mine. Here!"

"We don't want your jewels."

"But you wanted them before, in Egypt — why not now?"

"Tainted, they are tainted."

"How can that be?"

"You are a foreigner. A stranger. We don't want you among us, touching our holy objects — be gone!"

The thing seethed in her. Jennat wasn't even sure why she wanted so desperately to work with the Israelites. Was it to be near Jesse? Yes, but there was more. She needed to hold those treasures in her hands, to dispel the filth and dust of the wilderness. She wanted to feel the things of civilization surrounding her again. She wanted to share with the others their pleasantness, their pride and accomplishment. And she recalled her days in the caravan, when she was three. Once she had thrust her hand into the wares and the coins, trying to help. The caravaneer had kicked her in the side so viciously that she vomited and could not straighten up for hours.

Week after week Jennat watched the building of the tabernacle, the making of the great menorah with its almond-blossom cups, the sewing of the vestments. Daily, the Israelites brought their wares as offerings — metals, precious stones, purest olive oil for the lamps, ram skins and processed hides, fine goat's wool and lamb's wool and linen. Goods piled up, and Moses sent out word: "Enough! Let no man or woman bring any more material for the sacred offering!"

Jennat, fetching water, saw Nathan, amid the procession of volunteers, bringing one last load of hides and also a bulging goatskin sack. Loudly he proclaimed his offering, and scribes noted it on parchment, counting every piece as Nathan presented it.

"For Moses!" Nathan called out as each piece was noted. "For the tabernacle, praise God!"

Now it was nearly dark. Jennat finished scrubbing out a large pot with coarse sand and put it with the other utensils. She wound her shawl tightly around her head and body, bracing herself against the evening cold. She would hurry to Shepset and the other young people. Maybe they had found some kindling for a fire.

A few Israelites were still about, finishing up, putting their tools away. They stored their works inside a rocky enclosure around which dozens of guards kept watch in the night. But it was not nightfall yet, and the guards were eating and laughing loudly together.

Out of the corner of her eye she saw Nathan, moving

slowly, looking first to one side, then the other. He stepped lightly toward the enclosure, and, making himself narrow, slipped inside. When he emerged, there was a bulge under his robe, and Jennat knew, as if she had seen it with her own eyes, that Nathan had stolen back his offerings.

Jennat whirled about. Where were the guards? But then she wondered, What do I care? It has nothing to do with me. Still, she was filled with loathing and resentment.

Nathan turned and saw her, and his eyes narrowed instantly, his nostrils flared.

"What do you think you're doing here?" he growled. "It's after work hours — what are you sneaking around here for? Dipping into the Lord's treasure, I'll bet."

"I saw you," she flung out, her heart pounding wildly.

"What did you see? I took my own goods, the things I'd brought — Moses declared that too much has been offered. These are not needed. Is it my fault we are all too generous?"

One of the guards, hearing the shouts, ran toward the two. The man grasped Jennat by the shoulders and gave her a rough shaking; she bit her tongue and tears stung her eyes. "What's going on here?" the guard demanded. "What have you done?"

"Nothing."

Nathan made a gesture, rubbing his fingers together. He lifted his brows. "Hard to resist temptation," he said.

"We'll take her to the elders," the guard barked. "They'll decide what to do with her."

"Leave her to me," said Nathan with an easy nod and a smile. "I know the girl — I'll see to it she stays away from the workers."

"Don't know why they even allow this rabble near," muttered the guard.

The other guard came. "Found yourself a woman, eh, Ari?" He peered at Jennat, pushed the shawl from her face. "Not bad-looking, this one. Sweetheart, is it that you fancy yourself in the arms of an Israelite? Warm and sweet? Is that it?"

The men roared with laughter as Jennat broke away and ran.

Moments later Nathan overtook her, panting. He caught her by the arm, yanked her close, too close. The shape of his eyes, the slits of his nostrils repelled her, and also the scent of him — it seemed impossible to Jennat that this was Jesse's father.

"You're lucky I spoke up for you," he rasped. "Now, get this into your head." He grasped her by the hair and pulled her head back, so that he spoke into her upturned face, his breath hot and stale. "I don't want you near my son. We don't want you in our camp. Jesse is betrothed. He is sitting in the seat of honor now, with respectable men, leaders of the people. He has no desire for you."

"How do you know that?" Jennat screamed, hurling out the words, her face burning.

"I'm his father. I know what he called you — that little Egyptian harlot!' He laughs to tell how you came after him. He and Talia laugh about it."

"You lie."

'Test me! Ask him!" Nathan challenged.

He looked down at her, and a familiar hatred beat in her breast. The caravaneer, In-hop-tep, Nathan, and Jesse, all seemed superimposed in her mind as one person, one evil, malicious man.

In that moment Jennat made a decision, and she knew it was right. She would set out as she had started, alone. And let all the rest of them go to the netherworld!

After many months of careful labor, the ark and the tent of meeting and all its furnishings were finished. When everything was done, Aaron, the high priest, and his two eldest sons, Nadab and Abihu, were anointed.

Aaron was dressed in his splendid new garments. Precious gems — topaz, sapphires, carnelians, and emeralds — were set into his ephod and breastplate. His robe was of pure white linen, and at its hem were artfully embroidered pomegranates in blue, purple, and scarlet, alternating with small bells made of pure gold. The little bells rang delicately when he walked. Aaron was dazzling. Every eye was upon him as he approached the altar to perform his priestly rites.

Carefully Aaron and his assistants gave the sacrificial offerings, exactly as they had been commanded. Smoke rose from the offerings, rich and fragrant, pleasing as the good deeds that the worshippers vowed to do.

For seven days the rituals continued, and the people crowded around to witness this culmination of all their work. A flash of fire came from the heavens, a clear sign that Adonai had accepted their offerings, and they raised their voices in song. They were forgiven for all their sins. Now, surely, Adonai would lead them home to Canaan.

Jesse stood with his people, rejoicing. He had helped to polish and mount the jewels in Aaron's ephod. As he watched and listened, taking pride in his labor, Jesse felt an overwhelming sense of belonging to this entire people whose God was the Lord, and whose strength, therefore, was eternal.

No matter what happened from now on, Jesse thought, nothing would ever remove this solace and strength from him. He glanced about at his nearest kin — Rimon, Avi, Nathan, his cousin Seth, his father, and Talia with Shira and Channa — all one family, one clan. Talia came close to him. Her hand touched his. Now a glow surrounded him, as on that morning of Adonai's appearance on the mountain, and Talia seemed part of that radiance.

Aaron stood at the altar, his worship completed. His sons Nadab and Abihu rushed forward. Each of them carried a fire pan, already filled with flame, and they brought them to the altar. Suddenly, from above, a tremendous shaft of flame shot forth, beamed at the fire pans, instantly consuming and killing Nadab and Abihu, the sons of Aaron.

Talia let out a scream. Jesse turned to Avi, shocked.

Aaron, the father, seemed to stagger. His face went dead white. Dazed, deep in shock, Aaron took a step back, then reached for his dead sons, motioning for help to take them away.

But Moses stopped him. Moses' face was unveiled and shining. Strange glow — it seemed unearthly, un-human. "No, Aaron. You must stay here and serve Adonai, to glorify Him. Do you understand? Your sons were specially chosen to worship Adonai, to bring sacrifice, but they did not heed His instructions. They brought their own fire — a strange ritual. It was not acceptable to Him."

And Aaron remained and was silent.

Jesse and Avi, watching, murmured to each other. "Why? Why?"

Rimon led them all away, far from the tent of meeting and the tragedy. They sat together long after nightfall, trying to understand what had happened.

"Every time we come to rejoicing," said Seth, wiping his mouth with a cloth, "we fall to weeping. What did they do wrong?"

Rimon sighed. "Ah, poor Aaron, to be struck this way on the most glorious day of his life, to be brought to grief." He pulled at his beard. "Those nearest to Adonai," he explained sadly, "are held to the highest standard. Nadab and Abihu were arrogant, bringing their own fire, consulting with nobody else, making their own ritual, and not what Adonai prescribed."

"But they did it in praise," Avi objected.

Rimon replied, "Look, this is the way the heathen worship, inventing all kinds of ghastly rituals with which they think to please their gods — to make them do man's bidding."

"But there was nothing ghastly about this," Seth objected.

"It was not correct," said Rimon.

"People make mistakes," said Channa, his wife, but Rimon silenced her with a glance.

Nathan chewed his lip. He muttered, "Moses does rule with a heavy hand."

"Moses did not make that fire," said Shira. "We all saw. It came from heaven." She looked upward, then shielded her eyes.

"But what did they do wrong?" Avi persisted.

"Aren't you listening?" Rimon demanded. "If each man goes his own way, we will have chaos. There must be order in worship, as in life. The priest must be the most careful to do everything properly, to set an example for the people."

"But they meant well," Avi argued. "They came in love."

"Love isn't always enough," Rimon said. "There must be obedience."

"It is a tyranny." Avi leapt to his feet.

"God decrees," retorted Rimon. "Man obeys. How many times will it take for you to understand? We did not leave Egypt to run wild, like cattle. We exchanged the yoke of Pharaoh — evil and capricious Pharaoh — for the yoke of heaven, which is pure and good."

"Oh, I understand!" shouted Avi, fists clenched. "There is no love, no freedom, nothing but death and force, and it is all in the name of God — I don't believe it. I don't believe you."

"Avi, Avi," his mother said soothingly, trying to intercede.

Avi brushed her away and turned to Rimon, his eyes blazing. "This is horrible, Father! I wish I had never worked on the tabernacle."

"Silence!" cried Rimon. "You will bring disaster upon yourself and upon me. You are arrogant and stubborn, always running your own way, never obedient — "

Avi turned, and Jesse could see the hatred in his face. "How do I know this is God's will and not your way of chaining me down?"

Jesse didn't want to watch, but his eyes were riveted to the two as Rimon fell upon Avi, wrathful as a storm and as merciless.

The next day Avi vanished. The family members tempered their fear. Avi was angry; he had gone to be alone for a while.

But two days passed, and Avi did not return.

All over the encampments Rimon looked for his son, and then he brought Jesse with him to search and inquire.

At last Jesse and Rimon heard the truth from several men out hunting, who had seen three young people — two girls and a lad — hurrying with bundles on their backs to the wild land dominated by Midianite tribes.

Jesse and Rimon had walked for hours, searching. Hopeless now, Jesse sank to the ground, exhausted. His eyes ached from the raw sun on the granite surfaces, and from the dust that blew constantly into his face. His skin felt parched and leathery; his hands were swollen from the elements.

Gone. Avi was gone, and with him, Jennat and Shepset. Jesse looked out over the desert, and its emptiness accosted him. "How long must we wander in this wilderness? I don't want to go on, Uncle. Whatever lies ahead, I don't want to see it."

Rimon only groaned.

"I remember what they said in Egypt," Jesse continued, his voice low and bitter. "Moses was going to lead us to a new land. We went with him. If we'd known he'd leave us sitting in this cursed wilderness . . . It's been a whole year!"

"A year," Rimon echoed. "Time again now to observe the Passover night, as Moses commanded."

"Why won't he bring us to Canaan?" Jesse cried. "What about the promise?"

"We move when Adonai signals us — you know that. Otherwise, we wait. Maybe He does not want us to arrive in the land too soon."

"It can't be too soon," Jesse said bitterly. "Already we have lost — "

"We have all lost a great deal, Jesse," Rimon said, his voice rumbling, still firm. He sat down upon a rock beside Jesse, his head down, hands on his knees. "You," he said gravely, "are the only one left to me. Nephew. Child of my sister — we are of one flesh, Jesse. Avi has chosen to go his own way. I did everything I could so that he would follow the path to Adonai. Now my son is dead to me — but you, Jesse, are my hope."

"You said I'm a sinner."

"We are all sinners. The difference lies in who is willing to change."

"I'm not sure, Uncle. That's the truth."

"At least you care about truth."

"But you were right! I lusted after the Egyptian girl. And now she is gone, and I still think about her all the time, all the time, and I have these dreams. . . ." He shuddered. "Why is it that women can torment us so?"

"It is nature," said Rimon, almost smiling. "You're a good lad. Soon our clan will need a new leader. They will need you."

Jesse felt his uncle Rimon's arms around him. A sense of trust and power lifted him up: he would be heir to Rimon, a leader of his people.

Miriam and Aaron spoke against Moses because he had married a Cushite woman. They said, "Hath the Lord indeed spoken only with Moses? Hath He not spoken also with us?"

And the Lord heard it . . . and He said, "Hear now My words: if there be a prophet among you, I the Lord do make Myself known to him in a vision; I do speak with him in a dream. But with Moses do I speak face to face, so that he sees a true picture of God. How can you not be afraid to speak against My servant Moses?"

And Miriam was punished for her rebellion, banished from the camp for seven days and her skin made leprous, white as snow.

CHAPTER 15

Slowly the Israelites made their way across the wilderness, following the shimmering cloud. They traveled when it rose and they camped when it rested. After ten months in the desert of Sinai, they moved out, with their tents and their animals and all their possessions, through the desert of Paran. And as they wandered, they began to grumble against Moses, saying that he was too powerful, too ambitious, and that all the laws he had taught them were beyond endurance.

Everyone was aware of the rift. Korach, Moses' cousin, held meetings with the men, first in secret after dusk, then in the open daylight. Korach had seethed in resentment from the beginning. And then seeing Aaron in his splendid bejeweled priestly garments had filled him with envy and loathing.

Korach told a parable he had invented: "Look, a poor widow owns a field. When she goes to plow it, Moses forbids her to hitch an ox and an ass together. When she sows, Moses forbids her to sow with mingled seeds. At the time of the harvest, Moses forces her to leave the fallen grain for the poor. When she reaps her grain, she must give a portion to the priests as a tithe. The poor widow, in despair, sells the field and buys two lambs to get wool and food for herself and her orphan children. But again Moses comes. He demands the firstborn lamb for a sacrifice and the first shearing for the priests. At last the poor woman, overwrought, slaughters the sheep, but Aaron appears and takes a portion of the meat. 'Alas!' exclaims the woman. 'Even killing my sheep did not deliver me from these oppressors — take everything, take it and be gone.' This," said Korach, "is what is happening with Moses and Aaron. Soon we will be paupers in our own land. And they do this all in the name of the Holy One!"

Moses, hearing, trembled with grief. "I have taken not one ass from them!" he retorted. "Is it not enough, Korach, that you already were given priestly duties? Do you need more glory?"

Korach retorted, "Do you?"

Like a fire, the rebellion burst out from several sides at once. Dathan and Abiram, two men of the Reuben tribe, also made demands. Shouldn't the priests come from the house of Reuben, the oldest clan? "We are the firstborn of Israel," they protested, when priesthood was given to the Levites. "As the oldest tribe, we should be the high priests, not Aaron and his kin."

Korach inflamed his listeners. "Why should Moses have authority over us? We all heard the voice of Adonai. The Lord performed miracles not only for Moses, but for all of us!"

Someone took the other side, remembering, "It was Moses who went up onto the mountain and brought us the tablets of the law — the Torah."

"Take back your Torah, Moses!" shouted the rebels. "You said you gave us the law so that we might live. And yet we die."

They counted all who had died on account of the law — those killed by the Levites for worshipping the calf, those killed by plague, and lately, a man found gathering sticks on the Sabbath, despite the commandment against doing work or kindling fires on the day of rest and worship. What should be the punishment? None had been specified. Moses consulted Adonai. The man was to be stoned to death.

It was a slow death, inflicted by the entire community. The man's cries, his panic, and his final agony, all seared the hearts of the people.

"Why does Moses decide who shall die, and how?" Korach challenged. "Who will be next? Is any of us so perfect that we can't make a mistake?"

Jesse stood beside his uncle Rimon, listening. The speakers were powerful men, and convincing; still, Jesse felt torn.

Uncle Rimon tugged at his beard, raked his hands through his hair. Then he spoke out. "But God chose Moses to lead us."

"How can we be certain of that?" Korach responded. "Moses himself tells us that he talks to God — but Moses makes all the rules." He pointed to Rimon. "God also gave us a brain so that we can use our own judgment."

Abiram stood up beside Korach. "Moses gathers all the wealth for himself," he accused, "claiming he needs it to build the tabernacle."

Rimon wavered. Jesse could see it by the way his eyes flickered and his hands grappled with his cloak. "Perhaps you are right, Korach," Rimon said, "at least to ask these questions. Moses himself said that we are a nation of priests. So each man must judge what is right, what God wants of us."

"Exactly, exactly," cried Korach, pointing to Rimon. "You, Rimon, have led your clan for years. Why shouldn't you lead now?"

While Korach and Moses negotiated, the people waited and pondered. Moses called for Dathan and Abiram; they could talk this out. The two men refused to come. "Isn't it enough that you brought us out of a land flowing with milk and honey," they jeered, "and you leave us in this wilderness, and now you want to make yourself a prince over us?"

While the arguments raged, Jesse felt the new joy of basking in Rimon's shadow. The father he had always wanted was suddenly his, as Rimon treated him like a son. At dusk they walked together, pondering over the arguments. At midday, when the animals languished in the hot sun, they rested in a spot of shade, and Jesse wondered what it would be like if Rimon were truly a leader of many men, and he, Jesse, his right hand.

As always, Rimon led the family in prayers and in talk. Distant cousins drifted by with their wives and children, and in-laws and brothers. They sat together at night, having built themselves a break against the wind, and they squinted into the embers from their meager fire while they debated.

"Let's just get on with it!" exclaimed Seth. Impatiently he thumped his fist against his thigh. "We're withering away in this confounded desert, while those at the top have nothing better to do than quarrel about who is king!"

Old Uncle Jacob nodded wisely. "Too much power in the hands of a single man always leads to corruption."

"Corruption?" exclaimed Shira. "You say Moses is corrupt?"

At times like these, when all were gathered, Jesse felt the pain of loss most deeply. He knew that his mother would have sided with Moses. Efrem would have leaned first one way, then another, and Avi — Avi would have been sullen and angry, eager to be off and doing something, anything, to get away from talk.

"It is a matter of how we shall be ruled," said Rimon, tapping the tips of his fingers together, his brow furrowed.

"Shall we all be equal? Or shall one leader dominate and instruct us?"

"Someone must rule," whispered Talia, her eyes large and lustrous in the firelight. Jesse watched the way she moved her hand, pushing her hair back, the way she shook her head. All her movements were familiar to him, her opinions predictable.

"Rimon, why do you involve yourself?" said Nathan, leaning forward, his eyes piercing. "If Moses leads, you will be his follower. If Korach leads, you will be *his* follower. You have nothing to gain by rebellion. Wait it out! See what happens. Don't choose sides. If you want to live," he added in an undertone.

Jesse was astounded. His father seemed almost wise — a selfish kind of wisdom, to be sure, but it made sense. Jesse started to speak, but thought better of it and bit his lip.

"The question is," said Seth, "does God speak only to Moses?"

"No," said Rimon. "No."

The thing could not be contained. Secret plans were laid bare. People chose sides.

"Leave it alone, Rimon," Nathan warned. "If you are going to continue in these meetings, that's one thing, but I will not let you take Jesse with you."

Rimon's dark eyebrows shot up. "You say this to me? Why not let Jesse decide for himself?"

"I want to go with Rimon," said Jesse, breathing heavily. Until this moment, he had not made up his mind. Indeed, he did not want to go against Moses — Moses with the magnificent gaze, the teachings, the strength. His uncle Rimon was a fine leader, yes, but Jesse had to admit it — Moses was different. One could see it in the glow of his face, and by the light in his eyes. Moses had spoken face to face with God.

But there was this lifelong battle, with Nathan on one side and Jesse on the other. Now Nathan's insistence settled it.

Nathan pushed Jesse aside and addressed Rimon. "Look, Rimon, if you want to endanger your own life, so be it. But I don't intend to bury my son along with you."

"What's this about my life?" Rimon gave an exaggerated laugh. "One has a right to speak one's mind, after all. We are not prisoners of Moses."

"Moses has called Dathan and Abiram to come to him; they have refused. Moses is furious. Surely you know, Rimon, that no leader can tolerate this kind of thing. Moses must act, and he will act strongly, I assure you."

"What can Moses do to us, when we are strong in number?"

"You are going against him, then?"

Rimon did not answer.

Jesse stood between the two men, gazing from one to the other. Earlier, he had been outside the tent of meeting, listening to the ruckus.

"It will be settled in the morning," Jesse said, and both men looked at him in surprise.

"What do you know?" Nathan turned sharply. "Why are you hanging around those men? You're to watch the animals, get them to fodder, and what about the lambing? Lazy good-for-nothing!" Nathan lunged at Jesse, as if to catch him and thrash him. Rimon put out his hand.

"Leave off," he said heavily. "Nathan, let the boy alone."

"As you let yours alone?" Nathan shouted.

Jesse broke in. "Tomorrow morning Korach and his followers are to assemble outside the meeting tent with their fire pans, to stand before Adonai. They will make sacrifice, like the priests. Adonai will decide between them — who is acceptable, who shall lead."

"So, Moses calls for a test," said Rimon.

Jesse went on. "If Moses is indeed chosen to rule, there will be a sign."

Nathan said heavily, "Death is the only sign that the rebels will heed. Listen! You stay away from them."

Rimon swung his arms and strode about, his steps firm. "What can Moses do? Kill every dissenter?"

Encouraged by Rimon's confidence, Jesse said mockingly, "Father, you see death around every rock, always death."

"Yes, I see death!" Nathan shouted. "I've saved you from it often enough."

"Now, Nathan —" Rimon temporized.

Nathan pointed a sharp finger at Jesse. "I don't want you out of my sight until this dispute is over, do you hear? You're to sleep beside me tonight." Jesse turned away. Nathan followed after him, shouting. "Listen, there is plenty to do. The tent must be mended, a new pole made. And one of the she-goats is big and bloated. . . ."

Jesse stared at his father, eyes narrowed, but he did not reply. Darkness was his own best cover, and Nathan's nightly jug of wine would put him to sleep.

He found his uncle sitting beside a mound of stones, some marker probably set there by a passing nomad. Around Rimon half a dozen goats and as many sheep nuzzled at the sparse vegetation. They moved silently, intimidated by the power of the night.

"Your father bids you to stay, but still you go out," said Rimon without reproach.

"I am not a boy anymore, Uncle."

"So I see." Rimon sighed.

"Besides," Jesse told him, "one of the she-goats was giving birth. I heard her groaning and — it was a breech. I had to help."

222

"Ah, a difficult thing," said Rimon, nodding slowly. "But rewarding."

"At the time I didn't think so," said Jesse. "My whole arm went numb; I thought I'd break the kid's leg." He sat back, remembering the moment immediately after the birth, when the kid opened its mouth and stood on its own four legs, wet and bleating, looking up at Jesse with those enormous eyes, full of astonishment.

"So now this will be your charge," said Rimon. He smiled. "Did you name it?"

Jesse nodded, smiling at his own indulgence. "Of course. Not a very fancy name — I call him Yeled."

"Yeled. 'Little boy' — not bad. I was just thinking," Rimon said, "how few in number we are."

Jesse gazed out over the plain with its rows of tents, tribe by tribe assembled under their banners, thousands of men, women, and children. Yet Jesse understood his uncle's meaning.

"Three gone in our small family alone," Jesse murmured.

"Four," said Rimon, "counting Avi."

"Avi isn't dead," Jesse pointed out. Rimon didn't respond.

"Our families used to consist of ten, twelve sons, not to mention daughters," Rimon said. "My great-grandfather had sixteen children."

"We will have large families again," said Jesse. A sudden lump came into his throat. "In Canaan."

"I'm counting on that," Rimon said softly. "You and Talia —"

"Why is it only Talia and I who must build this family?" Jesse inquired, though without anger.

"Because the two of you are the best we have. Seth's children are too young. The other cousins, none of them count for much. You and Talia —"

"What are you going to do about tomorrow, Uncle?" Jesse asked him. "Are you going with Korach? Are you going against Moses?"

"I don't know." Slowly Rimon shook his head, and while he spoke he drew his fingers through his beard. "It is true that if each man decides to make the rules for himself, there is no rule at all. Power goes, then, to the strongest, usually the most cruel. The question is, did Adonai truly give all these laws to Moses? Or did Moses invent them?"

"We heard the voice of God," Jesse said softly.

Rimon said, "We should have remained to hear the entire covenant, but we were afraid, and I rue it."

"We were being ripped apart," Jesse objected.

"Now, I have to think," said Rimon. "Korach is right about one thing: we must use our own brains."

"What about faith?" Jesse asked, thinking of his mother.

"I must have faith in myself," said Rimon, still frowning deeply.

Jesse settled himself on a stone beside his uncle. A small goat came to snuff around him; Jesse gave it a slight kick, and the goat skittered away.

Rimon stretched out his legs. He groaned softly. "I have been sitting here since sundown. They say that Moses wandered in this same wilderness. But he came upon a bush that burned. A miraculous bush, and from it came the voice of Adonai, calling Moses to service."

Jesse nodded; everyone knew the story of the burning bush.

"Do you know what Moses did?" Rimon asked, nodding his head and stroking his beard. "Moses objected that he wasn't fit to lead; some say that he was humble. But I ask you — was it humility? Or was it lack of desire?"

"How can I know?" Jesse said. "I have never spoken with Moses face to face. I've never even stood near him. What do you think, Uncle? He has led us out of Egypt. He brought about wonders and miracles —"

"No. Adonai made the miracles. Moses only showed us," Rimon went on. "I have prayed every day of my life. When my children were taken from my wife's breast, I still thanked God for my blessings. When they harnessed me to a barge like an animal, to pull the stones along the banks of the Nile, I thanked God for my life and my limbs. When we came to the sea, did I hesitate? No. I leapt into that foam. And now I have tried with all my heart to follow His commandments and to teach them to my son. And does He know me? Does He answer me with even the merest whisper, the slightest puff of wind?"

Jesse sat motionless, accosted by the deep blackness all around him and the hard, bright stars high above. The darkness and the air oppressed him, for he had no words. None.

Rimon groaned again and clasped his hands upon his chest. "Every day I watch from the doorway of my tent, and I see Moses coming from his tent. I see how he walks. The ground seems to roll under his feet. I see his face, how it shines. And I say to myself, This Moses killed a man! He killed a man and ran away to escape punishment — and this is God's chosen?"

Jesse heard his uncle's agony as word after word tumbled out, unbidden, bursting.

"I watch Moses walk to the tent of meeting. He goes inside. Sometimes I see a cloud hovering there. And I stand and I try to listen. My whole body inclines to listen, to feel — oh, if once I could feel what Moses feels. Hear what he hears. But there is this terrible, hard silence. Whatever I say, however often I bless Him and call His name — I hear only silence."

Jesse stared out over the desert, marveling at how many shades of darkness the night possessed — the deep darkness of sky, the purple-black trees, the paler blackness of leaves, the shadows within shadows of the rocks, the dim paths, where the feet of humans and animals had scattered the stones and beaten away vegetation. All of it hung together in great sorrow and yearning, and Jesse could find no words for it.

At last he heard his uncle weeping. Quietly Jesse stole away.

Grimly and in silence the two hundred or so detractors stood behind Korach, Dathan, and Abiram. All night they had gone from camp to camp and tribe to tribe, to enlist people in their rebellion. They offered easy slogans.

"Each man his own priest."

"Each man answers his own heart."

"Moses is no better than any of us."

Jesse stood beside his father, fastened in his father's firm grip. Since early morning, Nathan had not left Jesse out of his sight, and now Jesse felt his father's fingers digging into the tender hollows at the back of his neck.

"Let me go!" he gasped harshly. "Leave me be."

Nathan's grip loosened, but not entirely. "You will stay with me," he muttered, his teeth clenched. "Fools," he spat. "Do they really think they can exist without a leader? In no time they'll kill each other — or starve to death for their constant bickering."

Rimon stood just beyond the rebels, like a man who straddles the balance line. And Jesse could see, by the furrows of his forehead and the clouded look in his eyes, that Rimon had spent a sleepless night, without reaching any conclusion.

"Let's go to him," Jesse urged his father. "Call him away."

A terrible premonition drummed in Jesse's chest, growing stronger with each beat of his heart.

"Rimon!" shouted Nathan, his cupped hand to his mouth. "Come to us. Beware, beware of —"

Even as he spoke, Korach, Dathan, and Abiram held out their fire pans, waiting for the Lord's flame to flash down upon them, to sanctify them.

"Believers of Adonai!" Moses called, and Jesse saw the veins throbbing in Moses' throat, and he saw the knotted muscles of Moses' arms as he stood, hands outspread and imploring the people, "Get thee far from these men and from their tents. Move away from these wicked men, lest ye be swept away in their sin!"

A rumbling rose softly at first, like the distant roll of thunder. Then, with a terrifying crash, the earth split apart. Huge boulders were hurled aloft. The ground cracked wide, wide, with flame bursting out. Black soot and smoke, red-hot fire consumed all but the stones. The flame scorched trees and shrubs, and as swiftly as it had ignited, so swiftly were screams of terror raised high, higher. Then suddenly all was still.

Gone were Korach, Dathan, Abiram, and all their followers. Jesse, trembling in terror and awe, believed the unbelievable, for he had seen it. The earth had opened her mouth and swallowed them up. And Rimon, standing on the edge, had been consumed along with the wicked.

The next day the congregation murmured against Moses and Aaron, saying, "Ye have killed the people of the Lord."

And the glory of the Lord appeared.

And the Lord spoke to Moses, saying, "Get you up from among this congregation, that I may consume them in a moment."

And Moses said unto Aaron, "Quickly . . . make atonement for them, for there is wrath gone out from the Lord; the plague is begun."

And Aaron made atonement for the people and stood between the dead and the living, and the plague was stayed.

CHAPTER 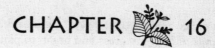 16

This time a sense of desolation came over Jesse. With Shosha's death he had felt guilt and sorrow. When his mother died, there had been a terrible sense of loss. Now Rimon was gone, and it left Jesse without a future.

"Rimon wanted us to marry," Talia told him. "He would have performed the ceremony. Now we must find someone else." She spoke breathlessly, for she was holding the lamb that Jesse was trying to shear. Woolly fibers clung to his mouth and nose, making him sneeze uncontrollably.

"Here, wipe your face," said Talia. She handed him a cloth. "I'll get you some water," she offered.

Jesse glanced up at Talia, then released the lamb, letting the mounds of wool fall around his feet. He brushed himself off and took the jug Talia held out to him, thinking how like a wife she already made herself, always present, serving him. Since Devorah's death, Talia and Shira had settled themselves close to Nathan and Jesse, camping beside them at night, moving out together in the morning.

"Who should do the ceremony?" Talia persisted.

"Do whatever you want," Jesse replied, wiping the sweat from his face.

"I thought maybe my second cousin Jonathan."

"That's fine."

"We can do it right after we get to Canaan."

"All right."

"We don't need a house right away," Talia said. She picked several strands of long dry grass and began to plait them together, making a band for her hair. "We can live in a tent."

"No!" Jesse leapt up. "I will not live in a tent one moment longer than I have to. We'll build a shed, a shack, anything."

"All right," Talia exclaimed. "You don't have to growl at me."

"Sorry."

"You are upset," Talia murmured. "I don't blame you. It is grief."

Jesse put his head in his hands, and he kept silent. Yes, he was bowed with grief, but his bad humor held more than that. There was this terrible boredom of wandering through the parched wilderness, with its constant rubble of stones underfoot, and the eternal dry wind that burned the eyes and stung the skin. It made one feel like a beast, with eyes only for the horizon, thoughts only for the night and its rest.

Occasionally a string of nomads happened by with their packs and their animals. They were braced against the desert wind, walking slowly, for their wandering was endless, and their destination forever changing. How could they stand it, Jesse wondered, never to know a home?

Now, having been so long without a roof, Jesse began to dream at night of houses and streets, of cisterns and olive groves, of being clean again and sleeping on a floor, in a room with walls.

The nomads were mostly Moabites, generally friendly and

230

curious. But other, hostile tribes also roamed the desert, and memories of Amalek still burned in Jesse, who, with his tribe of Benjamin, brought up the rear.

Seeing the nomads approach, Jesse's heart would beat madly, first with fear, then with expectation. If they were Moabites, he would wonder, and curse himself for it — is Jennat with them? Always, there was that plunging disappointment and then utter emptiness. Jennat had vanished, and it served him right. He had been cowardly. He should have brought her by the hand before his people — yes, before the priests — and declared his intention.

Again and again, while he tended the animals or plodded onward, and especially when he lay out under the stars on his mat, he relived every conversation he had had with Jennat. He relived the few kisses, the times of touching her hand, her cheek. He reinvented the words, making them more to his liking, with the consequence that she would now be here beside him. Then, even Rimon's death would not pain him so.

Every morning and every evening, Jesse joined the other men of his clan as they prayed to Adonai for the soul of Rimon, that he might be forgiven for his sins and accepted into the kingdom of heaven.

The fervor of Jesse's prayer, he knew, had little to do with love for Adonai, but everything to do with love for Rimon. Tears would stream down his face, and his hands would tremble as he remembered Uncle Rimon, how he had loved him, how he had treasured these last weeks beside him, almost as a son.

Nathan, seeing him one evening after prayer, held out a jug.

"Some wine," Nathan said abruptly, "may ease you."

"I don't want wine," said Jesse, his head down.

"Drink it!" Nathan held out the wineskin. All about them

231

people were tossing sand onto fires, hobbling their donkeys, bedding down.

With a sigh, Jesse took the wine flask and put it to his lips. The liquor was heavy, a brew concocted from dates and pomegranates, too sweet for Jesse's taste. But the drink seemed to soothe his blood, and a strange languor pulsed through him from his chest and head down to his fingertips.

"It's beastly hot tonight," Nathan muttered.

"The liquor makes one hot," replied Jesse.

"There is a spring beyond," said Nathan. "We could bathe."

Jesse was startled. It was not the sort of camaraderie he and Nathan had ever enjoyed. In fact, Jesse did not like the sight of his father's naked body, lean and bony, the back slightly crooked. Rimon, on the other hand, had been staunchly upright, his shoulders broad, his legs solid and thick.

"It will cool us," Nathan urged, his voice almost coaxing as he borrowed back the wine flask and took a long draft.

"All right," Jesse said.

Several other men were bathing at the spring. They nodded and muttered greetings and soon left, so that Nathan and Jesse, having dried themselves, sat quite alone, Jesse flat on the ground and his father above him on a large rock.

They sat without speaking, and Jesse tried to count the stars, imagining that each had a name, imagining that each was the soul of a dead person, knowing it was not so, but feeling strangely comforted by the notion that Shosha and his mother and now Rimon looked down upon him, giving him their light. He sat thus for a long time, hardly aware of his father's presence.

At last Jesse reached for the wineskin.

Nathan nodded in heavy slumber, holding the flask tight against his chest. A thin ribbon of spit ran down the corner of his mouth. It showed silvery in the moonlight.

Jesse pulled the flask from his father's hands. It was empty. Nathan's breath stank of decay. Nathan's voice suddenly cracked through the stillness. "You weep over that man as if he were your father."

Nathan's eyes, half open, gleamed malevolently, and Jesse moved away.

But Nathan's hand darted out, grasping Jesse by the sleeve.

"Did he ever save your life?" Nathan demanded. His tongue sounded thick, and he smacked his lips together with a sucking sound.

"You're drunk, Father," Jesse said.

"I'm drunk, Father," Nathan repeated, and he began to laugh, his hands and shoulders shaking. "I'm drunk."

"Let's go," said Jesse, rising.

"Saved your life," Nathan called out, his head rolling from side to side. He lifted the wineskin to his mouth, head back, sucking out the last drops, and then he flung it down. "Not once, but again and again and again. Oh, yes. You never knew. If you knew, you'd show a little respect for your father. Maybe even a little love. If I died, would you pray for me?" Again, he laughed, a coarse sound.

"Yes, I would pray, Father," Jesse said woodenly. He would pray to be forgiven for his hatred.

"Ah, but your thoughts!" Nathan cried, beaming and triumphant. "I can read your thoughts, you know, because I am a savior — yes! I saved you, and that makes you mine, as if you were my flesh. I know everything about you, Jesse."

Despite the heat of the night, Jesse shivered. He began to walk, but his arm was grasped from behind so violently that he fell back to the ground.

"Sit down!" Nathan stood over him, his face bent nearly to touching Jesse's face, the hiss of his words striking Jesse's flesh.

233

"Leave me be," Jesse cried, twisting away. "You're drunk and disgusting. I didn't even want to come out here with you. You make everything foul and —"

"I do? I make everything foul? Who do you think made you what you are? Who do you think got you that post with In-hop-tep? Did you think your Uncle Rimon did that for you?"

"I don't know — I never —" Jesse stammered, trying to back away, but his father crouched beside him now, one knee on the ground, his hands grasping Jesse's arms, pinning him down.

"It was me. Me! I got you that post, and it took every bit of cunning and a pile of silver to do it. Let me assure you, my fine son, that everything you ever got cost me a fortune. A fortune!"

Jesse's throat went dry, and he struggled against his father's weight, until finally Nathan let go. But Jesse remained beneath his father's shadow, Nathan's face still above his. "I — look, I'm sorry. I shouldn't have said that." He thought of Rimon's admonition: "Honor your father!" How was it possible to honor such a man?

Nathan persisted. "But you said it. 'Foul,' you said. When all I ever did was break my back for you, risk my neck for you."

"Thank you, thank you, Father." Jesse gritted his teeth.

"You should know the details — how I paid the official who spoke of you to the teacher, who planted the thought in the mind of that young Egyptian woman that she might have an assistant, a young slave to do the heavy work, the firing —"

"You arranged it?" Jesse gasped.

"I arranged it, to have you safe in a household. To teach you a skill. To make you rise above the common quarry slave, so you would never have to heave those stones . . . and then, you idiot, you stole the gold and you ended up in the quarry anyhow, and again I had to save you."

"What? You?" Jesse edged away, scraping himself backward along the ground, and still Nathan pursued him with face, body, and fist arched over him.

"Yes, me! Not Rimon, your precious uncle. What was your uncle doing while you were working in that quarry, half dead already from exhaustion? Skin and bones, you were. I've seen the look plenty of times — the throat gets tight and bony, and then the eyes, the eyes cloud over and sink back into the skull. I saw that look on you, and I took three beautiful gems, ah, you should have seen them! A topaz and two garnets ... and I arranged with the gang leader to throw the spike to wound you — "

"I might have been killed!" Jesse cried. "Did you also arrange with Jennat to call the physician?"

"No. That was good luck." Nathan was perspiring. "I had to risk it."

"I don't believe you," challenged Jesse. "Where would you have gotten gems?"

"From the Israelite mothers," Nathan spat. "From the fathers. Those who could afford it. The Egyptians had their quota of Israelite boys to kill. They drowned them in the Nile. Sometimes they took them and bricked them up in the walls. The babies made fine mortar, they said, their blood making the bricks a rosy color."

"Stop it!" Jesse shouted. "Stop it!"

"Oh, it's not so pleasant to hear the truth," Nathan hissed, and he grasped Jesse's ear and held it, tight, and with the other hand Jesse's robe, and he shouted into Jesse's face. "Not so pleasant as pretending that Rimon — handsome, smart, and pious Rimon — was your father! Well, look what happened to the holy Rimon. His precious Adonai killed him, so he must not have been so holy after all. And look who yet lives? Nathan! Nathan the savior, Nathan who saved you as a baby, bought your life from the Egyptians — "

"You bought my life," Jesse cried, "and traded another baby! You decided who would live and who would die!"

"Yes! Someone must decide, why not me? I saved you for Devorah — it was all she ever wanted, a boy. A baby boy, you. She promised me everything, anything if I would save you. She promised me her hand, her body . . . anything, even her love. But she betrayed me, didn't she? I never got her love. Or yours, either, because you were always arrogant, screaming when I tried to hold you, kicking me away from the very first — "

"What do you mean?" Jesse broke in, dazed. "She promised you her hand, her body . . ."

Nathan drew back. He sat down, his knees drawn up tight against his chest, arms clasped around them. And now Jesse pursued him. "How could she give you your hand after I was born — how could she? Weren't the two of you — wasn't she . . . ?"

"Devorah was — she had another husband. Before me."

Jesse heard his breath whistling out, like a distant wind. He glanced up, saw the stars flashing and streaking as if they were racing away across the sky. "My mother was married before?"

Now bits of conversation came back to Jesse, hints from the past, Devorah's threat when they were about to leave Egypt, "I'll tell Jesse everything!" and her dying words, "Nathan never told him."

"You," Jesse said, standing up tall, firm as a tree, rooted at last to the truth, "you are not my father."

"I am your father! By right, by purchase, by my life, I am your father."

"But she was — already pregnant with me, from the other man, my real father." Jesse's words were a shout of gladness.

"Oh, you are so smart. Yes, yes, you were already in her

236

belly when he died. Want to know how he was killed? Knifed by another Israelite — he was not so pure, not so precious, your real father. A cousin of mine, I knew him from childhood. He was a quarreler and a fighter, always bashing people over the head, quick-tempered and sullen. Your mother," Nathan sneered, "was not so good at choosing men. But I wanted her." Nathan's mouth was slack, and he breathed heavily, with a faint rustling in his lungs.

"She was lovely. Delicate and gentle. Wise. I wanted her from the moment I saw her with that fellow. Lucky for me, he was killed. I saw the fight. I saw his blood seeping into the ground. And I knew it was my luck, for she would need me if she wanted to keep that child growing in her womb. A widow-woman was the first to be assaulted by the guards, and they would surely take that child the moment it was born.

"I went to her," Nathan continued, and Jesse watched his every move, strained close, as if the words themselves were objects that he might catch and keep forever in his hands. "I told her I would marry her and take care of her, and that I would save her child. She wanted to know how. I showed her the gems and gold I had collected, not only from the Israelites, but from the Egyptians — "

"The Egyptians also paid you? Why? Why would they?"

"To tell them who had given birth and when. They were rewarded, don't you see, for filling their quota — "

"You sold Israelite babies, for gold?"

"For you! For Devorah! Someone had to have the courage to decide, to save lives."

"But who were you to decide? Who appointed you?"

"Oh! You think that every messenger has to be sanctified, chosen by Adonai!" And Nathan laid back his head, so that the moonlight fell on his face, and he called out mockingly, "Adonai, Adonai, thank You for appointing me!" Laughing,

237

Nathan swayed deeply to and fro, imitating piety, and he pounded his chest. "Here I am. Nathan, judge of who lives and who dies. I, Nathan, allowed Jesse to live."

"No." Jesse rose. Now it was he who stood over Nathan, hands clenched, looking down. "No. This is wrong. It makes no sense. You try to ensnare me, as always, with your lies. Why would you have to pay the Egyptians? We were slaves in Egypt. They could take whatever they wanted."

"What do you know about it?" Nathan's voice was low, but filled with derision. "Yes, we were slaves. But even Pharaoh had set a certain order. Even a tyrant must seem, before the people, to do justice. He gave reasons for killing our boy babies. He said we were spies and traitors and by sheer numbers we might overwhelm the Egyptian people. So it was understood that some boys would be killed — a certain number. Pharaoh's men even made it seem humane — they took only their quota. And didn't you hear the rumors? That we Israelites bred like spiders, so a few more or less babies didn't matter.

"As for the money, some of our people had family jewels, handed down. We had our flocks, brought to Egypt in the early days. Our flocks multiplied. Of course, the Egyptians took their quota of hides and milk, but they didn't eat our meat — you know that — they held the lamb as sacred. So we had something to trade with other tribes now and then. We were poor, but there was always something — a ring, a coin, a jewel."

"And these you hoarded for yourself, from the blood of babies."

"These I used," Nathan said, "for my work."

"Filthy work."

"It's a filthy world, my son."

"I'm not your son. I never was and never will be."

The Israelites journeyed and pitched their tents and came to the territory of the Amorites and the Moabites. The Amorite king would not let the Israelites pass through his land. He sent out his army against them. The Israelites smote him and took over his land.

Then Og, the king of Bashan, went out against the Israelites, and the Lord said to Moses, "Fear him not, for I have delivered him into thy hand, and all his people and his land."

When Balak, king of Moab, saw all that Israel had done to the Amorites, he was sore afraid and overcome with dread. He called up Balaam, his prophet and sorcerer, saying, "Curse for me these people, that I might smite them and drive them out of the land."

But Balaam would not curse the Israelites, saying, "I cannot do anything beyond the word of Adonai; I must curse whomever He curses and bless whomever He blesses."

CHAPTER 🌿 17

"Tell the story again, Jennat," begged the Moabite women. They had finished their day's work of gathering fuel, tending the goats, and preparing bread and yogurt for supper. Now they sat together outside the large tent, laughing and gossiping. Many had infants clinging to their breasts. Girl children sat on their mother's laps or slept on straw pallets by their sides; little boys went soon to their fathers, to learn manly arts from an early age.

The Moabite women glittered and shone. When they went to the men, their faces were veiled. But now, among themselves, their cheeks glowed from the application of rich oils. Their arms and necks shimmered with layers of gold chains and spangles.

Jennat settled herself among them and spread out her robe, feeling queenly. She had few jewels, but her stories made her the center of attention, at least for a while.

"Well, Osiris was once a living king of Egypt," Jennat began. "When he died, he became a god, and he married his sister, Isis." It was their favorite story, a tale of murder and revenge. The Moabite women never tired of it. They rubbed their hands together when Jennat got to the bloody parts.

Jennat continued. "The other brother, Seth, was terribly jealous of Osiris and decided to murder him. Seth tricked Osiris into stepping inside a golden coffin. When Osiris's feet were planted within — whoop! Seth slammed the lid shut, and Osiris was smothered. Dead."

"Ah," exclaimed the women, slapping their thighs in appreciation. "Don't forget the part where Seth rips the body into fourteen pieces!" one coached.

"I'll get to it," Jennat said with a sigh and a twist of her lip. She glanced at Shepset, who sat opposite her. Shepset was big with child. Her movements were graceless now, and she groaned and heaved from side to side when she walked.

Several Moabite women crowded close to Shepset. They gave her goat's milk to drink and sweets to eat. They had welcomed the two young women, eager for new faces, and especially for new stories. And the men, of course, immediately adored Shepset's grace and her dancing. It had driven Avi to distraction, until now he was in despair.

Jennat had heard them fighting about the child.

"How can you think such a thing, Shepset?" Avi implored. "To give it away to the priests — it's my child, too!"

Shepset had tossed her head, laughing. "What makes you think so, Avi? What makes you think you are the only man in my life — or in my tent?"

"You might as well murder the child at the outset!" cried Avi. Furious, he threatened to leave Shepset, to go back to Egypt. For the past weeks he had remained secluded, and when Jennat called to him, he would not respond. She did not want Avi to leave. He was her only link to a future that, however dim, promised something better.

When she went to Shepset, there was only more anger, for Shepset refused to explain anything, repeating, "It's nobody's business what I do with my child."

"But a baby needs its mother," Jennat argued. "Shepset, maybe when the child arrives, you'll change your mind. You'll want to hold it and keep it."

"Leave me alone, Jennat. I won't change my mind. I've always planned that if it should happen, the child will be given to priests, trained for temple service." Shepset smiled slyly. "What better way for me to win the favor of the gods than to give them my firstborn?"

"Shepset," Jennat begged, "let me help you take care of the baby — you'll grow to love it, I know."

Shepset gave her a hard look. "Don't think I am one of your slobbering Israelite mothers," she said.

Now Jennat finished the story of Osiris and his son Horus, of family treachery, murder among the gods, eyes torn out, bellies ripped open. Fine examples, Jennat thought grimly, but the women sat forward, mouths wide open in attention, taking in Jennat's words.

"Horus wanted to avenge his father's death, and he did battle with his uncle Seth. His mother, Isis, refused to help Horus. So Horus took a sharp blade and — "

"Cut off her head!" the Moabite women shrieked in unison.

"Yes," said Jennat. "While she slept."

A heavy, almost sick feeling came over Jennat. She wished she had not told the story. She thought of the tales Jesse had told her, of his ancestors, Abraham, Isaac, Jacob, and Joseph, tales of courage and faith, in which goodness was rewarded.

By contrast, the stories of these gods were horrible, degrading. How could they serve as examples for people to follow? They only excited the women and stimulated them to treacheries of their own.

The Moabite women whispered together behind their hands, their eyes flashing. Laughter pealed forth. Several young girls moved near. "What are you whispering about? Tell us! We're all sisters here, with no secrets."

"Everyone has secrets," the others laughed, pushing the young ones away.

"We'll tell you our secret if you tell yours."

"What's your secret?"

The secrets always had to do with men, with petty thefts, deception, humiliations.

Shepset, in their midst, rocked with laughter, and Jennat heard her say, "But you must bring only the most beautiful women — I know these Israelite men. They are not so easy to persuade, especially if they have been at prayer."

"We'll show them something better," exclaimed one of the women. "What man in his right senses would choose prayer over possessing a woman? Surely the Israelites are human, too."

Jennat strained to listen. The Israelites, it was rumored, were camped nearby, almost at the border of the Jordan, within sight of their destination, Canaan. The word sent a shiver across Jennat's back, as she remembered how Jesse had looked when he said the word *Canaan*.

Jennat felt as if she been swept away by some terrible wind, blown here into the Moabite camp without warning and without wishing it. She was still a stranger among them, and the things they applauded and desired were also strange. All their attention lay on the accumulation of jewels and betraying their husbands, finding lovers, escaping from toil. She recalled, with a pang, how the Israelites had toiled for their tabernacle. She remembered the awe in their faces when their God spoke; she remembered their ardent resolve when they cried out to heaven, "All You have commanded we have heard

243

and we will do!" They had promised their God faithful service and obedience, even before they knew exactly that would be expected of them. Faith and love had moved them to make this covenant. The Moabites knew no such thing, for they fashioned little gods that they kept in their pockets — just as Jennat had once done herself.

Now she shuddered, partly in shame. She had lost her idol of Hathor on the way in the desert. Better, she thought, if she had tossed it away on purpose.

The Moabite women seemed tense tonight; their laughter had a hard edge to it. Jennat drew in their words, suddenly alert.

"So, we will tempt them — they will utterly succumb."

Jennat shifted uneasily. "You plan to go to the Israelites? To the men?" she asked. "What about your husbands and fathers? Will they let you go?"

The women looked at each other mockingly.

Cozbi stood up, shaking her head, making her long earrings dance. She was of noble lineage and bright, their undisputed leader. "It's our husbands and fathers who are sending us," she said loudly, "and for a good cause."

"What cause?" Jennat asked.

Cozbi whispered to several others — Marit, her cousin, Zela and Zippora, her friends.

"Don't tell her," said Marit. "She would not understand."

"She understands," said Zippora. "Jennat ran away from the Israelites — don't you remember? Because of the treachery of a man."

The women consulted once again, talking swiftly, glancing out at her. "She is not one of us," Jennat heard whispered.

"She is only a guest — we tell her nothing."

"Perhaps I can help you," Jennat said, "knowing their ways

as I do." Her heart pounded, and she forced herself to breathe deeply to keep her voice calm.

"It is to defeat the Israelites," said Cozbi, nodding toward her companions. "They are overrunning the land. They are warlike and evil — they will settle here and soon take over everything."

"But tell her the plan," Zippora said breathlessly.

"We will invite them to a festival," said Cozbi, "give them fine food and drink. We will bring up our gods and we will dance. We will make them bow to our gods and do all the things they say they abhor." Cozbi tossed back her hair, smiling. "Pleasure," she murmured. "They call it sin."

"The Midianite women are joining us," added Marit.

Cozbi laughed and stretched her arms with self-satisfied languor. "Balaam, the prophet, suggested this brilliant plan. There is no other way to overcome this horde. Balaam was supposed to curse them, but he refused. He would not go against Adonai."

"A Midianite priest knows the Israelite God?" Jennat asked. "How can this be?"

Cozbi shrugged. "Why not? There are many gods in the world. We all know that. So now we will not rely on prophets or on gods, but we will be the instruments for Israel's defeat. We, the women."

The women clasped each other's arms, smiled into each other's faces.

Jennat's hands trembled. "But how will your plan defeat the Israelites?" she managed to ask.

Cozbi shook her head impatiently. "Look," she said, straining toward Jennat, speaking distinctly, as to a child. "If we can make them sin, then their own God will annihilate them. It has happened before, when they made a golden calf.

Thousands were killed. This time their God will be even more furious, because he gave them a second chance. So" — she brought her finger swiftly across her throat, and Jennat could almost imagine blood gushing out.

Without his uncle Rimon, there was nothing to hope for. There was no reason to stay.

Jesse waited until the wine took hold and Nathan was blubbering in his sleep.

During the day Jesse had put aside several necessities; goat-skins for warmth, several flasks for water, an earthenware jar filled with legumes that they had gotten from a wandering merchant in trade for Devorah's sandals.

Jesse had resented the trade most bitterly. To see Nathan toss his mother's shoes onto the trader's cart with such gross carelessness had made Jesse's blood boil.

In the past two days, since Nathan's revelation, Jesse had re-called a thousand insults, old grievances that he had repressed, thinking he had to forgive them because it was his *father*.

All that was over now, and with each memory Jesse felt the sting again. And it wasn't only Nathan's deceptions that ate at him like a gnawing worm; it was everything that had hap-pened since the escape from Egypt — the heat, the hunger, the screeching wind, the assaults and rebellions, and most of all, Rimon's death.

Jesse could not forgive Moses. Moses had brought a hor-rible death down upon Uncle Rimon.

"I cannot stay with such a man," Jesse said aloud; he was half startled by the sound of his own voice, and he realized that he meant both Nathan and Moses.

As night settled down over their encampment, Jesse stole away, a pack on his back. He had decided not to take the donkey, to do nothing for which Nathan could curse him, but he would take his due.

He did not relish the thought of having to worry about animals, but a person alone in the desert might quickly starve to death. With a few goats and sheep, he could at least sustain himself until he reached a town. Then he would barter the animals for something else.

He would have to keep watch over his small flock. At night one heard the preying jackals, hyenas, and wildcats — their gleeful cries of meat-lust and finally the long howls of full-bellied satisfaction.

Now Jesse stood among the small herd — about a dozen goats and twice as many sheep. He selected seven — three sheep and four goats, including the nursing mother with the kid he had delivered. For some reason, this kid appealed to him, making him laugh with its antics, its stubborn will. Besides, the nanny would provide Jesse with milk to make *laban*, the soft, curdled yogurt that he enjoyed. Will there be manna along the way? he wondered. Will there be quail?

The process of planning his departure had all but erased the realities of leaving from Jesse's mind. But now, as he stood in the moonlight with the animals he had separated out, Jesse looked back.

How peaceful, how quiet, was the encampment. Moses had taught them most recently of harmony, of every man respecting his neighbor. And he had told them the true story of a pagan sorcerer named Balaam, who, when asked to curse the Israelites, would not. He stood, instead, upon a mountaintop and raised his voice in praise, saying, "How goodly are your tents, O Jacob, your dwelling places, O Israel."

Now those words reverberated in Jesse's mind, and he almost laid down his staff and led the animals back to their enclosure.

But the goats had skipped forth, and the lambs followed, their dumb faces set, their stiff legs taking them awkwardly into the unknown.

Yes, the tents were beautiful and the wilderness all about most peaceful — when Israel slept. When she awakened, this nation was a hub of dissension and bickering, of petty cruelties, force applied against neighbor, against brother, against son. He had to leave. He was right to go.

The night was miraculously mild, the breeze slightly warm, spreading its secret fragrances aloft. Alone, Jesse felt as if he were entering a separate universe. His path was lit by the moon, and silence lay in layers over the earth, with now and again a small fissure of sound breaking through — the chirp of a bird, the clatter of a burrowing animal jumping out from its burrow and confronting the world in surprise.

Never in his life had Jesse felt so entirely alone, like Adam, the first man in creation.

Out now on the empty plain, Jesse walked and walked. He turned toward the immense granite mountains that tossed down layer upon layer of stony residue, and he suddenly felt lifted. It took courage to set out alone!

The animals followed. He brought them to a small wadi filled with tough grasses, and they immediately foraged and grunted out their little bleats of gratitude. And Jesse sat down, leaning on his staff, and from force of habit he counted, scratching the marks on his staff with his thumbnail — four goats, three sheep, and the nursing kid, and soon Jesse, despite his best intentions, fell asleep.

He dreamed of Talia. She screamed at him, "Coward! You're always running away to hide, just like your father, only worse. Coward. Coward."

Talia wore a bridal veil; it covered her face and entire body. Someone intoned the sacred words, and they were married.

Jesse moved near to her and lifted the veil, and as he did so, the bride's head fell to one side, and he saw that it was a bony skull.

He bolted awake, hearing his own muted cry and the sharp bleating of a lamb. The goats, too, added their discontented murmurings. Jesse saw the sun peering out over the horizon.

Well, he told himself, stretching and taking a drink of water, it was only a dream. Talia would be better off without him. He did not love her the way she wanted to be loved. She would be angry and hurt at his disappearance, but all in all, it would be better for her, too.

Jesse stood, squinting at the sun, and he headed north, where, the scouts rumored, there lay several cities, numerous kingdoms. He would settle in one of them, follow the dictates of the local king — why not? None could be more demanding than Adonai.

He recalled the awful dream, and he shuddered.

The question that kept singing like a dirge through his thoughts every day came suddenly again: Why did Rimon have to die? Moses had said to them, many times, "Adonai is just and merciful. He is full of compassion." Then why had the earth opened its mouth and swallowed up Rimon? Why would a man like Rimon have to die, while Nathan, the seller of flesh, still lived?

A terrible heaviness clutched at Jesse's heart, as sorrow followed sorrow. Why had Devorah died? And Shosha? Why had Jennat left him? Jennat. The name was like a twisting claw in his breast. Jennat. He did not want to think her name, but still he said it aloud and let its sound swell around him.

"Jennat!" he shouted out to the empty desert. "Jennat!" The lambs turned to gaze at him in dumb surprise. Chagrined, Jesse looked about and counted the animals. The mother and kid were missing.

With a groan and a sigh, Jesse walked, then ran, in ever-widening circles. At last, on the verge of panic, Jesse saw the two, hunched together in the sparse shade of an overhanging ledge.

Jesse prodded the ribs of the mother goat. It brought both animals struggling to their feet, and with piercing objections the goats leapt out.

"Come, or I'll leave you here," Jesse shouted at the animals, clutching his staff high in his fist. "Stay with me. Don't stray, I tell you, if you want to live."

The kid stared up at him, then trotted nimbly over and butted its small head gently against Jesse's hand.

In spite of himself Jesse laughed and fingered the bony head, the soft shafts of the ears.

"All right. Come on, Yeled. I wish I had a bell for your neck, Little Boy. Well, we'll rest now and walk late afternoon and evening."

Jesse flung his robe over a small branch, creating shade, and to his amusement the little goat crouched in beside him, lying at Jesse's feet. The mother, glad for respite from her charge, wandered some distance away and stood chewing at a bush, flicking away insects with hardly a glance at her kid.

And Jesse sat out the heat of the day, wishing for a flute or some instrument with which to pass the time, wishing for some companion to talk to, and again the awful questions rang through his thoughts: Why did they have to die? Why is everything so hard, and suffering so common? At last he was exhausted and once again fell asleep.

He awakened this time to a sky gone cold and gray. The wind whipped around his body and assaulted his face. Walk, his mind told him. Rest, his body commanded. Walk while it is yet light, he decided.

Jesse gathered himself up, whistled sharply to his small

flock, and forced himself to trudge again, planting his staff down step by step, braced against the howling wind.

He walked until his legs trembled and his fingertips felt numb with cold. Then, as the icy blue light slipped away at the edge of the horizon, Jesse hastily contrived a small tent from the several goatskins he had brought, teeth chattering and hands shaking as he worked, and he huddled inside his shelter.

He realized he had not eaten all day, but he was too tired to bake flat bread, and the wind was too strong to build a fire, and his bones ached, as if with fever. He lay down in a ball, covering himself closely, and he murmured, "Let me die, then. Take me as You took my mother," and again he slept.

Dreams held Jesse locked in darkness, as in a coffin, and he dreamed of holding down the lid against the night marauders, baying wolves, and screeching wildcats coming to kill him, to tear his limbs and eat his flesh while he still lived.

The sounds pushed him deeper and deeper into the wells of sleep, and jolted him, finally, to stark wakefulness. He burst forth from his makeshift shelter to confront the bony, hairy face of the nanny goat, her udders shaking with the force of her bleating.

If a goat could speak, Jesse thought, his heart throbbing in alarm, this one would take credit for a warning cry. He ran out, already knowing deep down that disaster had struck, but still making himself imagine otherwise.

Then he saw the bodies, widely scattered — one neck cavity a bloody gash, limbs torn off, some half eaten, a head pulled asunder, a belly slit open, organs ripped loose, mostly gone, tails and hooves lying loose, abandoned.

Blindly, as if he were seeking a human adversary, Jesse ran back and forth, clutching his knife, screaming, "Murderers! Killers! Damnable killers!"

Back at the site, he stared at the carnage, then heaved, but his dry stomach contained nothing for vomit, and he felt the cramps of his empty agony and stood counting. Three carcasses, one lamb and two goats. Two lambs and the kid were missing. The kid!

The kid might yet be alive.

Jesse ran from rock to rock, to this fissure, that wadi, to a tiny oasis of three stunted trees, and the mother goat staggered behind him, sometimes leaping as if in play, her blank face suggesting no knowledge of the catastrophe, no awareness of right or wrong. Yet surely, Jesse thought, surely she had known of her kid's disappearance, and by some grain of intelligence or instinct, had summoned him awake.

He began to shout, "Yeled! Yeled!" His cries echoed from the hills and rocks and returned to him, "Yeled! Yellll-ed!"

It was an absurd, useless effort to call a goat by name, yet he could not stop himself, as if he were looking for a child.

The sun rose high; the bright day stretched before Jesse, endless and futile.

On and on he staggered, searching for the kid, with the nanny goat tottering behind him, both Jesse and the goat stumbling in exhaustion.

At the bottom of a ledge, nearly concealed from view by a sticklike tree growing straight out of a crack in the rock face, lay the kid. Its mouth was open, tongue hanging out. A thin ribbon of bloody saliva flowed from its mouth.

"Yeled!" Jesse screamed. "Yeled!"

He assessed the slope, the depth and width of the ledge. The mother goat looked down, head hanging over, and pawed at the rock.

Slowly Jesse lowered himself down the escarpment. His foot slid. He grasped the jagged rock above him, felt the gash on his shoulder. He stretched out his legs so that his body swung down at full length, and then he dropped to all fours, landing beside the kid, bruising his cheek against the side of the rock.

He felt the pain of it, and now he heard the dull breathing of the kid. "Yeled," he whispered, reaching out to touch the goat's head.

The kid blinked. Now Jesse saw that both its hind legs were broken. One dangled down over the ledge; the other lay oddly contorted, the bone piercing through the hide.

"Oh, Yeled," Jesse whispered, his throat constricted, "what have you done? Why didn't you stay with your nanny? I should have watched you, kept you — why did you stray? What can I do with you?"

Carry it up, bind its leg, express milk from the teat of the mother goat, for the kid could not stand up to nurse — keep it alive — yes, yes. He would do it.

Jesse gently put his hand under the kid's shoulder.

The animal cried out in pain. The sound cut through Jesse's own body.

He could place the kid in a sling fashioned from his robe, heave it upon his back, lift it up over the ledge, and then he would tend it, carry it — yes, he would heal it.

Even as he planned the rescue, Jesse reached into his waistband and brought out his knife, flicking the sharp point against his thumb from long habit, making sure that the blade was adequate for the task.

Tears blurred Jesse's eyes, so that everything before him seemed to run red, a river of blood, the spurt of it mingling with the kid's scream, the last gurgle of breath rushing out to meet Jesse's own cries.

Jesse raised his head and looked up from the canyon to the precipice where the nanny goat stood, into the bright sunlight and far beyond. He closed his eyes against the glare as he shouted out, "Forgive me. I had to do it, don't you see? I didn't want to kill it. I had to." The nanny goat would not understand his reasons, could not, because she was a mere beast.

As Jesse sat crouched on the ledge, bent over the body of the kid, many visions and voices pressed in upon him. He remembered the words of Moses, "God's ways are not our ways — we cannot understand. We can only praise Him." Death comes, and with it grief. Somehow it is arranged that man must bear these burdens. But with all this, there is a constant source of love.

His mother's last words, "Love him. Love him!" he now understood. Love Nathan. Love Adonai, both of them, man and God. To love one, you must also love the other.

And Jesse understood the greatness of Moses, for Moses had killed a man and had moved from arrogance to complete humility. With humility he had grown to love his people, all of them, those who strayed and those who were steadfast. And Jesse wept at his own ignorance and doubts. If he could love a goat, something he had not created, how much more, then, must Adonai care for him?

"Adonai, Adonai, forgive me!" Jesse called. "I didn't know. . . ." There was so much he still didn't know. He had to return to his own people to learn the rest.

Flies came buzzing around the carcass. The kid's blood began to dry to a thick rusty color. Birds of prey circled overhead and cried out for their booty. The sun baked down upon Jesse, bringing a terrible weakness to his limbs, a throbbing into his ears, so that at first the sound was deceiving. . . .

"Jesse! Jesse! Jesse!"

The sound of his name. How was it possible?

Two voices mingled together, how did they know his name?

"Jesse! Jesse!"

He looked up.

A face looked down upon him — red, round, worried, strained.

He almost laughed. It was a vision, one of those last visions before death, an illusion caused by hunger and heat and grief.

"Jesse! Wait, I'll get you up — we heard you shouting, 'Yeled!' Who is Yeled? No matter — we found you, thank heaven."

"Avi? Avi? Is it really you?"

"Of course, you idiot," came the happy cry. "Who else would find you in this forsaken wilderness at the bottom of a ravine? Who else but another idiot worse than you?"

The reunion of the two cousins was almost more than Jennat could bear. She stood apart, trying to rule her emotions. The two cousins embraced, shouted, spoke, and interrupted each other, and in few words the entire past was brought up to the moment. Jesse heard about Shepset and the child, and Avi learned that his father had died, and how.

In amazement and grief, Avi repeated, "My father — undecided? In doubt? He always seemed so sure of himself. I used to think he knew everything."

"He wanted greatness," Jesse said. "He wanted to be like Moses. For me, it was enough that he was Rimon, my uncle. I loved him, Avi. I think he was a great man."

"But he was always for obedience," Avi said, his fists pressed into his cheeks. "And in the end he himself did not obey Adonai's chosen leader."

Jesse shrugged. "He was in doubt. My father, on the other hand, is always certain. Oh, he knows there is no God at all, only human treachery and deceit, buying bodies, alive or dead. Which is better?" he asked bitterly. "To wonder about God, or to deny him completely?"

"Jesse — did Nathan tell you that he — "

"Yes. He told me. He is not my real father. But it is also true that he did save me, more than once. I owe him something for that."

Jennat glanced between the two of them. She was afraid to speak; they were relatives, and she was an outsider.

"Then what brought you out into this wilderness?" Avi asked.

"I ran away," Jesse said. "I thought I could be free. Separate. I should have remembered what your father once said, that we are bound by the yoke of heaven. If we want to be truly human, that is."

Jennat stepped near. She looked at Jesse, and her heart pounded. His clothes were caked with blood from the goat; his hair was matted and his face bruised. She had seen his weakness when he had stood. But something else showed through, a look in his eyes, like a beacon.

"I have brought some meat and bread," she murmured.

"Thank you," Jesse said, and she felt his eyes upon her.

Jennat gave him the food and a flask of water. She watched him eat and drink. It filled her with yearning, as if he were a child and she the mother. Then he looked up at her and said, "I never thought I would see you again, Jennat. In the night — I was sick. I prayed to Adonai that I would see you again."

"So did I," she said.

"I thought you were dead, Avi," Jesse said. "How is it possible that we found each other?"

"Jennat and I are on the way to — "

"To warn the people," Jennat broke in.

"We left the Moabites undecided, I thought," Avi said,

with a look at Jennat. "There is always the possibility that we can return to Egypt."

Jennat stood firmly and said, "I am not returning to Egypt. Never."

"To Egypt, Cousin?" Jesse smiled. "We can't go back there."

"You can smile about it?" Jennat could not take her eyes off Jesse, the traces of a beard on his cheeks, and those eyes, darkly bright, as if he knew something now that he had never known before.

"I smile," Jesse said, "because I know Avi doesn't mean it." He reached for his cousin's arm. "He is like me. We are bound to our people, because we love them, the worst along with the best."

Avi stood up, his face flushed. "What makes you think I feel the way you do?"

"Because you are here, and not with Shepset."

"We heard you yelling, we were only on the way — "

"To warn the Israelites of the Moabite plot," Jennat put in. And now she told Jesse all that she knew about Cozbi and the other women, that they had in fact already left their various encampments to converge upon the unsuspecting Israelites, hoping to cause their doom.

"After you warn the people," Jesse asked, his eyes now fully upon her, "what will you do, Jennat? Will you go away again, looking for a caravan?"

Jennat met his gaze. "I will stay with your people," she said, "and hope someday to settle among them in Canaan."

"In Canaan?" He sang out the word.

"I want to tell you," she said, "that I have gotten rid of Hathor. I lost her, but if I hadn't, I would toss her away now."

"Why is that?" asked Jesse.

"It is only a thing of wood, without power. Oh, people

make stories about those gods, but they are no different from men, no better. How can we worship such things? Your God," she said softly, "asks that you live well and do justice."

"Justice." Jesse sighed. "That is the trouble. I don't know how to do justice."

"Maybe no man does," said Jennat. "But at least your God commands you to try."

"You two stand there talking," said Avi, "while we have a task to do." He swung his arms, ready for action.

"Right," said Jesse, and he whistled loudly for the nanny goat and the two remaining sheep, and he took Jennat's hand in his.

She was about to ask him about Talia, the betrothal, and what he now intended to do. But for the moment, it was enough just to be walking with Jesse hand in hand.

And Moses went up to Mount Nebo . . . and the Lord showed him all the land . . . and said unto him, "This is the land which I swore unto Abraham, Isaac, and Jacob, saying, 'I will give it to thy seed; I have caused thee to see it with thine eyes, but thou shalt not go over thither.' "

So Moses the servant of the Lord died there in the land of Moab . . . and he was buried in the valley of the land of Moab . . . and no man knows of his grave to this day. And Moses was a hundred twenty years old when he died; his eye was not dim, nor his natural force abated.

The children of Israel wept for Moses in the plains of Moab for thirty days. And since then there has not arisen a prophet in Israel who was like Moses, whom the Lord knew face to face.

CHAPTER 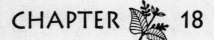 18

Jesse stretched out his legs and rolled his shoulders, stiff from sitting so long in one position, and tired from telling this long tale. The two boys, however, had not moved from the spot. They had watched him intently the entire time.

Now Jesse smiled and handed them each a round cake filled with sour goat cheese. The boys ate eagerly, and they plied him with questions.

"But what happened after that, Father?" they asked. "Why didn't you all cross the Jordan? You said there were spies. What about the spies, Father?"

"One at a time," said Jesse, smiling indulgently. These two were his youngest sons; five others were already grown, and his two daughters were married.

Jesse had brought the boys out to the edge of the encampment today for this very purpose, that they might learn the full story of their heritage, before the fateful moment of crossing into Canaan. They must never forget that their people had once been enslaved in Egypt, and that they were saved. Because only those who remember their slavery will appreciate their freedom.

Now it was time for the boys to hear everything. Well, almost everything, thought Jesse, smiling to himself. He had skipped over a few things about himself and their mother.

"Eat and then we'll go," said Jesse, passing around the water flask and taking a long drink himself. "Of course, you know the story, that by the time we got back to camp, the Moabite women were already there, and the Israelites, many of them, had fallen under their spell. Well, Pincas the priest rushed out and killed the sinners — many, many of them. Even the princess Cozbi was put to the sword. You see," Jesse emphasized, "we must keep God's word in our hearts always, and resist temptations."

The boys chewed their cakes thoughtfully. Ten-year-old Aaron nodded in agreement, but Elias, at fifteen, seemed skeptical.

"Why, then," Elias asked boldly, "does Adonai place temptation in our way?"

"Ah, that's another story, my son," said Jesse. He thought of his own youth, his own questions.

"Tell about the spies," called out Aaron. "How they saw giants in the land, and how Adonai said we must all remain in the desert until the old ones had died, the ones who were doubters. That's why all the grandfathers are dead, isn't it, Father?"

"Yes," said Jesse, sighing. "We were camped at this very spot thirty-eight years ago. We were ready to cross over the Jordan to claim the land that God had promised us. Moses sent scouts to spy out the land and tell us of its inhabitants and its vegetation. The scouts were gone for forty days. When they returned, they brought back enormous bunches of grapes." Jesse gestured with his hands, showing the size of them. "They said it was a goodly land, and fertile, but that

261

the inhabitants were fierce giants, who would destroy us in a single blow."

"Was it true, Father?" Aaron asked excitedly. "Were they really giants?"

"Of course not, you dumb donkey," said Elias, giving his brother a punch. "They were just men, warriors, and the spies were scared."

"They did not trust in Adonai," said Jesse, nodding. "They were afraid and fainthearted. The new land, the promised land, was not for such as they. Men must show the courage and the will to claim what is given them — or they will lose it. So" — Jesse stood up and retied the sash at his waist — "Adonai decreed that we must remain here in the wilderness for forty years, one year for each day that the scouts were spying out the land, doubting God's intentions. It happened two years after we escaped from Egypt. So, thirty-eight more years would pass. All the old ones would die, and the young, those with spirit, would claim the promised land."

"You are not young anymore, Father," Aaron pointed out.

Jesse laughed. "True," he said. "But you are, and it is you who will build the land for your people. That is why I brought you here to tell you the story. Now, let's go back to camp. We've been out more than half the day, and your mother will be wondering what became of us."

A small patch of dust stirred at a distance, seeming to blow toward them like a tumbleweed. "It's Mama!" cried Aaron, running toward her. "Mama! Father told us the story, the whole story of how you all followed Moses and crossed the sea — "

"He told you the whole story?" Their mother smiled, looking doubtful. "Sometimes he leaves out parts of it," she said.

"What parts?" asked Elias, catching up. He took his

mother's arm, and she touched his hair for a moment, hair that curled and shone, like his father's.

"Well, I will tell you," she said, settling herself down on a rock. She motioned for the boys to come near, but Jesse stood at a distance, watching, thinking how beautiful she still was. The gray strands in her hair seemed to accentuate her large, beautiful eyes. She still painted them with kohl; that was one of the old habits Jennat would never give up — and he was glad of it.

"Well, when we got to the Israelite camp," Jennat said, speaking swiftly, excitedly, "there was a great crowd at the tents, and ferocious noise, singing and dancing, clapping and wild music — wicked music, my sons," she said, looking stern. "The women of Moab and Midian had come to tempt the men, and they were dressed in their style, immodestly, without — "

Jesse cleared his throat and shot a glance skyward.

Jennat bit her lip, then continued. "They had brought their idols, and they urged the Israelites to bow to them and pray to them and bring sacrifice. Into this we came, and Avi — your uncle Avi — and your father shouted that it was a trap, that they must send these wicked women away, put out their ceremonial fires and . . . and then someone caught me, held me by the throat, and the next thing I knew there was a sword at my belly, the tip nearly piercing through."

"Ah, Mama!" Aaron gasped, and Elias sat wide-eyed and red-cheeked, listening.

"Well, they dragged me away, thinking I was one of the temptresses, one of those women — " She glanced at Jesse.

"They put her in a holding tent, her hands tied with ropes." Jesse shuddered, remembering. "I screamed, and I went to everyone, begging them — I even went to your aunt Talia."

"Talia?" The boys looked at each other, astonished.

"Well, your aunt Talia and your father were once betrothed," said Jennat with a wave of her hand. "Your father went to her and begged her to help, to intercede with the elders, for one of her cousins was a priest, a man of some power — "

"And did she help?" asked Elias.

"Not at first," said Jennat. "At first she resisted. . . ."

"But then she saw," Jesse added, "that your mother and I were — "

"In love," said Jennat. "Talia saw that we would never change. So she brought your father to the priests, those who were to be the judges at the trial."

"You had a trial, Mother?" Elias exclaimed. "How exciting. I never knew anyone who had a trial."

Jennat laughed, then pulled her lips together, looking stern. "Better not to know such things," she said. "But your father — that was the thing that you must know, how your father seized the moment, when they proclaimed the charges against me — that I was a spy, a wicked woman come to bring death to the people — your father rushed up — "

"They tried to restrain me," said Jesse, remembering. "My father and his friends tried to hold me back."

"Nobody could hold you back," said Jennat, gazing at him. "You were like a wild bull, like a lion. You charged up to the judges, and you stood there, and I tell you, boys, I have never heard anyone speak in such a voice or with such power. 'If you find her guilty,' he shouted to them, 'then you must kill me, too, because we came here together. If she is a stranger, so am I!' And your father, a boy of seventeen, stood there with his hands uplifted, and he challenged them, 'Don't you remember the words of the Torah?' "

"Father said that to the judges?" Aaron cried. "To the judges?"

Jennat nodded. "Yes. He told them the words, those words that we have taught you and the other children: 'Justice and compassion you shall show to the stranger, for ye were strangers in Egypt.'"

The boys ran to Jesse, hugged his arms. "Is it true, Father? Really?"

Jesse coughed, then wiped his face with a cloth, his eyes peering out at Jennat. "Your mother does not lie," he said.

"The best part," said Jennat, "you haven't yet heard."

"What? What?" clamored the boys.

"Moses came just then to the judging tent, and he heard every word that Jesse had said."

Jesse nodded, his eyes misting with the memory. "Ah, yes. Moses had been listening to all of it, and he — "

"What did he do?" Elias whispered. "What did he say?"

"He came over to me," Jesse said, his voice grown soft now and husky, "and he laid his hand on my shoulder, and he said — he said" — Jesse took a deep breath, and he half closed his eyes as if to see it all again — "Moses said to me, 'Well done, lad. You have truly heard the voice of the Lord.'"

"And so, you were married," summed up Elias.

"Married, and the parents of many fine sons and daughters," said Jennat with a smile, putting an arm around the shoulder of each boy. They began walking back to the camp.

"Wasn't Talia angry with you, Father?" asked Elias.

"Your aunt Talia is a wonderful woman," said Jesse with a grin. "A forgiving woman."

"Besides," said Jennat, "she married her second cousin, and he is a Levite. It was much better for such a wonderful, pious, and forgiving woman to marry a priest, don't you think?"

The boys skipped ahead, and Jesse and Jennat walked slowly now, their steps in rhythm, arms linked around each other's waists.

"Well, tomorrow we cross the Jordan," Jesse said.

"If only Moses could have come with us," Jennat murmured.

"Joshua will lead," Jesse said. "We needn't fear." It had become a refrain among the people, a way of numbing their grief, for their beloved leader had died here on the mountain, within sight of the river that he would never cross.

"I hope the boys understood the importance of the story you told," said Jennat.

"Oh, they'll understand it in time," said Jesse.

That night, while he and Jennat lay sleeping, Jesse was awakened by a stirring sound, and he rose to investigate.

The darkness of the desert, its vast sky overladen with various shades of black and deep blue, broken by the light of millions of stars, held him entranced. He breathed in the night air, overwhelmed by his own feelings of love and joy and, yes, even reluctance to leave this wilderness.

A moving shadow at the edge of his vision broke Jesse's reverie. He heard a whisper, a rustling of leaves, a male voice, the light laughter of a girl.

Jesse moved noiselessly across the earth in his bare feet, and in the faint starlight, he saw the two young people standing close, moving into a kiss.

Jesse turned, his heart pounding, and he went back to the tent to lie down beside his wife.

"What is it?" Jennat whispered, startled. She sat up and looked all around.

"Nothing, nothing," said Jesse.

"It is something," Jennat insisted, "to get you up in the night." She pushed back the cover, but Jesse took her arm and drew her down again.

"Let it be," he said softly. "It's only Elias, out with a girl."

"A girl?" Jennat confronted him. "What sort of girl?"

"A young woman of the desert tribes," Jesse said softly. "A Moabite, probably. They've been meeting at night."

"And you never told me?" Jennat exclaimed. "She is a heathen!"

Jesse smiled, but did not reply. Jennat, the convert, had become more ardent in service to Adonai than many of the Israelite women.

"Our son is being tempted," Jesse said. "It is always so."

"But we escaped Pharaoh and Egypt so that we could go to a better place, where we could serve God."

"It is true," said Jesse, slowly fingering his beard, aware that the gesture was much like his uncle Rimon's. "But Egypt is also within us, Jennat. Whatever we become in Canaan will depend on our choices. Elias, too, must choose, as we did. Be happy, my dear one, and have faith in our children."

He felt her relax beside him, but Jesse lay awake until the dawn, preparing himself for tomorrow.